Praise for

IMPOSSIBLE CREATURES

'There was Tolkien, there is Pullman, and now there is Katherine Rundell. Wondrous invention, marvellous writing. This book is her best yet, and that's saying something'

Michael Morpurgo

'Katherine Rundell is a phenomenon. She not only understands what fantasy is for and why children (and the rest of us) need it, but she crafts original and brilliant books that delight readers of all ages and kinds, while stretching our minds and filling our hearts'

Neil Gaiman

'I love Katherine Rundell's writing ... Readers who already know her books will seize this with delight, and new readers will love it and demand all her others at once'

Philip Pullman

'A marvellous imaginative fantasy told with great style and sparkle – a book to race through in a day and keep for a lifetime'

Jacqueline Wilson

'Fantastically exuberant, wildly imaginative, impossibly brilliant. Rundell's best, which is something to be marvelled at. It made me want to yell, or laugh, or bite something'

Kiran Millwood Hargrave

'Between the covers of *Impossible Creatures* is a world as enchanting, as perilous, as richly imagined as Narnia or Middle Earth'

Frank Cottrell-Boyce

'A soaring odyssey of burning fierce heart and wit'

Piers Torday

'A menagerie of delights. So packed with magic you'll want to take notes. *Impossible Creatures* is a world you'll want to move into'

Patrick Ness

'I savoured every moment of *Impossible Creatures*. An absolutely magnificent story!'

Abi Elphinstone

'A rare and remarkable feat of glittering imagination from a truly masterful storyteller. The best thing since Pullman'

Catherine Doyle

'A thrilling and page-turning epic ... My Book of the Year'

Lauren St John

IMPOSSIBLE CREATURES

IMPOSSIBLE CREATURES

KATHERINE RUNDELL

Illustrated by
Tomislav Tomić

BLOOMSBURY
CHILDREN'S BOOKS
LONDON OXFORD NEW YORK NEW DELHI SYDNEY

BLOOMSBURY CHILDREN'S BOOKS
Bloomsbury Publishing Plc
50 Bedford Square, London WC1B 3DP, UK
29 Earlsfort Terrace, Dublin 2, Ireland

BLOOMSBURY, BLOOMSBURY CHILDREN'S BOOKS and the Diana logo
are trademarks of Bloomsbury Publishing Plc

First published in Great Britain in 2023 by Bloomsbury Publishing Plc

A catalogue record for this book is available from the British Library

ISBN: HB: 978-1-4088-9741-6; TPB: 978-1-5266-6789-2; Export
PB: 978-1-4088-9740-9; Waterstones: 978-1-5266-6898-1;
eBook: 978-1-4088-9742-3; ePDF: 978-1-5266-6160-9

4 6 8 10 9 7 5

Typeset by RefineCatch Limited, Bungay, Suffolk

Printed and bound in Great Britain by CPI Group (UK) Ltd, Croydon CR0 4YY

MIX
Paper | Supporting
responsible forestry
FSC
www.fsc.org
FSC® C171272

To find out more about our authors and books visit www.bloomsbury.com
and sign up for our newsletters

In memory of Claire Hawkins, my great-aunt,
who lit my childhood

'The griffin is both a feathered animal and a quadruped; its body is like that of a lion, but it has wings and the face of an eagle.'

Isidore of Seville, *Etymologies* (c. 600)

'His mouth is death and his breath is fire!'

The Epic of Gilgamesh (Mesopotamia, c. 2000 BCE), probably the earliest written reference to dragons

'I sing the progress of a deathless soul.'

John Donne, *Metempsychosis* (1601)

THE
GUARDIAN'S
BESTIARY

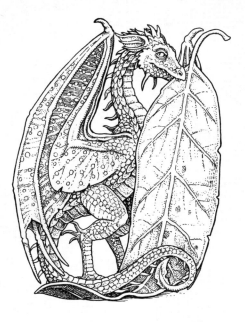

There is a secret place in our world that is carefully hidden, to keep it safe from us. It's a wild magnificence of a place: a land where all the creatures of myth still live and thrive. It is known as the Archipelago: a cluster of thirty-four islands, some as large as Denmark, some as small as a town square. Across the islands, thousands of magical creatures run and fly, raise their young, grow old, die and begin again. To us they're half forgotten, and were long ago dismissed as children's stories. But we have not destroyed them; they survive. They are plentiful, and shining, and real. It is the last surviving magical place.

Al-miraj

Al-mirajes are horned hares of dazzling beauty. Their ears are long and pink on the inside, and their horns pure gold. During the mating season, where the al-miraj treads, fresh shoots of greenery rise from the earth; they can carpet a barren field with grass within an hour. The al-miraj is said to seek out the valiant, the wise and the good. Queen Arian of Lithia once sought to give one to her fiancé, only to see the creature shun her suitor and joyfully greet her maidservant. She married her maidservant instead and they lived happily ever after, with a garden full of gold-horned hares.

Avanc

The avanc is a swamp-dwelling carnivore, resembling a fanged beaver. The teeth of the avanc, which are bone-white and pointed like pins, grow an inch every day, and they keep them trimmed and sharpened against rocks, trees and occasional humans. The softness and lustrous beauty of their fur can lead children to take liberties. Those children who do so, do so only once.

Borometz

Also known as the 'vegetable lamb', the borometz grows from a green stalk, to which it is tethered by a tendril. The lamb reaches one foot in height; its skin is green and its wool is white. If the lamb eats all the grass within the reach of the tendril, both the lamb and the plant will die. For this reason, many people in the Archipelago carry seeds, to plant around the borometz's stalk if they see one. Their wool, given freely to those they trust, makes the softest cloth in the known world; cloth which lasts hundreds of years, and smells very faintly of the earth.

Centaur

(female: **centauride**)

Centaurs have the body of a horse and the torso and head of a human. While they are skilled artisans in a variety of crafts, much centaur culture focuses around food, because they must eat a dozen times a day, to fuel the needs of their bodies and tremendous brains. They are great culinary inventors, and centaur feasts take place at every full moon, spread out under moonlight. They serve forest fruits, piled three feet high, and ferocious crab-apple spirits, and the feasting lasts all night and into the next day.

Chimaera

The chimaera resembles a lion, but has a second head, that of a goat, and a tail which ends in the face of a snake. These three faces all have individuated brains, nervous systems and strong opinions. This makes it difficult for the chimaera to achieve as much havoc as it otherwise might, as it generally fails to agree with itself as to what to do next.

Dragon

There are thirty-seven species of dragon in the Archipelago. The largest – the red-winged dragon, which is black with a scarlet under-wing – is as large as a cathedral. The smallest, the jaculus, can sit comfortably on the joint of your thumb. The yellow dragon, slim-winged and long-tailed, is the fastest in the sky, while the bronze-tailed aquatic dragon is able to breathe underwater, and has been known to spend its entire adult life beneath the ocean, erupting to the surface only to hunt occasional sailors. The silver dragon, which can live up to four thousand years, is thought to be the oldest creature in the world. It is unpredictable in temper, as befits one who has seen so much.

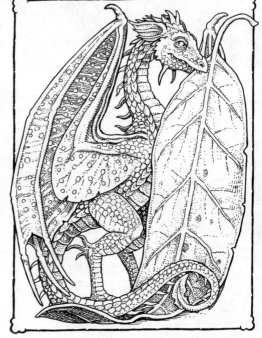

Griffin

Griffins have the body, tail and back legs of a lion, and the head, wings and front claws of an eagle. Though they do not speak aloud, they learn astonishingly fast, and can understand the entirety of a human language within days. When fully grown, their wingspan is broad enough to shelter a child underneath it. In cold weather, their bodies radiate warmth. The griffin is more reliant than any other creature on the glimourie in the soil and the air; they are among the world's most magical creatures. [*Addendum, by Frank Aureate: For the last five years, griffins have become rarer and rarer. The reason is unclear, but it is possibly connected to a fading in the glimourie. Their status now is believed to be near-extinct.*]

Hippocamp

Hippocamps are the true sea-horses of the oceans. They live in herds of ten to twenty; the male is larger than the female, but the female is swifter. They range in colour from emerald green, to grey, to, in the north-west, the shining pink of coral. Some are tamed and ridden by nereids. All boats in the Archipelago must, by law, run on wind or sun, so that the water will remain unpolluted, and the young hippocamps (known as 'hippolines') can grow into their full lustrous beauty.

Kanko

A foxlike creature the size of a mouse, the kanko's tail is split in two, allowing it to perform extraordinary feats of balance. Also known as 'lightfoxes', their saliva has luminescent properties, and has been used in paintings, particularly in Japan, where they originate. They have a rich, attentive intelligence despite their size, and are known to bring luck. The nest of a kanko, therefore, mustn't be disturbed; but they have been known to nest in inconvenient places – in shoes, hats, pockets, and, once, in the beard of a gentleman on the day of his wedding.

Karkadann

Karkadanns resemble unicorns, if unicorns had vicious souls and canine teeth. One of the few creatures in the Archipelago who kill for sport as well as food, they eat meat, preferring human flesh, and grass, for digestion. The hide of the karkadann ranges from pure black to purple, and the skin sags from their bones. The horn is black, and the tip carries a poison which can cause agonising gangrene, paralysis and death. They can be kept at bay with the horn of a unicorn, but, as you are extremely unlikely to have a unicorn to hand, that is frankly of limited help.

Kludde

A dog the size of a bear, the kludde is black except where, in place of ears, it has a pair of flames. It uses the lights of its ears to attract its prey – largely deer, wild cattle and al-mirajes – and then devours it. It can be identified from a distance by its breath, which resembles the shriek of metal on metal. The only way to kill a kludde is to extinguish its flames with wet earth or sand. Kluddes live primarily on islands uninhabited by humans; very few Archipelagians will see one in their lifetimes. Those who see them do not forget. [*Addendum by Frank Aureate: unless they have been eaten, in which case they presumably do.*]

Kraken

The oldest of the sea creatures, krakens have been traced back as far as the Cretaceous period, co-existing with the Tyrannosaurus rex. Their tentacles range in number from eight to forty-six, depending on the sub-species. They are terrifying in their moments of hunger: there have been accounts of krakens consuming as many as four hundred sailors in a single day, and the whirlpool created by their tentacles can pull ships of enormous size to the sea-floor. Krakens do not in general migrate, and remain in the body of water they were born in, so sailors in possession of good maps can usually evade them; but those who sail without maps take their lives in their hands.

Lavellan

The lavellan looks like a small water shrew. It features in the satirical song: 'Let him not go away from the houses, to moss or wood, lest the Lavellan come and smite him.' This is not a good song, but it is a good warning. The lavellan can poison a water source by swimming in it, and can, despite its small size, kill an adult human with its teeth. The lavellan has no interest in harming humans unless provoked, but its definition of 'provoked' is a broad one and can include sniffing, laughing and all forms of interpretive dance.

Longma

A winged, scaled horse – often green or brown with a black underbelly – of breathtaking beauty and strength. Some longmas go their entire lives without touching the ground. Sky-ready like no other creature, they wash by seeking out rain clouds and flying slowly through them, their scaled wings outstretched. A longma is the only creature in the world that gives birth in the air: the mother flies as high as she can into the sky, so that when the foal falls from her womb, it has as long as possible to unfold its wings before it hits the ground. Longmas should be treated with caution: only a very small number develop bonds with humans. Even then, those humans occasionally wake to find themselves being eaten in small ways, which are nonetheless inconvenient – a finger, for instance, or half an ear – because there is no such thing as a truly tame longma.

Manticore

The manticore has the tail of a scorpion, the face of a human, the teeth and body of a lion, and the personality of a self-righteous politician. Some sub-species are winged. Manticores, like karkadanns, are one of the very few creatures who will attack humans on sight, even when not in need of food. They lie and kill for the pleasure of it. They smell of decay.

Mermaid

(cf. also **merman**, **merfolk**; a newborn merchild is a **merbaern**)
Most mermaids live in the northern waters of the Archipelago. Some clans, such as the Marian tribe, grow tails as long as thirty feet, and each mermaid tail, whatever their length, has 40,000 muscles (humans, in comparison, have about 650 in their entire bodies). Many merfolk are musicians, and have invented a range of underwater instruments of great sweetness and beauty. Some of their songs, shared with humans, have entered human tradition: Vivaldi is thought to have borrowed many of his compositions from the merfolk.

Nereid

It is unwise to mistake a nereid for a mermaid; they object, and their objections can be perilous. Although they live underwater, they have no tails. Their hair and fingertips are silver, and their pale skin has a silver sheen. Their speaking voices are famously mesmeric – they're said to have taken their language straight from the music of the sea. Although they are entirely capable of walking on dry land, they do so only in cases of urgent need. Found primarily in the south seas of the Archipelago, they are a fiercely logical people, but their logic is the logic of the ocean, beyond the understanding of humans. The human populations of the Archipelago treat them with awe, and keep their distance; the expression 'as unknowable as a nereid' is a common one in the islands.

Ratatoska

(pronunciation: *rata-TOS-ka*.
Alternative spelling: **ratatoskr**)
Akin to large squirrels, green-furred with a short horn, the ratatoskas spread news across the Archipelago. They know more of the world's secrets – the gossip, the tall tales, the truths and half-truths and quarter-truths – than anyone else. Though physically harmless, they can, when young, be giddy chaos-merchants with a liking for mischief. If you wish to spread a piece of news, and are not too concerned about accuracy, tell a ratatoska.

Sphinx

Sphinxes are gifted mathematicians and scholars, ruthlessly loyal allies and implacable enemies. The tooth of a sphinx, held in the mouth of a human, allows its owner to understand any language; a lick from a sphinx can heal most wounds. Originally found primarily in Northern Africa and South-East Asia, sphinxes migrated across the world before coming to rest on the mountainous peninsula of the Island of Lithia. Those wishing to visit the sphinxes' mountains should be aware that, if you should fail to answer the riddle they pose, the sphinx has an ancient right to eat you.

Twrch Tryth

(pronunciation: *twOOrk troeeth*)

A blue-black boar, said to have been ridden, once, by King Arthur. Its fur shines iridescent in moonlight. The boar can grow as large as a rhinoceros, and is capable of crushing those who frighten or anger it, but is gentle and sweet-tempered with children. It has been known to shelter swallows beneath its belly and in its armpits during rainstorms. Known as the warrior-boar, the twrch tryth will fight for those it loves. Clumsy on the ground, they are exquisitely elegant in the water, and can swim the length of the Archipelago without pausing for a single minute.

Unicorn

Born coloured pure gold, unicorns turn silver in their second year and white in their fourth. They prefer wooded areas, and soft turf underfoot. Able if left untroubled to live more than three hundred years, unicorns can thrive on grass and shrubs, but they love herbs – lemongrass, thyme and, most of all, mint. Their breath can endow humans with courage. Hairs from their tails and manes can, when woven into bandages, cure fatally infected wounds; they have been known to walk battlefields, breathing life into the fallen. There have, throughout history, been accounts of people riding unicorns, but it is vanishingly rare; most who have tried have found themselves carefully and politely trampled into the ground.

THE BEGINNING

It was a very fine day, until something tried to eat him.

It was a black dog-like creature, but it was not like any dog he had ever seen. It had teeth as long as his arm, and claws that could tear apart an oak tree.

It says, therefore, a great deal in Christopher Forrester's favour that he refused – with speed and cunning and courage – to be eaten.

THE BEGINNING, ELSEWHERE

It was a very fine day, until somebody tried to kill her.

Mal had returned home from her journey, flying back from the forest with arms outstretched and coat flapping, buffeted by the wind.

Mal Arvorian could fly only when the wind blew. The weather that day was perfect – a westerly breeze that smelt of the sea – and she was sky-spinning, twisting in the cold air. Her flying coat was thick, and too big for her, and she wore it with the sleeves rolled up four times. When the wind was up – it didn't need to be strong, but some wind was necessary – she could catch at the corners and open it, like wings, and feel the breeze lift her off her feet.

That day she had flown over treetops, her shoes brushing the tips of their branches, and swooped low, causing a herd of unicorns to scatter.

In the kitchen, her Great-Aunt Leonor had grumbled at her cold hands, and given her a cup of hot cordial, when there was a knock on the door.

It was the murderer.

ARRIVAL

The day before the attack, Christopher sat on a bench outside the ferry terminal, waiting for his grandfather. He had travelled alone from his flat in North London to Scotland, and he was cramp-legged and ravenously hungry.

A squirrel leaped on to the bench, and watched him. Slowly it edged closer, quivering, until its whiskers were touching his knee. It was joined by another, and then another, until there were seven of them, clustering around his feet.

A woman waiting at the taxi rank turned to stare. 'How's he doing that then?' she said to the man next to her.

One squirrel darted to crouch on the toe of Christopher's shoe. Christopher laughed, and the squirrel ran up his shin bone to his knee. 'All right there?' he said to the squirrel. 'Nice day.'

'Feeding them, no doubt,' the man said, then called over to

Christopher: 'You shouldn't feed wild animals! It's bad for their guts.'

'I know,' said Christopher, and he smiled half a smile. 'I'm not.'

It was a joke among his friends that wherever he went, animals sought out Christopher. Cats on the street came to wind figure-of-eights around his ankles; dogs leaped up at him in the park. Football games had been interrupted when a small chorus of yowling foxes tried to get near him; there had been a day when insistent pigeons dive-bombed him during a school trip, and swimming in the outdoor ponds in Hampstead was almost impossible. The lifeguard had ordered him out of the water, because the sudden arrival of a phalanx of swans was making the smaller children scream.

Christopher had smiled, whistled at the swans, and led them out of the pond and into some nearby bushes. One young swan had tried to fly on to his shoulder, scratching at his skin with clawed, webbed feet. He had the marks for months afterwards. He didn't mind the scars: he knew that the attention and love of animals were no gentle thing. It often involved a certain amount of blood.

'Something in his smell,' his father would say stiffly. But Christopher didn't, as far as he could tell, smell significantly different from other boys his age. He washed, though not unduly.

As a small child, it had been the great delight of his life. As he grew older, it still gave him tremendous joy, but he learned to hide it – because his father hated it. The animals drove him into an inexplicable anxiety. 'Get away!' he would say, and he would chase off the cats, the birds, the occasional mouse or rat on the underground. Christopher and his father never went to the countryside now, because there was always an outside chance that hares would chase him across fields, and swallows would want to nest in his hair.

It hadn't always been that way. Before his mother's death, he remembered his father differently. Animals had come to his mother too. He had a photograph of the three of them in Richmond Park, surrounded by deer, his father laughing with a baby Christopher on his shoulders. But she had died, nine years ago, and his father had contracted, as if a weight had settled on him and concertinaed him downwards and inwards. Everything in the house had felt smaller – diminished and less brave – after that.

So Christopher secretly opened his windows at night to let the birds in. He wore a long wool navy overcoat, and occasionally let sparrows investigate the patch pockets. He made detours to greet crows if he saw them, and allowed them to stalk on clawed feet up his arm and on to his shoulder. His friends were wary – 'They'll peck your eyes out!' – but he only smiled and shook his head.

'Nah.' His voice around animals became softer, lighter. 'They won't,' he said – and they didn't. His face around them took on the look of a drawn bow: ready, waiting.

The crows brought him silver buttons and paper

clips, and coins which he dug holes in and strung on to a shoelace and wore round his neck. Some of the seniors at school jeered at him for the necklace, but it didn't stop him wearing it. It was a way of saying his allegiance was to wild and living things.

And so he grew older and taller – they were a tall family, with gangling legs and finely made hands – and he waited.

What he was waiting for, Christopher couldn't have explained: he only hoped, in a way that burned in his lungs and stomach, that there was something more than that which he had so far seen. The animals felt like a promise.

(He was right. It was an astonishment that would change his life forever.)

ARRIVAL, ELSEWHERE

The murderer arrived by boat. He came gently, with a soft tread and beautifully clean hands. He strode past a group of men and women hauling in a catch of fire-fish, his knife out of sight in his pocket. They glanced round at him, but he only nodded at them, and they forgot him as soon as he passed out of sight, which was as he intended. He was a professional: he had spent years perfecting the careful art of forgettability. His hair was neither long nor short, and his shoes had been polished to exactly the shine that attracts no comment. His eyes, which were as dark and cold as the bottom of the sea, settled on nothing for very long. Until, that fine day, they settled on Mal.

It had been easy, in retrospect, for the murderer to find her. It's easy to find your quarry if you've been told to hunt down a flying girl and then you see a child, twenty feet up, weaving through a flock of seagulls. Human flight was an unusual sight, even in the Archipelago.

It had been years now since Mal had first learned to fly. A travelling seer had given her the flying coat soon after she was born. He had named her, and laid the coat at her small feet. He tried to say more – to explain why he had given the coat to her and her alone – but the house was in mourning, for Mal's mother had not survived the birth, and he'd been sent abruptly on his way.

So it was with no instruction at all that Mal took to the sky. The nearest neighbours had laughed at her, a small girl swamped in a coat running into the wind; so she'd flushed, and woken earlier the next day so nobody would see her. At first, when the wind dropped, she used to thump down to the ground with a bone-breaking crack; she had fractured both her ankles at different times, snapped a wrist and bent her little finger backwards to the wrist. Her big toenail had turned an interesting green-black and fallen off. But she had tried again, and again, licking the blood off her skinned knees, climbing up trees and jumping out of them.

And she had proved her neighbours wrong.

'No, I *will* do it', she said, when the neighbour's boy laughed at her. 'You don't know anything about it.' She wore her chin high, on those days. People were difficult – she felt herself grow spiky around them, liable to say the wrong thing and blush right up to her forehead – but the sky made perfect

9

sense to her. She might be grubby and awkward on the ground, but in flight, the locals said, Mal Arvorian was a thing worth seeing.

By the age of nine, she'd learned to glide to a gentle stop. By ten, she could land on the tips of her toes, or on one foot. By twelve, she could tuck her chin to her chest and throw herself forwards, somersaulting in the wind. That spring morning she had flown over the sea with her bare feet skimming the water, her boots in her pockets, the ocean spray flecking her ankles, laughing with the speed and joy of it.

The murderer had watched her, and smiled an unlovely smile.

Mal was forbidden to fly anywhere except around the garden or across the fields: her Great-Aunt Leonor would have been horrified had she known how far Mal went. But her great-aunt forbade an immense, book-length list of things, and she couldn't obey them all.

'I can't,' she said to Gelifen, 'just stay indoors and sit on a chair all day. That's how people turn to stone.'

So, forbidden to cut her own hair, she had given herself a fringe with a pair of nail scissors. It came out a little erratic and drunken, but she liked it, and plaited a gold thread she had pulled from an embroidered tablecloth into her braid to set it off. Forbidden to go to the forest, she flew there in the thin light of the sunrise, before Leonor was awake. She longed to know the green squirrel-like ratatoskas, and gradually came to be on speaking terms with them, listening to their gossip. She told them stories in return, of how she'd found Gelifen (an egg, washed up close to the shore: 'I ran fully clothed out into the waves for it, and I hatched him in my own bed. He sleeps on my pillow now'), and heard it repeated by one young ratatoska, high and shrill, to another ('She swam halfway out to Lithia, she did, in full evening dress; had to battle a nereid for it, she did').

She spent hours running through the trees with Gelifen, looking for unicorns and gorging on waterberries. She had seen a family of al-mirajes go loping through the sun-dappled undergrowth, a trail of fresh shoots of grass marking their progress behind them. She had been bitten, once, by an avanc – entirely her own fault, Leonor scolded, for getting too close – and it had gone septic, and her great-aunt had had to sit up with her for seven nights running. As soon as she was allowed out of bed, she'd gone back to the forest. She had work to do there.

Most of all, though, there was the sky. If, as occasionally happened, someone in town shook their heads, and told her she was a little scrap of chaos, a burden to the old woman – then Mal would glare, and redden, and run to take refuge in flight.

The sky was Mal's freedom. She would angle herself to fly up through the clouds, soaring higher and higher in the white blur of them. She would open her mouth and stick out her tongue, and come back to earth drenched and red-cheeked and victorious. 'Cloud-eating', she called it. Some clouds tasted different from others; a different chill and flavour to different shades of grey and white. Gelifen couldn't yet fly alongside her, so she tucked him into her jumper, his beaked face protruding from the blue wool at the top.

A few people, over the years, had suspected that the girl was rare in some way. Some of them thought it with a spike of jealousy for their own children, and others with a thrill of pleasure. But they were busy, and people mostly let her be, to run and eat and fly.

Except, that day, for the murderer.

FRANK AUREATE

A car horn hooted, and the squirrels scattered. A battered Ford drew up next to Christopher's bench and a man in his seventies leaned out. 'Christopher? Is that you?'

On top of the roof of the car were four seagulls.

'They follow me around, whenever I come to town,' said Frank Aureate, gesturing to the gulls as Christopher approached. His voice was deep, Scottish. 'It's always been that way, with the animals. I wouldn't mind, you know, with the gulls, except that they make eating outside a task. They take an aggressive interest in my sandwiches.' He unlocked the passenger door.

Christopher grinned, and got into the car. One of the seagulls tried to follow him. When the seagull had been removed, and his grandfather had wiped the bird's weaponised poo from his hands and dashboard, Christopher said: 'There used to be a fox that tried to chew its way through the window latch of my bedroom, when I was seven. When I met it in the street it would lick my knees.'

They looked at each other, and a flicker of something sharp and warm passed between them. Frank looked away first. 'Good,' he said. 'Aye. That's good.'

'Is it? My dad doesn't think so.'

His grandfather made a noise that was somewhere between a snort and a cough. He smiled half a smile – a smile that looked like Christopher's – and began the four-hour drive to the hills, and to the house.

Nobody had meant Christopher to come to Scotland: Christopher least of all. He hadn't wanted to come to the middle of nowhere to spend the holiday with a man he hadn't seen for nine years. His grandfather had not, it seemed, particularly wanted to take him. But his father had been summoned away for work, and there was nowhere else to go. Urgent calls had been made. Christopher had argued very hard and loud to be left alone, but his father said it was probably illegal. And so now he was here, being driven through the town, past the small cinema, the supermarket and the bank, and out into the Scottish Highlands.

The buildings began to thin, and the trees to thicken. Frank produced sandwiches, and home-made honey flapjacks, and black coffee from a flask. Christopher spat the coffee out of the window when his grandfather wasn't looking – it tasted like a melted shoe. But the sandwiches were excellent, on thick fresh bread, and the view outside the car grew greener every minute.

'We've no neighbours; the next nearest house is a good twenty-one miles away. It's a long way yet,' said Frank Aureate. 'Sleep, if you want to.'

But Christopher didn't sleep: of course he didn't. He watched. Eventually the houses at the roadside stopped altogether, and they were driving along mountain roads, past lochs and heather. The way grew steeper, and the earth darker, a peaty black dotted with gorse. The air began to smell different – richer, and deeper, and wilder.

BEFORE THE MURDERER

Mal's town of Icthus had, a few thousand years ago, been the largest trading city in the Archipelago, with a long high sea-wall and a raucous port, before the enchanted islands were separated and hidden away from the rest of the world. Now, though, Atidina, cut from stone, proud in her rugged shoreline, was a place on the way to nowhere, lying at the far south-east edge of the Archipelago, and Atidinan citizens were glad to keep it so. Occasionally a herd of hippocamps would come and swim alongside the boats, or a mermaid would approach a fisherman, playing a tune on a flute made from a razor clam. Otherwise, there was just the business of the sea and the steady living of life.

On the morning of that day, Mal had been shopping. She had flown over a portion of the forest to a cliff, which led down to a sandy cove where boats often moored. In the cove was a large sailing boat, rusty and ocean-battered. Painted in flaking letters on its side was its name: *The Sailsman.*

The wind whipped Mal's hair into her face, and she let out an audible thrum of happiness. She landed with barely a noise on the sand. The boat had a long gangplank lowered to the shore, and Mal ran up it.

The boat wasn't, technically, a place she was allowed to be. Nicely brought-up children did not visit the Sailsman's boat. It was a shop, but you couldn't be sure that everything it sold was what it said it was, or was strictly legal. People had been cheated. Pure-gold bracelets, polished just once, showed the tin underneath; some of the beauty creams gave you vivid red pustules all over your face.

But enough of the objects were genuine for some to think it worth the gamble, and there were a dozen people on board. Mal ran down the stairs, to the room below deck. It was bursting with things for sale: piled on shelves, tied to the wall, hanging from the ceiling in baskets and hammocks. There were richly carved boxes which opened only under a full moon, and teapots that never grew cold, made from fire-clay forged in the eastern islands. There was a dagger which – claimed the handwritten label – could cut any material in the Archipelago. The label, printed in laborious capitals, read: THE GLAMRY BLADE. Mal longed to run her thumb along the tip of it: it came to a point so fine it seemed to fade into invisibility. She reached out a hand – but a man, a great rock of a person, nearly seven feet tall, with gold hoops in his ears and a burn scar on his neck, stepped closer to inspect it. He smelt strongly of alcohol; she darted past him, further in.

There was a wall of blue glass jars, containing sweets from across the Archipelago. There were balls of soft gum, harvested from the sea by sylphs, which gave you brief bursts of great physical strength, but if you chewed too long gave you a rash of scales across your hands. There were ruinously expensive candies called voulay-drops, made by centaurs in the mountains of Edem. They tasted of that which you craved most; but also, if you ate more than one, made you vomit something black for days afterwards.

She shook herself, and moved on again; it was not sweets she had come for. A young man in overalls eyed her suspiciously, and asked if she needed help.

'No,' she said, and added when he raised his eyebrows: 'No, *thank you*. I know exactly what I'm looking for.'

And as she spoke she saw it, among the shelves of smaller, cheaper, dustier wares. She had first spotted it six months ago and coveted it instantly, but hadn't had nearly enough gold. She had been saving ever since. She'd been haunted at night by the idea that someone else might buy it, before she had enough.

It was more tarnished than it had been half a year ago. It was small enough to fit easily in her palm, an engraved thick silver lid over the glass, which clicked open to show a quivering needle. A small pocket-compass; except it wasn't.

She held it, as carefully as if it were alive, and watched the needle spin a full circle, until it pointed back up the cliff, back exactly the way she had come.

'Do you know what that is?' The Sailsman's voice came from behind her, and she jumped. The ship's owner's clothes were sea-stained, and his skin hard lived in, but his eyes under the heavy brows were not unkind. People said he treated the taxation laws as entirely optional, but he would make a fair deal, where the need was real.

'Yes.' It had no label, but she did know. She'd read about them, in four different books. 'It's a casapasaran.'

'And you know what it does?' His voice was low, and grainy, as if he'd eaten the sand his boat was moored on.

'I think . . . wherever you are, the needle points you home.'

Mal had plans for the casapasaran. She had what might be called, generously, a unique sense of direction. It was a difficulty, being a person who could unfailingly point to the west and say, 'That's north', and then journey for hours in completely the wrong direction until the sunset was right in front of her. It was a hindrance for someone with such a longing to fly. But this device would mean she could go anywhere her coat would take her, knowing it would always point her home again.

'And can you afford it?' The Sailsman took the casapasaran from her and held it up, wiping the dust from it with his shirt.

The Sailsman's actual name, she knew, was Lionel Holbyne, though nobody had ever been known to call him Lionel. (Understandable, Mal felt, in the circumstances: *Lionel!*)

'Yes.'

'There are no discounts for youth or winsome faces – and no sympathy reductions for badly cut fringes.'

'I've got enough money! I've been saving.' She reached into her coat pocket and pulled out the coins, counting them in her palm: two gold, nine silver.

He looked at her, long and hard, and then he nodded. 'Fair. We don't give receipts, and we don't take returns.'

'I know.' She hesitated – then, because she did urgently want to know, it burst out: 'You know the dagger over there, where it says on the label that it can cut anything in the Archipelago? If that's true—'

'Not *if*,' said the Sailsman. 'It can. The *glamry blade*, is its proper name.'

'I wanted to know, what if you tried to cut another of the same kind of knife with it? Which would cut which?'

'There isn't any other, and there never will be. The blade is ancient; it was centaur-made, for the Immortal.'

'But how do you know it can cut everything? Have you tested it on *everything*?'

The question was a mistake. The Sailsman's eyes hooded in distaste, like shutters coming down.

'Are you calling me a liar?'

'No! I'm not,' said Mal. 'I was just curious.'

'Safer not to be,' said the Sailsman. He held out a palm. Hurriedly, fumbling, she put the coins into it. He waited a long, hard second, then flicked a smile at her, and gave her the casapasaran.

'Go, then – quick, before I change my mind. I shouldn't sell it for so absurdly little. But you recognised it for what it was, and that counts for something. Perhaps, anyway. Who knows. These are strange days.'

Mal grinned. She half ran off the boat.

As she reached the sand, the wind was stronger. She would go to the forest. There was a spot, deep in the woods, that she wanted to see; without the casapasaran, there was every risk she'd end up lost for days, circling the same tree. With the casapasaran, everything was different.

She flew there, twenty-three feet up in the sky, the wind buoying her, her feet pointed behind.

She did not see that the murderer watched her go.

THE FORBIDDEN HILLTOP

Frank Aureate's house had clearly once, long ago, been grand – the kind of house with attics and wine cellars, and oil paintings of disapproving-looking women holding small, disapproving-looking dogs – but now it wasn't grand at all. It was so overrun with ivy that the windowpanes were splintering. One of the windows was cracked, and carefully patched with paper and tape.

The house was at the foot of a steep hill, surrounded by a shin-high lawn spotted with daisies and clover. Trees rose halfway up the hill and then stopped, and the hill went on alone, a great dark swell of land against the scarlet setting of the sun.

Frank gripped the edges of the car to climb out of it. He walked with a stick, and Christopher handed it to him. He watched his grandfather move, with painful stiffness, towards the house. The old man was surprisingly beautifully dressed in a green corduroy suit, patched at the elbow. He had heft to him: large hands, a belly, broad in the shoulder and jaw and wrinkled neck. His eyebrows were so bushy they would, Christopher thought, enter a room several seconds before the rest of him.

'No need to stand there on one leg like a cormorant,' said Frank. 'Come in.' Christopher followed him in, bag in hand, breathing in a scent of wood smoke and cooking. 'The house is crumbling at the edges these days, but it's clean, and most of the walls stay up.' He looked around, suddenly uncertain. 'I haven't had a child here since your mother was a girl. Is there anything you need?'

'Is there phone signal?' said Christopher.

'None at all, I'm afraid,' said Frank. He did not sound remotely apologetic.

Christopher's heart sank. 'Then ... could I drive your car, to where there would be?'

The old man looked hard at him. 'I think you're about four or five years off being old enough, aren't you?'

'But the car's an automatic – and there's nothing I could hit, round here, except the trees. And the trees aren't going to make any sudden movements. Please?'

His grandfather raised one eyebrow so high it brushed his white fringe. 'First you get to know the area; then we'll talk. But the place first. It matters.'

Christopher followed him into the sitting room. He was assailed by the sight of a life-size oil painting of a man in uniform with enough facial hair to stuff a small cushion. 'Nice moustache,' he said.

His grandfather smiled. 'Aye, it's a proper horror. A distant ancestor of ours; I think my father said he was Belgian. But the house and its contents were never the point. The point –' and his eyes ran over Christopher like a bus – 'is the land outside the house.'

Frank showed him the kitchen, the boot room, the larder stocked with herbs and jars of preserves and beans, and a startling number of tins of anchovies.

'You can go anywhere in the house, and anywhere out towards the road. But there's a condition your father insisted on. *You don't go near the top of the hill.* D'you understand, lad?'

Christopher looked out of the window at the slope rising behind the house. Instantly, he wanted to run up it.

'You can go as far as that ridge of trees, halfway up, but no further.'

'But why? What's up there?'

'It's dangerous.' Frank led him down a corridor and up a flight of stairs, thumping hard and fast with his stick.

'What sort of dangerous?'

'It's not something you need to think about. Only do as you're told. Promise me.'

'But I can swim, and climb. And I'm not a little kid – I'm not going to get lost or fall into a mine shaft or eat poison berries or anything like that.'

Frank did not look round. 'It's not something we're going to discuss further. It's what your father wants, so it's the one place you may not go. If I find out you went beyond the trees, there'll be a price to pay.' He opened a door to a high-ceilinged, white-painted bedroom, with a double bed and a shelf of books in languages Christopher couldn't begin to recognise. There was a dark red jumper on the bed. 'This is your bedroom. Make it entirely your own – move the books around, draw on the walls if you want to. I knitted you a jersey.' A slight flush rose on the old man's neck. 'Aye. But, you know – feel no need to wear it.' He cleared his throat. 'Dinner is at eight. You're welcome here: you're my grandson, and it's right that you should come. But don't forget what I said.'

He left. He didn't notice – for even the wisest of the old forget, sometimes, the care and subtlety of the young – that Christopher had made no promise.

THE DYING OF THE LIGHT

Mal flew for four miles, deep into the forest, her feet skimming the treetops. It was here, where the trees grew thickest and the light was dyed deep green, that she planned to set up her experiment.

As she landed, though – as carefully as she could, so as not to snag her coat – she stopped short. At the foot of one of the trees was a ratatoska, the size of a cat, lying on its side. Its fur was dark green, not the grey-green of mature adulthood, so it was still young.

She was suddenly cold. Mal knew several of the forest's ratatoskas: she bent closer, holding her breath, but this one's face wasn't familiar. With the tip of her finger, she touched its coarse fur. It didn't move. She knelt, and put her hand to its nose, feeling for its breath. Very gently, she turned it over; its body moved stiffly, like a puppet. It was dead.

Mal rocked back on her heels, breathing hard and fast. For months now, she had been coming across dead creatures in the forest. A gagana – a bird with an iron beak and copper claws – dead in its nest with its young. A seabull, washed up on the shore, too far from where it ought to swim. Two weeks before, unforgettably terribly, there had been a unicorn foal, pure-gold, stillborn.

Swiftly, her teeth gritted, she dug in the soil with her hands, and lifted the ratatoska into it, covering it with earth, so that the lavellans wouldn't eat it.

She ran her hands along the ground. The soil here was patched; some was still rich brown, but some had changed to a grey-black silt. Atidina's forest was one of the most ancient in the Archipelago; it was supposed to be rich brown forever. When she was seven, or eight, or nine, all the soil had been brown. Now, though, it was changing.

She had a tangle of sticks and string in her coat pocket – she pulled them out. She began to mark out the patches of grey, with the sticks jammed in the ground, and the string looped around them. This was her experiment: careful, earnest, painfully home-made. She inked the sticks with dates, in her spiky handwriting, biting her tongue in concentration.

She had been doing this now for half a year: to prove to herself that the swathes of grey soil across the forest really were growing larger. She had tried to bring her great-aunt out to see that the patches had outgrown the stakes: that they were creeping across the woods. Her great-aunt had refused to come:

'My legs won't carry me, and I've better things to do than look at the dirt.'

Worse, though, than the soil – worse than everything – were the griffins. Griffins had always been delicate; they'd always been rare, for thousands of years. But for the last five years, they had been disappearing; slowly at first, and then fast, in a great and terrible rush. A traveller had found the whole colony on the Island of Wings dead. Some said it was a fluke – a tragedy, yes, but connected to nothing else. Others said it was a sign of something dark; an evil augury, the beginning of worse.

A report had gone out that summer, from the City of Scholars: no griffins had been seen for twenty-four months. They would therefore, in the Book of Living Things, be marked: *Presumed extinct.*

She had thought about writing to them, to tell them what she knew, but had decided not to. She could not bear to risk him being taken.

She shivered, hard. She tucked her hair into her navy fisherman's jersey, and prepared to fly home.

THE ONE PLACE YOU MAY NOT GO

The next day, Christopher went up the hill. Frank's black Labrador, Goose – a dog whose primary characteristic seemed to be an enthusiasm for putting her tongue on Christopher's face – followed him. It was a cold blue day; he wore the red jumper – his grandfather had knitted it thick as armour, with a broad rollneck – and his navy coat. The air, he thought, smelt different up here: rich and unfamiliar. It smelt like a concentration of growing things, green and earthy – like life distilled.

He reached the ridge of trees, and stopped, leaning against a pine. He peered upwards, to the peak, and felt his chest tighten. His father trusted him with nothing, he thought bitterly; not even with his own safety. He was nervous about everything; always assessing the world, every stick and stone, every car and street, every instrument in the kitchen, for how it might harm Christopher. He warned against potato peelers and tin openers; he viewed birthday candles as deadly weapons. Christopher loved his father, but it felt like being nailed down, pinioning them both to the ground.

There was a sour taste in his mouth. It would take him barely five minutes to run to the peak.

He hesitated, his skin prickling. Goose spent the time trying to investigate the entirety of his ear with her tongue. He'd be back before anyone knew. What could possibly be so dangerous? It was ridiculous and unfair, he thought, not to tell him, and he flexed his feet in his shoes.

There was a bang, and he jumped. Down below, a gust of wind had sent a shutter slamming against the house. His grandfather could glance out of the window at any time and see him. If he was going to go, he should go now.

'Come on, Goose.' He faced up beyond the trees to the peak. 'You only get the best view if you climb to the top'. And Christopher, with the dog beside him, struck out beyond the treeline, walking fast for the top of the hill.

He had not gone far when the ground began, infinitesimally at first but then quite unmistakeably, to shake under his feet.

THE MURDER

It was the casapasaran that saved her life.

Mal flew home, landing in the garden. Her house was small and plain, but the garden was large and lush, and beautifully tended by her Great-Aunt Leonor, Mal's only living relation. The end of the garden was marked by a high wall. On the other side there was a drop, and a river. Mal had been told, at an average rate of once a day for a decade, not to climb the wall. The river was deep and swift-running, flanked on the far side by brambles, and lavellans – poison shrews, whose bite was deadly – were found in the water.

Her great-aunt looked at Mal as she came into the kitchen, and sighed. Leonor had once been tall and elegant; now, at seventy-six, she was bent. 'Your hands are freezing – and filthy, Mal! What have you been doing?'

'I was in the forest. I saw—'

'Well, wash them – with soap, please – and come to the table. I baked.'

The table was laden with food. There was a beautiful, moist nut cake, and fresh cinnamon twists, and a plate of biscuits still hot from the oven. Leonor was grey-haired, untalkative, unsmiling – but she showed her care in her cooking. She was the finest baker in the whole of Icthus: it was there that she put her patience, and her love.

She cut Mal an immense slice of cake. Gelifen nipped Mal in greeting, and then crouched over a bowl of full-fat milk, his long tail twitching, his wings fluttering with pleasure.

Leonor gave Mal a cup of hot spiced berry cordial. Leonor made it herself, spending hours bent over the stove, stirring until it was sharp and sweet at once, exactly as Mal loved it. The old woman sighed. 'That hair! It's a disaster. You should let me fix it.' She gently touched Mal's uneven fringe.

There was a knock on the door. Leonor went to answer it.

At the same moment the casapasaran suddenly began to shake in Mal's pocket. She took it out. It had been steady, pointing a little to the left, towards her bedroom. Now, though, the arrow twitched; it appeared to stutter, juddering back and forth – and then began to spin, slowly and then faster, until it was vibrating in her hand.

'It's broken!' she said to Gelifen. 'But I only just bought it!'

She stepped backwards to look at it in the light – and so it was that when the door burst open and the murderer lunged into the kitchen, she was far enough away to miss the sweep of his knife-hand as it came down.

Leonor, who had been pushed roughly aside, screamed. She ran into the kitchen, and threw herself in front of her great-niece.

'Get away!' she cried. 'Get away from her!'

The man let out a hiss of surprise. He lunged and swiped again, this time at Leonor.

There was a terrible cry, and her great-aunt looked down at her chest. Red was flooding across the front of her apron. She dropped to the ground. 'Mal! Run!'

'Leonor!' Mal screamed, and darted towards her. Gelifen screamed too, a high animal shriek, and flew at the man, talons outstretched. The man cut at Gelifen in mid-air, twisted, and sprang at Mal. The tip of his knife slashed down the back of the coat, grazing her skin. She grabbed the edge of the table and upturned it, scattering glass and crockery across the floor.

Mal seized Gelifen and sprinted out of the house and into the garden. The wind still blew. She ran forward, spread out the coat, and tried to leap into the air – but the wind billowed through the cut in the back. She tried again, her breath shuddering in her chest. Flight did not come.

Earthbound then. There was sour metallic dread in her mouth, dread in her blood, taking over her chest. She could not breathe. Where? She ran first towards the garden shed, then, changing her mind, towards the wall at the end of the garden.

The murderer came round the corner of the house. He was tall, but there were men in town who were taller; there were none, though, whose faces were so hard. She had no doubt he would kill her.

For one moment, they stood and stared at each other. He called out to her. 'Stop! Stop!'

She turned and made for the wall. He was just a few steps behind. She turned to look and saw his knife thrust towards her – she swerved – she could hear him breathing.

There was a cry from behind him, and he twisted: Leonor, her red-stained hand pressed to her chest, came round the corner of the house, holding the firewood axe.

Her voice came out high and thin and burning: 'Get away from my girl!' She threw the axe, overhand, as hard and straight as she could: not hard, not straight, but with an awesome fury.

The murderer roared and ducked, and it caught him a blow with the blunt edge against his shoulder. He ran at the woman, who staggered back behind the house. There was a high shriek, and then silence.

Mal stumbled, winded with horror, and fell forwards on to her hands and knees. Her blood turned to concrete. She tried to scream, but it came out a croak. There was no breath in her lungs.

Gelifen pecked at her, trying to shake her. Mal hauled in breath; it tasted of acid. She forced herself to run. She reached the wall and clambered up it, the stones cutting into her hands and Gelifen clinging to her back. She stood at the top, looking down at the river roaring below her. In the far-off distance, she saw a unicorn grazing at its bank, and a green herd of rata-toskas. Even further away, a longma swept down to drink – too far to help. Close by, three little shrew-like creatures swam up the river, against the current. If only, she thought, she could just fly, up and out of this nightmare.

'There's a river on the other side,' she called out to the man. 'If you come one step closer I'll jump. It has lavellans in it. They'll kill you if you follow me.'

'They'll kill you too. Come down.'

'They might not. They know me.' Panic and horror and misery had taken hold of her, but her numb lips formed words, tried to keep him talking. 'Tell me why you're here and then – then I'll come down, OK?'

The man snorted. 'I'm not paid to make conversation.'

'What are you paid for then? And who paid you? *Why are you doing this?*'

The murderer's eyes flicked over her, and she could feel his contempt. 'Have you noticed the creatures dying? The earth drying? The glimourie failing? It's a sign of his power.' The murderer was breathing hard, moving closer. 'He will give everything, he says, to the men who join him early: those who join him now, before his rise. I have lost enough times. I am choosing now to win.'

'But none of that has anything to do with me!'

'He told me to find you. He sent me a message: find the flying girl. Now come down.'

'Who? Who is *he?*'

The murderer shook his head. For a moment, dread passed over his face. He set his hands on the wall, his fingers searching for handholds. Mal looked down at the river. It was fast – fast enough to toss her against the stones below. A lavellan looked up at her. Its small poison teeth were bared.

Her voice came out high, and desperate. 'Wait! What have the dying creatures – and the glimourie – got to do with me?'

He looked at her, and his eyes were hungry. 'They have *everything* to do with you.' He hauled himself on top of the wall.

She held Gelifen tight to her chest. The man stepped closer. His knife was in his hand.

Mal jumped.

She dropped eight feet into the water. The surface closed over her. She saw, underwater, sudden darting flecks of phosphorescence. It was ice-cold and churning; she braced to be thrown against the rocks, or to feel the bite of the lavellan on her face. Gelifen was torn from her grasp. Then there was only water, roaring past her, and a great jag of terror. And then nothing.

THE STAMPEDE

The sun had come out and it was very fine, as Christopher half walked, half ran up the hill. Fine, at least, until the ground began to quake.

He was nearing the top of the slope with Goose at his heels when she stopped short and gave an anxious whine. He bent to stroke her. 'What is it, girl? Are you hurt?'

Then he heard it: a rumbling, deep in the earth. He bent to touch the ground, and felt it shake under his palm. An earthquake? Goose's hackles rose along her back and she began to bark in high, terrified yaps.

Then there was a wild whinnying cry, and a huge green horse covered in shining scales thundered straight towards him. Christopher yelled. He tried to pull at Goose, but she was rooted to the spot, flattened against the dirt, so he lifted her in his arms and ran. She was heavy, but terror gave him speed; he

37

darted behind an oak tree and crouched, gasping for breath, over Goose.

The horse tore down the hill, its eyes wide and rolling. He could see the muscular gleam of its green-scaled flank as it came. As he watched, it spread vast scaled wings and took flight, flapping above the treeline.

And then came the stampede. First a cascade of shrew-like creatures with canine fangs, soaking wet, a dozen of them, and then a great horde of what looked like large green-horned squirrels, wailing and crying out – 'Run! Run!' – as they went. Goose struggled in his arms, but he held on to her.

It was impossible. Wild incredulity rose in him – had he been drugged? He pinched viciously at his skin to wake himself, but his nail drew blood and he felt the pain course down his arm. Fear roared through his body.

Before he could move, a high neighing rang out, and down the hill galloped a horse with a horn of pure-bright silver. It went charging past him; its tail, white as moonlight, was tangled with weeds.

'A *unicorn*,' he breathed to Goose.

As fast as they had come, the creatures had gone, vanished into the trees below. Christopher's hands and feet were ice-cold despite the sun. He felt winded with shock.

His first instinct was to sprint home to his grandfather. But then from the top of the hill there came a noise: a high, peeping cry. It was a desperate, terrible noise: the noise of something struggling to live.

He hesitated only for a second; and then he sprinted, faster than he had ever run, up the forbidden hill.

He could not have said what he expected to find – but it was not what he saw. The hill flattened at its peak into a small lake. It was forty paces across, and a blue so dark it was almost black. In the centre of the lake, something was drowning. The water was churning and white, and something with wings and a tail was flailing. Shrill peeps of terror came from it.

Christopher didn't stop to let himself think; if he stopped to think, the madness and impossibility of it would envelop him. He threw his coat and jumper on to the grass, and tore his shoes off and ran in.

The cold was like leaping into a brick wall: it kicked the breath from his lungs. The creature let out another desperate cry. Its short forelegs weren't made for water, and though its wings flailed hard, it was going under.

The water was deep, and Christopher swam fast. The splash of the lake was in his eyes, and when he reached the place where he thought the creature had been, he couldn't see it.

He spat out water tasting of mud and silt, and dived under again, deeper. And there it was: its eyes and beak closed, sinking fast. Christopher's stomach lurched and he kicked downward – the pressure tightening on his ears, the cold burning on his skin – and seized it by the back leg.

He shot to the surface and gasped for breath – but the creature did not breathe. He waded out of the lake, grabbed his coat and wrapped the creature in it. Its eyes opened, and it vomited a quantity of half-digested whatever-it-ate on to his sleeve.

Christopher let out a burst of laughter that was also a choke. 'Nice', he said. 'Thanks for that.' His teeth were chattering so badly he could barely speak. But his whole body was shining with relief, and with a dizzying, unbelieving awe. Because he knew now what he was holding in his arms.

The creature had the hind legs of a lion cub, and the wings and forelegs of an eagle, white-feathered and tufty. His face was that of a young bird, with large green eyes, but his ears were like a horse's, brown and pointed and much too big for him.

'You're a griffin', Christopher said.

There was no question but that it was real, because it twisted in the coat and scraped panickily at him with two different kinds of claws. The lion's hind claws were sharper, and dug further into his skin, and despite the pain Christopher's heart gave a bound.

'Hey, hey!' There was blood coming from somewhere; warm, new blood. He caught with difficulty at the griffin's forelegs. He lifted its tail and turned over its soft hind paws in his hands. There it was: a deep cut on its left back leg. He wrapped his sock around it. The creature writhed in protest, slippery as an otter, but did not bite.

He pulled his shoes back on to his soaking wet feet. His fingertips were blue with cold. Then he picked up the griffin again. 'Let's get you somewhere warm, quick', he said.

The griffin seemed soothed by the sound of his voice. It

nestled its beak into the crook of his elbow. It smelt of wet fur and wet feathers, and under it the musky, soft, growing smell of young animal. It was, he thought, the most beautiful thing he had ever seen in his life.

'I'll protect you,' he said. 'Don't panic. I won't let anything happen to you.' The creature bit him lightly on the thumb.

This was, some might say, a foolish and dangerous promise to make to any living thing, given the chaotic unpredictability of the world. But, equally, that's the thing about griffins: they are persuasive.

THE GUARDIAN'S SECRET

Most men, if their grandson burst into a room dripping water and clutching a mythical creature to their chest, would begin by asking questions. But Frank Aureate was not most men.

His grandfather was dozing in an armchair by the fire when Christopher flung open the door. He sat up, took in the scene – Christopher, blue at the lips and a wild look in his eyes, and the bundle in his arms, and Goose at his heels – and rose to his feet.

'I need a bandage,' said Christopher. 'For the griffin.'

'You went to the lochan then,' said Frank. 'To the lake. When you were told expressly not to.'

'I had to,' said Christopher, and he held out the bundle in his arms. 'He was drowning in it.' As fast as he could, he told his grandfather what he had seen.

Frank stood in the centre of the room, breathing hard, his

face full of unreadable calculations. Then he crossed to the kitchen. He came out with a glass of whisky and a roll of bandage. 'Give me the griffin. Go and shower, as hot and fast as you can, and come back down.'

When Christopher returned, Frank was tying off the end of a bandage around the hind flank of the griffin. There was a cup of hot chocolate by the fire.

'Come,' he said. 'Sit. You can feed him.' He looked very old, and his body creaked as he sat down. He gave Christopher the griffin, and a tin of sardines. 'Aye. So. I see that an explanation has become necessary.'

'But – there was a *unicorn*. Aren't you going to—'

He was quelled with a look from Frank that almost frightened him. '*Sit*,' said the old man. 'Listen.' It was a look that made clear, for a moment, the force his grandfather had once been; and still was, under the old paper skin and the crooked hands. 'It won't have gone far – there are fences. It's more important that you hear what I need to say.'

Christopher sat. He opened the tin of sardines, and the griffin pecked at his hand in excitement.

Frank sighed. 'I would've told you eventually, Christopher. But you're too young. Your father and I agreed on that.' He drank deeply from the whisky. 'We were going to wait till you were at least eighteen; your father was arguing for twenty-one, or twenty-five. In truth, I think he'd rather you never knew.'

'Tell me *what*? Never knew *what*?'

43

Frank took a key from his pocket and unlocked a tall wooden cupboard. From it he took another key. He took down from the wall the oil painting of the man in uniform.

'It really is a gargantuanly hideous picture. I chose it to hide the safe on the reckoning that nobody could possibly want to steal it.'

Christopher gave the griffin a sardine; it swallowed it whole, trying to take his fingers with it. 'Steady,' whispered Christopher. 'My fingers aren't on the menu, thanks.'

Behind the painting there was a metal safe. Frank Aureate unlocked it, and drew out a much-folded document and a small book. He thumped them both on the table, and unfolded the paper. Christopher leaned forward. It was a map, painted in exquisitely small brushstrokes on thick vellum.

'This is the Archipelago.'

Frank Aureate ran his fingers over the map, slowly, lovingly. 'Let me remember the words my mother used.' He drew breath. 'There's a secret place, Christopher, in our world – hidden from us, to keep it safe – where all the creatures of myth still live and thrive. The people who live there call it the Archipelago. It is thirty-four islands – some as large as Denmark, some as small as a town square. Across these islands, thousands of magical creatures roam, raise their young, grow old and die, and begin again. It's the last surviving magic place.'

'Magic? You can't really—' said Christopher, incredulity rising in his voice. Frank held up a hand.

'Stop. The world has always had magic in it, Christopher.

Aren't you holding a griffin in your arms? The magic grew with the Earth's first tree; from the tree it flowed into the soil, into the air and the water. In the Archipelago, they call it the glimourie.'

Christopher felt the weight of the griffin; its animal warmth. He gave it another sardine, and felt its small tongue flick against his fingers. 'And that's the magic? The glimourie?'

'Glimourie, aye. Or glamarie, some of the islanders call it. Glawmery, glamry, glim, glimt. It's all the same: it's the name they give the first magic. Long ago, it was everywhere. For thousands of years, magical creatures lived freely over the whole Earth. But gradually, as we humans began to build our civilisations, we realised we could use the creatures; that we could farm and kill and trap them, for the ease they could give our lives. And they became rarer, and rarer. It's not a story to make you admire humanity. But there was one place – a cluster of islands, in the North Atlantic Ocean – where that first tree grew. There the glimourie in the Earth and air was at its strongest. And one day, a few thousand years ago, those islands disappeared.'

'Disappeared?'

'Aye. And everywhere else in the world the creatures died out, as we hunted them to extinction. As the next thousands of years passed, we forgot, slowly, that once the world had been lit by the shining of a unicorn, or the dragon's fire – and we came to believe that the true accounts we had were myth. Just children's stories. Nothing important. We're a forgetful people, humanity.'

'Where are the islands? The Arki– what did you call it?' The griffin tried to bury his beak in the tin; Christopher fended him off, and gave him the remaining fish.

'Ar-ki-pe-la-go. An old word, for a cluster of islands.'

'Where did they go?'

Frank's face shone: like the fire beside him, it glowed. 'That's the thing, boy. They're exactly where they always were.'

Something was rising in Christopher's body: a hot roar in his blood, from his face to the soles of his feet; a burning swell of excitement. And yet still – even with the griffin, who was scratching his feathered ear with his hind leg, heavy in his lap – it felt impossible. It felt *too much*. It was too much what he'd always longed to be true.

'But if they're there, why don't we know about them? With radar, and surveillance drones, and all that?'

'No boat can get close; the glimourie pushes them away, so gently that they never notice. In the same way planes can't fly overhead, but they never know it. It's unchartered and unchartable.'

The griffin seemed full now, and its eyes were fluttering with tiredness. He buried his beak under Christopher's red jumper, up against his chest, and Christopher stroked his tufty wings, calming him. He leaned over him to look at the map. 'Show me?'

Frank pointed. 'This one – Lithia – that's the largest, and has the densest population of humans. This one – Arkhe – is the furthest north: that's where that first tree grew. Down here,

46

to the south-east, are the wildest parts – where people live alongside dragons. About a dozen are inhabited by a mix of humans and creatures, the others by creatures alone.'

'Unicorns?'

'Unicorns, aye. There are huge herds – in the thousands – on the island of Ceretos, and on Atidina and Lithia.'

'Centaurs?'

'Yes, centaurs, on Antiok. And many, many more – all the less-known creatures that were in the stories of old – karkadanns and manticores, krakens and kappas and seabulls. It is a riotous, glorious place.'

Christopher's heart was beating so hard that the griffin, disturbed by its racing thump, backed out of the jumper and cast him a look. 'Is there any way to get there?'

'Not unless you know how.'

Christopher rocked backwards, dizzy. He looked up at the mustachioed Belgian. 'But – how do *you* know all this? And how do you have this map?'

The griffin clambered on to the cushion next to Christopher and closed his eyes. The old man's eyes, though, were very keen.

'Haven't you guessed? Because I am a guardian of the way through.'

'*You?*'

'No need to look so jaw-dropped,' Frank said drily. 'I was a strong young man before I was a weak old one, you know.' He smiled. 'Aye, me. Though you can't get there by boat, yet there are routes – at least one, and I believe there are more elsewhere in the world. The way opens once a year, for a single week, at the fourth full moon, when—'

'The lake! Is it the lake?'

'Exactly so. The lochan.' He pronounced it *lock-en*. 'At the bottom of the lochan – it's deep, that lake, a hundred feet and more – grows an ancient tree. Three thousand years it's been there, its branches spread underwater. It was grown from the seed of the apple of the Glimourie Tree. It is my job to protect it from theft, from ruin, from time. My Charlotte – your mother – would also have been a guardian. She –' and there was only a single second before he said – 'cannot, of course. So it will go to you.'

'To me?'

'To you. Did you ever wonder why animals flock to you?'

'I thought maybe it was ... I don't know, something in my skin. My smell.'

'That's not so far off the truth. They feel that you are a place of safety. Living so close to the waybetween, some small part of the glimourie has got in the blood of this family. When I was a boy, I would wake to a flock of crows on my doorstep every morning. They would bring me gifts – pins and buttons.'

Christopher put his hand to his necklace, and his grandfather smiled a dry smile.

'And your mother, Christopher – your lovely mother was suspended from school for keeping a nest of shrews in the pocket of her winter coat. There was an unreasonable fuss about fleas. It's a *pull*: between the guardian and living creatures.'

'But nobody told me!' He felt his astonishment turning to anger. 'Why didn't anybody tell me? All this time?'

'It was your father's idea.'

'But why should he get to decide?' To his shame, furious tears were rising in his eyes; he forced himself to push them down again. 'He doesn't trust me with *anything*! He never will! You said yourself! He wanted *never* to tell me.'

'*Wheesht*, Christopher. He's your father.' Frank handed him the book. 'Here. Take this. This is the Guardian's Bestiary. My great-great-grandfather began it; each generation adds to it. It's an account of some of the wild creatures of the Archipelago. Read it.'

Christopher's lungs and eyes were question marks. His heart beat like it was talking: as though it were saying, *What? What, how, what?* It was impossible that this was true.

'But ...' There were a thousand things he wanted to ask; a cacophony, rising in his throat. *Who else knew? How did it work? What did a guardian do?* So he said the most practical. 'It's not a full moon. There was no moon last night. But the griffin came through.'

'I know!' Frank folded up the map. He pinched the bridge of his nose, and the wrinkles on his face compressed and deepened and darkened. 'That's the root of my fear. The waybetween shouldn't be open. And there's worse too – I've heard stories, these last years.

'There is some darkness passing over the islands. Something corrosive, unknown and unseen. The creatures are dying.'

Christopher flinched towards the griffin, as if to protect it. 'Dying?'

'Aye. It seems – and only God knows how, because it should be impossible – that the glimourie is fading. And it's the glimourie that all magical creatures depend on. It's in everything – in the air, in the water, in the earth. But the creatures are suffocating in the ocean. There've been stories of longmas eating each other.'

'What's a longma?'

'A flying horse, bedecked with scales.'

'I saw one!'

Frank nodded. 'You said. I'll fetch it. That'll be a job, that will. Longmas are in our oldest tales, but they've been forgotten. They're related to dragons. But the worst is the griffins. I couldn't believe it when you came in, boy, with that bundle in your arms: there've been no sightings of griffins on the islands now for more than two years. I thought we'd lost them.'

Frank turned the map over in his hands. He touched it to his lips, and gave it to Christopher. 'Here. Study it. I wrote to your father, two years ago, to tell him; I thought he should know. He replied telling me not to write to him again. He was worried you'd see the letter. But something, somewhere in the Archipelago, has shaken the safety and the peace out of it. Something has gone darkly wrong. I don't know what, though I've been working in every way I know to find out. It's some-thing worth your fear, lad.'

THE DOG IN THE WATER

Half an hour later, Christopher had the griffin in his arms. He had wiped the coat sleeve clean of griffin vomit, and thrust the map deep into one of the pockets.

He was walking up the hill, as fast as the griffin would allow him to go, which was not fast. The griffin writhed and scratched in his arms. But if he set it down, it climbed up his ankle and dug its talons into his knee until he picked it up again.

'I'm trying to get you home!' he said to the griffin. 'But you're not exactly speeding things up, are you?'

'I need to find the smaller creatures, and the unicorn,' Frank had said. 'I may be a while. The unicorn will be simple – they crave mint, so she'll be easy to lure. But the others'll take some time, and then I'll have to take them up to the lochan to return them. Wait here and watch the griffin.' He took a jar of dried mint from the larder, and his walking stick from its place by the door. 'Don't leave the house – d'you hear me? God only knows what else might have come through. The griffin will be fine, as long as he sleeps.'

But shortly after Frank had limped out, the griffin had awoken. The creature's whole bony little body shook. He had refused to settle. He tore at the sofa cushion with his beak and claws, and, when Christopher picked him up, at his clothes and arms.

Fearing he was liable to be grated like a carrot, Christopher carried him to the door, and called – 'Frank? Grandfather?' – but the old man was nowhere in sight. He could be hours.

The griffin let out a cry, and launched himself into the air. He flew straight into a painting of a glum man on a glummer horse, put a claw through the man's nose and dropped to the windowsill, peeping in pain and fear.

'OK!' said Christopher. 'Stop! I'll take you back!'

The griffin appeared to understand. He returned to Christopher's feet, and bit hard on his shoe.

So it was that Christopher found himself walking up the hill, the griffin in his arms. The water of the lochan was dark, rippling in the breeze. The ground around the water was marked with chaos of hoof- and paw-prints.

Christopher looked around. The earth was still; no rumbling shook it. 'If I put you in the lochan,' he said to the griffin, 'will you know what to do?'

But as he spoke, the griffin froze, his ears flat against his skull.

'What is it?' said Christopher. And then he heard it too.

It was a shrill and hideous sound: metal screeching on metal. It was coming from the long grass and reeds at the water's edge.

Christopher looked around frantically for somewhere to hide the griffin. There was a big patch of bracken; he thrust the griffin into it, and the creature curled into a ball, quivering.

The noise came again. Slowly, stealthily, there stalked out of the reeds a creature as large as a wolf. It was black, built like a fighting dog, its teeth bared – but where it should have had ears it had two sparks of blue flame, and its breath, coming hard and fast, was a metallic rasp.

It crouched low in the grass. Christopher understood that twitch of the tail, that tense shifting of the hind legs. It was hunting. There was a limit, clearly, to the sympathy between himself and living creatures: the limit was here, and it had teeth.

White-hot fear flooded through him. Without moving his head, Christopher's eyes darted sideways. There was a stick, which would do as much damage as a toothpick. But there was a large rock at the edge of the lochan, sharp-angled and as big as his two fists.

He stepped towards the rock. The dog paced closer, low-slung and tail out. Its breath came again, like a shard of glass down a blackboard. Christopher crouched for the rock.

Instantly the dog leaped at him, its breath rising to a

screech as it sprang. Christopher ducked and rolled away, and as it shot past him he hurled the rock at it, hard, furious. It grazed skin off the creature's back flank – it twisted its head towards the wound – and a voice came from behind Christopher, high and terrified –

'The flames! You have to put out the flames!'

There was a girl, soaking wet, standing in the grass.

He heard, understood, bent to the water of the lochan – but she cried, 'Not water, idiot! It's a kludde! Earth – wet earth!'

She ran to him and dug her hands into the wet soil of the lochan: he did the same. The kludde turned, hackles raised in fury. It sniffed. It stalked three slow steps towards them, its tail low and angry. The shrieking of its breath rose, piercing, agonising, reverberating across the hill. The creature sprang – and as it launched itself, Christopher hurled the soil.

One handful went wide, spattering on the grass, but the other caught the creature in the eye, mid-air, and on the left ear-like flame. The flame flickered and went out; and the creature thumped to the ground with a howl of rage and pain.

The girl ran shin-deep into the water and threw handful after handful. Some missed, but a spattering caught the right flame; Christopher threw again, and again, bending to kneel in the wet dirt and hurl mud at the creature.

The kludde stumbled, its eyes turning bloodshot, and gave a high thin cry. Then it dropped down with a harsh thud, its side bleeding into the weeds at the edge of the lake.

There was total silence. Even the birds were stunned into abnormal hush.

'Are you OK?' he said. She nodded; she was gasping for breath. She seemed winded.

Christopher stepped closer. The creature was not moving. He nudged it with his foot, half expecting it to turn and lunge at his leg. 'It's dead,' he said. And then: 'What would have happened if there was no wet earth?'

She swallowed, caught her breath. 'I've never seen one – but we'd have been eaten. Face first.'

'Face first? Is that deliberate – like, the face as a starter?'

'That's what I was taught. Legs as the main course, I guess. Toes for dessert.' Her eyes swept over the hillside, the forest, the house down below. 'Listen – please – I'm looking for a griffin,' she said. 'He's very young, and he'll be scared.'

Christopher's head was still swimming. He looked at her face, to see if she could be trusted with the griffin, the finest living thing he'd ever met. She was, he saw, raw with panic and with love. He nodded.

'He's here,' he said. 'He's OK.' He parted the bracken, and there was the griffin, which huddled, shaking, in the greenery. He stroked him between the ears – 'You're fine,' he whispered, 'you're safe' – and lifted him out.

'Gelifen!' She was small but strong, and she clutched the griffin to her chest so hard that it gave a shriek of pain and clawed at her face, drawing blood and leaving three red lines along her cheekbone.

55

'I'm sorry!' She spoke to the griffin, her face buried in the feathers atop its head. 'I didn't mean to hurt. I didn't know what to do. If you had died – I couldn't bear it.'

She softened her grip enough for the griffin to move, and he began pecking at her in joy: at her ears, shoulders, hands, fingertips.

'Thank you,' she said, 'for finding him.' All the creature's unease had vanished: he gave a guttural *burr* in his throat, a turbine of delight. Christopher saw that her olive skin was covered in tiny bite and scratch scars, on her hands and wrists, on her neck and cheek.

She was, he thought, about his age or a little younger, and a full head shorter. She had long black wet hair down her back, threaded with gold. She wore dark blue trousers and a blue jersey, which were grass-stained and mud-stained and something-that-looked-like-blood-stained. Her dark eyes had a ferocious kind of focus to them. She looked at him, her chin high.

'What's your name?' said the girl. He told her. She held the griffin close, and it rested the side of its head against her jaw. 'Are you the guardian?' There was hope in her voice. 'You are, right? I was taught the waybetween has a guardian?'

Christopher wanted to say yes – but he had no idea what it meant to be a guardian. So he said, with perfect truth, 'My grandfather is.'

The girl nodded. She pulled at the neck of her jersey, tucked the griffin inside, put back her shoulders. And then she spoke the most powerful and exhausting, the bravest, most exasperating and galvanic sentence in the human language.

Some sentences have the power to change everything. There are the usual suspects: I *love you*, I *hate you*, I'm *pregnant*, I'm *dying*, I *regret to tell you that this country is at war*. But the words with the greatest power to create both havoc and marvels are these:

'I need your help.'

PHOSPHORESCENCE

oth stood, still panting. He looked at her: the girl, and her
griffin. She was shaking; quivering with wet and some kind
of shock – something even more, he thought, than the kludde.
There was something vivid about her, something tremendous,
as if she might be about to erupt.

'What kind of help?'

She looked at him: a boy, tall, with lake water in his dark
hair, white skin covered in mud and kludde's blood. His fingertips were twitching with adrenalin. He looked, at that moment,
ready to do anything: face or fight anything.

'I need you to come with me. To the Archipelago.' And
then: 'My name's Mal. Mal Arvorian.'

'You're from the Archipelago?' He had assumed that
people from the islands would look different; wizard hats,
perhaps. Wands, at the very least.

She nodded. 'And I have to go back, right now. But ...' She swallowed. He knew that look; had seen it on his own face. She was deciding whether or not to tell the truth. 'If I go back alone now, I'll die.'

He stared. She had to be exaggerating, he thought, but there was no flicker of humour in her face. 'Are you serious?'

'There's a murderer, OK? And he's looking for me. He killed my great-aunt, and he tried to kill me. I can't go back alone. But if I don't go, Gelifen will die, and maybe I'll never get back home.' Imperiousness rose in her voice. 'So you have to come, all right?' Beneath the haughty tilt of her chin, her eyes filled with tears, and her lips shook. 'You have to.' Her voice cracked. 'You have to, you *have* to!'

'Come to fight a *murderer*? "Please come to tea, and by the way you have to fight to the death"? Why would I say yes to that?'

'I didn't say fight to the death! We could run. We could make a plan. Together.'

Christopher closed his eyes; he tried to force his head into sense. 'Why would anyone want to kill you?'

'I don't know.' And seeing his face, she said, louder, 'Honest, I don't know! I've done stuff that might make people annoyed, but not that would make them murder me. He's tall, and sort of blond. He looks normal; that's what was so frightening. He could have been a teacher, or a doctor.'

'Isn't there someone else who could help you?'

59

She shook her head, wordless.

'The waybetween isn't supposed to be open,' he said. 'What if I come and it closes behind me? What if I get stranded in the Archipelago forever?'

She didn't move, didn't answer. She only stood there, the griffin tucked inside her sweater, waiting.

Christopher turned and looked at the dark water of the lochan. His heart was beating hard. Deep in the centre, there was a flicker of green light.

He thought of what his grandfather would say when he returned to find both boy and griffin gone; of his confusion, and anger. He had left no note. He thought of the fury and fear of his father.

'Quick! I have to go, right now,' said Mal. 'I can't stay here – Gelifen will die. Creatures need the glimourie. Will you come?' Gelifen pecked at her skin, urgent, panicky.

Christopher ran his thumb over the map in his pocket. Enchanted islands; unicorns, and krakens, and gold-horned hares. And the pushed-down-out-of-sight, what-if, hope-waiting portion of Christopher's heart rose up in his chest, and he felt it beating double time under his skin.

'Yes,' he said. 'OK. I'll come.'

She exhaled with a great rush, as if she'd been holding her breath. 'This way then. Quick.'

She waded into the water, splashing. Christopher took one last look around the hilltop, and one last glance towards his grandfather's house, and then he followed her. It was madness, extraordinary, impossible, he thought; he had woken that morning, pulled on his jeans and slung his crows' string around his neck with no inkling that he was going to an enchanted island.

Together, they swam out into the centre of the lake. 'We take a breath,' she said. 'A huge breath, all right? Fill your lungs. Now!' Together, they took a breath. Together, they kicked beneath the surface, swimming down, deeper and deeper: the lake seemed to have no end. His lungs were screaming when he saw it: amid the mud and reeds, a sudden flash of green; a small scrap of phosphorescence.

She turned in the water, her eyes open, her cheeks distended with the effort of holding her breath, and held out her left hand. He took it. Her right hand reached out, and she touched the spark of phosphorescent light.

ARCHIPELAGO

There was a crushing in his chest, as if he were being compressed under an opera house – and then suddenly he was in deep rushing water. He hadn't expected it, after the stillness of the lake – he was pulled along with the current; a rock struck him on the chest. He kicked to the surface, heaving for breath. Mal burst from under the water next to him and they swam side by side to the bank. She smiled at him as they hauled themselves up it – a brief flash of teeth, effortful but gallant – and tried to wring the water from her clothes. She looked at the wall that rose from the bank, and her hands began shaking.

Above their heads, three birds flew; eagle-sized and fire-red, with tails a foot long. He recognised them, instantly, for what they were.

'Phoenixes,' he said. The sight made his skin sting with

astonishment. His grandfather had been neither mad nor lying. He had told the clean, sharp, astonishing truth. This was the Archipelago.

'Yes! Leonor says—' but she stopped, and swallowed. She started again. 'That's my house, on the other side of the wall. I don't know if the – if the murderer's still there. But there's only one way out – back over the wall and through the garden. There are fields on the other side of the house, leading to a forest.'

'Why can't we just swim downriver, and find another way out?'

'The river's full of lavellans. We wouldn't make it five minutes in the water. This is the only way. And I need to see if … if Leonor's alive.'

He approached the wall, dripping, and climbed until he could just see over the top. There was a lawn, flowers, a rake, a willow tree. No murderer. But just as he breathed a sigh of relief, there was a movement in the house. A figure was walking swiftly past a top-floor window, and its face was contorted with anger.

He dropped down. 'He's in your house! Upstairs.'

A short, sharp wail, immediately smothered, broke from her. She pressed her fist to her mouth. He could see her fighting her terror; he tried to think.

'He doesn't know I'm here,' said Christopher. 'He thinks you're alone, doesn't he?'

'Yes. Me and Gelifen. He tried to kill Gelifen too.'

'So if we can't run, then we'll have to do something else …'

'Go on.'

'Take him by surprise. But ... we'd need some kind of bait.'

She looked from the griffin, to the wall, to Christopher. She swallowed, and clenched her fists; he did not know, yet, how characteristic it was of her. She was summoning bravery.

She tried to make her face into something confident and unconcerned. 'I'll be the bait.'

She crossed the lawn slowly, her step steady, her eyes down. She was wet, and her face was hidden by her hair. Her body looked fragile and defeated.

She reached two wooden chairs, partway up the garden, surrounded by flowers. She sank on to one. She curled up her knees; she looked very small.

In the house, the figure turned to the lawn, and then stiffened like a hunting dog. He disappeared from the window.

Her face, behind the curtain of her hair, could not be seen from the house. This was just as well: her face had large fear in it, but also fury, and knives, and ... *ready*. She glanced once at the willow tree, and gave what was clearly an attempt at a reassuring nod, and then away.

Christopher crouched in the willow tree, breathing hard. Gelifen, stowed above him among the leaves, gave a soft, strangled peep.

The man appeared at the corner of the house. Mal did not look up. It was as though she had not seen him. The man

64

drew his knife, as long as the girl's arm. The side of his mouth lifted, half smile, half rage. Then, silent, feet like a cat, he launched himself across the lawn –

And Christopher exploded from the tree. He sprinted to the rake, snatched it up and swung it as he ran. It connected with the murderer's shoulder just as he reached Mal. The man turned with a hiss and jabbed at Christopher with his knife.

It grazed his arm and Christopher jumped backwards, and swung again. The rake missed the man's head but collided with the knife and sent it flying. The man jerked the rake from Christopher's hands and in the same movement swung the end upwards, so that the wood cracked against Christopher's temple. Christopher staggered sideways, his vision blurred, a roaring in his ears.

The man seized hold of Mal, hard around the torso, and turned to stride up the garden. She screamed, and kicked, but he only gave a grunt. She sank her teeth into his jaw, and hung on. The murderer screamed, pushing at her neck to get her off.

Christopher ran to the garden chair. Breathing hard, he focused his whole strength on his one single chance: he swung the chair through the air in a great arc. He felt it make contact with a horrible thud.

The man fell, and Mal fell too. She scrambled away from him on her hands and knees, spitting, scrubbing at her mouth. Christopher helped her to her feet. Gelifen half flew, half ran over the lawn and across the flower bed, trampling flowers as he came.

Together they looked down at the man, lying inert on the grass.

'Is he ... ?' said Mal.

'Dead? I don't think so. No. He's breathing.'

'Should we – kill him?'

'No.' Horror for what they'd done was rising in Christopher. 'Do you have any rope?'

She ran into the house, and came back with a two-foot length of thin, fraying rope. She looked sick, colours gone haywire, red around the eyes and blue-white around the lips. 'This is all we had. I took all the money in the house too. Leonor used to hide it under the bathroom sink, in a soap tin.' Mal swallowed. 'She was there. I covered her with her favourite blanket.'

The rope wasn't long enough, and his hands were shaking, but he did what he could, tying the man's hands behind his back. He stepped back, and she leaned over the man to tighten the knot, pulling at the rope with a set face, her teeth bared.

'Come on,' he said. 'We need to run.'

THE ARRIVAL OF UNICORNS

They ran, the griffin in Mal's arms, through a field, and on to one with wheat, and another of grass, in which grazed a number of very small green-faced sheep, all of which – Christopher did a double take – were attached with tendrils to a green stalk. It was growing dark. Mal stumbled, and he caught her by the elbow.

'Gelifen,' she panted. 'He's heavy.'

'Shall I take him?'

'No!' she said. 'You can't. I need to carry him. He needs to be close to me.'

He saw the pain still etched into her face, and understood. It was she, rather, who needed to be close to the little griffin, whose warmth was radiating through his soft fur and feathers, and whose eyes watched her with a steady trusting gaze.

'All right. But we're going too slow. That rope won't hold him for long – come on.' He held out a hand, towards the one not clasped around the griffin's body, and she put her palm in his. He pulled, and it did help: they went faster, field after field, running through the long grass in the fading light.

'I can't see him,' said Mal, peering back in the dimness.

But Christopher barely heard her. His eyes were wide. Every drop of fear vanished, for one astonishing moment, from his body.

Ahead of him, emerging from the wood in the dusk like a cluster of ambulant stars, came a herd of unicorns.

Some were pure white, some white with silver manes, some silver with speckles of white across the neck and flank. The horns of the largest were as long as a walking stick, and opalescent. The horns on the smaller unicorns looked like solid silver.

They came towards him, trot-walk. He counted, fast: thirty-two of them. He had never in his life seen anything so shining.

'Their sense of smell's very sharp,' said Mal. Her voice was awed. 'They must've smelt something.'

What they had smelt was Christopher. Like the squirrels, and the cats and swans and foxes in London, they came galloping to him, clustering round, surrounding him and Mal in a great press of dazzling white bodies.

One unicorn, pure white with a silver blaze to its face, bent its soft white muzzle to his side. It tried to burrow its face into his coat, into his neckline, next to his skin. He ducked his head out of the way of its horn and stroked its long blaze.

'I've never seen anything like them,' he breathed.

'Of course you haven't,' Mal said. She spoke softly, running her hand along a unicorn's neck. 'There *is* nothing like them.'

He wanted to give the unicorn something: some kind of gift in return for its trust. Swiftly Christopher searched his pockets. The inside pocket had the map, damp, and half a packet of Polo mints. His grandfather had said that unicorns had a taste for mint. Quickly he tore open the pack and held them out in one hand. The unicorn dipped its mouth and sucked them from his palm, leaving it wet with unicorn spit.

Then it touched its muzzle to his face, and breathed. Christopher felt the warmth of it on his skin; it smelt of mint and animal and something else, something magnificently wild: the smell, he thought, of glimourie. It gave him a great swell of courage. It made him want to yell, or bite something.

But Mal suddenly gave a horrified cry. Christopher turned: the man with the knife stood at the far edge of the field.

'Run!'

But the unicorns, instead of parting, closed in around them, encircling them, butting against Christopher's chest with their faces. He pushed against them.

'Let us through!' he said.

'Christopher!' said Mal. 'They're letting us ride them.'

'Are you sure?' He looked at the tips of their horns: they were sharp as daggers. But they nudged their bodies against him, urgent. 'I think it's possible this is just a really vivid hallu-cination,' he said. 'But – yes. OK.'

She tried to climb up, Gelifen still in her arms, and slipped down. He bent and intermeshed his fingers. She set her dirty boot in his hands, and he heaved upwards, and she was up atop a pure-silver youngster.

He gripped the nearest unicorn around the neck, and half jumped, half scrambled on to its back. The unicorn reared up. Christopher dug his fingers into the white mane, and with a chorus of whinnies the whole herd took off at a gallop into the forest.

Tree branches whipped past them. He saw among the galloping herd three foals, their small flanks sweating with the effort of speed. Their coats were pure gold.

There was a shout behind them. Invisible, somewhere in the dark trees, the man with the knife cried out, his roar of fury echoing through the wood.

The trees thinned, and they burst out on to springy turf. The moon had risen, and ahead of them Christopher could see a cliff and the sea. The wind was growing, and the waves were high and violent. There were two ships, just dots on the horizon, and, much closer in, a single boat, its lamps lit for the evening, was making its way through the water, keeping as tight to the shore as depth allowed. Its name, rising and falling in the waves, was Neverfear.

With a great whinnying, the herd came to an abrupt stop, rearing and snorting. None would take a step closer to the cliff edge. Christopher swung down from the unicorn and stretched out his arms to help Mal and Gelifen. She bowed to the unicorns, so he did too – he'd never bowed to anyone before – a lowering of his head, and the unicorns vanished back into the wood.

'He's still coming!' she said. Fear was layered on fear across her face.

There was an overhang to the cliff, up ahead. It stuck out over the water, in a jagged spit. There were rocks immediately below. 'We need to get off the island. We're going to have to jump,' he said.

'Into the sea? We'll drown!'

'We could climb down the cliff edge.' He turned back towards the wood – thinking of the ivy he'd seen, thinking he could make a rope – when there was a crack behind them in the dark of the forest. The murderer and the knife, running through the thicket. They could hear him stumble, and gasp, and there was spitting and swearing. He was clearly in pain – but he was terrifyingly fast.

'There's no time!' she said.

'Then we'll have to jump on to that boat.'

'We'll break all our bones,' she said.

'We might. But look where the sail curls down from the mast.' Christopher pointed. 'There's almost an acre of sail to break our fall. If we jump out far enough, we'll fall against sailcloth and canvas.'

'*And what if we miss?*' The terror of the day had knocked the confidence from her. She tore at her lip with her teeth.

'Just make sure you don't miss! It's not that far down.' A lie. 'It's break our bones or be murdered, Mal.' He made his voice harsh, deliberately, to cut through her fear. 'It isn't a joke.'

She clenched her fists. 'It'll have to be Gelifen first. If I jump with him I'll land on him.'

'Quickly then!' His ears were straining for sounds from the forest.

'I *am*!' She whispered in the creature's ear and he gave a soft call in response. Then she swallowed – and threw Gelifen out and over the water.

'Fly, Gelifen! You have to *fly*!' The creature was bewildered, and half flew and half plummeted downwards, not close enough to the sail, landing with a thud on the wood of the boat.

She leaned over the edge, the dirt crumbling, trying to see the griffin in the dusk. 'He's not moving!'

'Then we need to get down to him. Fast,' said Christopher.

Together, they backed away a few paces. 'One,' he said. 'Two.'

He looked behind him – and saw the undergrowth part, and a man's shadow emerge from the woods.

They both cried out, a roar of shock and fear. Together, they ran at the edge of the cliff. His foot left the earth, and Christopher's stomach dropped, every instinct screaming at him to jerk backwards, to grab at the rock – but his momentum hauled him out, and he was falling through the air, the wind in his eyes, blinding him.

Mal's flailing elbow connected with his brow – and then they both crashed into the sail, their fingernails tearing as they clawed at the canvas slide, desperately trying to grab a hold, grab at the rigging, grabbing at halyards and reef points – anything to break their fall. With an agonising crash, they landed against the deck.

THE *NEVERFEAR*

You cannot expect to launch yourself out of a clear sky into someone else's life – and even more so, on to their boat – and hope they do not notice. The owner of the boat did notice. He was the diametric opposite of pleased.

'What, by the Immortal, is this?'

The man who stood above them was the kind of vast that makes other large men look petite and ballerina-esque. He had dark stubble, a gold earring in each ear and a burn mark on the left side of his neck. There were lines etched deep across his face, laid on it by the sea.

'What is this rainfall of children? Did I go sailing just to have storms of infants cascading down my sails at me?'

Christopher scrambled to his feet, and Gelifen, slightly dazed, clawed his way to hide in Mal's coat, and they stood staring around them. The sailing boat was large, mahogany wood worn black by time, with a cabin that led below deck. Its brass fittings were spiky with green rust, but it moved fast through the dark water. A second sailor, a compact grey-bearded man in his sixties, stared at them open-mouthed, a screwdriver in his hand.

'I'm sorry,' Mal said. 'We had—'

'*Sorry?*' The larger man breathed hard and angry on them, and his breath had whisky on it. '*Sorry* is for farting near the fruitbowl, girl! Sorry isn't good enough when you come erupting over the horizon like a pair of wingless chickens! You could've broken my cargo, you could have torn my sails – you could have cost me thousands.'

Mal was flushing bright red, a scarlet that rose up to her hairline. 'I don't know what else to say! And—'

'It's not – what we would have chosen to do,' said Christopher. He was still winded, and his words came out jagged. 'If we'd – had a choice – we wouldn't have – leaped off a cliff.' The man turned his bloodshot eyes on him, and he felt himself grow hot under their burning scepticism. 'But we had to – because ...'

'A man was trying to kill us!' finished Mal. 'Up there.'

Christopher looked back up at the cliff, but the murderer had vanished.

'And yet I see nobody.' The man gestured upwards; he had, Christopher saw, a bandage on one huge, scarred hand, heavily bloodstained. It did not make him look more welcoming. 'So why should I believe you?'

Mal was staring at the man with sudden recognition.

'I've seen you before!' she said. 'At the Sailsman's. I was there!'

'That's not a recommendation,' said the man. 'Lionel Holbyne is half-criminal, half-haircut. I wouldn't trust him further than I could throw him. In fact, considerably less far. Explain yourselves. *Now*.'

They exchanged looks. Mal nodded the smallest vestige of a nod. So together they told the story, talking over each other, talking fast; the whole truth, with nothing changed.

The man listened. As he listened, he sucked from a hip-flask, three long gulps that emptied it. He belched. 'And this man – this so-called murderer – what did he look like?'

'He was tall and white, with blondish-brown hair,' said Mal. 'And brown shoes.'

'Brown shoes are hardly helpful. Anything else?'

'No ... Wait, yes! He had this big mole on the side of his neck,' said Mal. 'I saw it up close. And he'll have a cut on his cheek now, from where I bit him.' She had one too, Christopher saw, from where she had embraced Gelifen too tightly; three curving lines, next to her eye and along her cheek. It had a rakish sort of beauty to it.

The man sucked on his teeth. 'A mole? Could be Adam Kavil. Could be Ricardo Mill. Both take on dirt for money; both too exhausted by life to care about a little more death. Mill would be better than Kavil; he's slower.' He tilted his rugged head and shifted his gaze out beyond them, looking past them, as if considering whether to share their danger or throw them to the sea.

'Can we just sleep here, on the boat? We wouldn't need beds – we could lie here, on the left,' said Christopher. There was a clear patch of deck, next to a pile of coiled ropes. And Mal would have slept, he could see, upright on a mountainside. 'You could put us on land somewhere tomorrow.' He did not want to walk any further that day. He had already come, he thought, so far: halfway across the known world, into the unknown one.

'No,' said the man. 'You'd attract the authorities – particularly with that griffin. I've no love for men with clipboards in their hands and regulations in their mouths.' He shook his head. 'I'll drop you at the first rock I see, and you can hail a boat when one passes.'

'Please,' said Mal. The look on her face was half-entreaty, half-glare. 'Just – *please*! For love of the Immortal, let us stay!'

Something in the last words made the man flinch; a ripple that ran across his brow and cheeks and jutting jaw. 'I should throw you to the nereids. But – just tonight – you can sleep on the deck.' He left them and slammed his way down into the cabin.

Christopher and Mal spoke in whispers. 'I think we're safe now,' he said. 'For the night, at least.'

'I don't know,' she said. 'He might still eat us.'

She said it louder than she meant to, and the man, returning with an armful of blankets, snorted, 'I don't eat children. No flavour. Take these.' He thrust the blankets at them. And to each he gave a fairing biscuit, spiced with cinnamon

77

and ginger. 'They're the last in the barrel, so don't ask for more, and don't wake me in the night.'

Sailors, Christopher knew, share the ship's biscuits grudgingly; when they do, it means something.

Mal dared to look at him, straight in the eye. 'Thank you,' she said.

He sighed. 'My name is Fidens Nighthand. You may call me Nighthand: I don't answer to Fidens. Yours?' They told him, and he nodded. 'The other crew are Warren and Ratwin. Treat them both politely, or Ratwin will bite you in your sleep.' Warren – the man with the screwdriver, who had since returned his jaw to its usual place and gone back to work – raised a hand, but they could see no sign of anybody else.

They didn't think of washing. They just lay down on the deck, and covered themselves with blankets. Gelifen tucked himself under Mal's chin. She whispered in the griffin's ear, something Christopher could not hear. Gelifen gave a soft peeping sound, and heat began to flow from him, hot and steady as a radiator.

After a few moments, Mal whispered: 'Are you sorry you came? Are you angry?'

Christopher looked up at the sky. The stars were so bright, here on the water, that he would have been able to read a book by their light. He was hungry, and still damp, and his whole body ached with exhaustion. But he had seen unicorns, and felt the cool of their horn against his palm. 'No. I'm not sorry.' He was the burning opposite of sorry.

'Good.' Mal's exhaustion was so great that her breath turned slow and rhythmic almost immediately, but Christopher lay for a while, looking up at the night sky. Far above, something – something vast, with massive wings – flew past the moon.

Mal cried out in her sleep; he turned to her, but she didn't wake.

Christopher's last thought was that he saw a creature – a large green shape, with a blunt, green, fur-covered horn – looking over at him with curious eyes, before he fell into a more exhausted sleep than any in his life. The boat advanced through the unknown ocean. But when he dreamed, it was of his father, searching for him with an angry and anguished face.

A STARK AND SHINING BLUE

The sky, when he woke, was blue. It was a blue so blue that it made all other blues look like they had been only the practice for this one shining sky.

The sea, when he crossed to lean over the rail of the boat, was a darker, deeper blue. There was no land in sight. But as he watched, there rose from the water a herd of horses; horses with long tails and fins, coloured silver and sea-green, leaping like dolphins from the water.

A thrill – of excitement and fear and high, burning astonishment – passed through him. He said it aloud, under his breath, testing the words: 'The glimourie. The Archipelago.'

The salt spray of the waves flew in his face; he caught some and rubbed it into his skin, his hands and wrists and forehead. That could count as washing for the day. He loved the taste of the sea.

Mal was sitting up when he came back. Sleep had healed some of her feverish look. She grinned at him – her eyes tipped up at the corners when she smiled – and began grooming the griffin's wings, who objected with both sets of claws.

'Ow! Gelifen! By the Immortal, that hurt! Here, you take him.'

She passed him to Christopher, and licked at the blood on her hands. The griffin clambered up on to his shoulder and began to chew at his hair. His beak was sharp, and he took off a good mouthful.

'If you're going to eat my fringe,' said Christopher to the griffin, 'you could at least eat it the same all the way round.'

'You look like you've been in a fight with a hairdresser,' said Mal.

'It's not half as bad as yours,' he said. 'Here, Gelifen – eat her eyebrows, go on,' and she ducked and snorted with laughter, and snot flew out of her nose on to her sleeve, and Gelifen ate it.

At that moment, Nighthand appeared. 'Breakfast,' he said. He rubbed bloodshot eyes. 'I have a headache the size of a western island. But I will not have it said that I don't feed my illegal stowaways.'

Nighthand's first mate, Warren, came up from the cabin, and peered across the wooden deck.

'Where's Ratwin?' he asked.

'She's fishing,' said Nighthand.'

Christopher stared about him for any sign of a woman with a fishing rod, but instead, over the edge of the boat there came a squirrel the size of a cat, with a blunt horn. It was carrying a large fish in its mouth, which it dropped at Nighthand's feet.

'This is Ratwin. She's our navigator. Ratwin, this is Christopher and Mal. They're our uninvited stowaways.'

The ratatoska gazed at them with bright brown eyes. 'If he welcomes you, I welcome you,' she said. She spoke very high and fast. 'If not, I bites you.' She looked at Nighthand. 'Which is it?'

'Neither.'

'I can think of no other options,' said the ratatoska. 'Shoulds I half-bites them?'

Warren's mouth twitched beneath its grey beard. 'Come to the cabin, Ratwin,' he said. 'I'll fry the fish.'

'She's a map reader,' said Nighthand, as they went down. 'Most ratatoskas collect gossip. Ratwin collects directions, compass points, water-routes. She knows the ways of the islands – where the krakens rise, and where the nereids swim – better than any sailor I've ever met. Come on. Breakfast.'

It was obvious that Nighthand believed in food. Down in the cabin there was a small table built into the wall, creaking with dishes. There was Ratwin's fresh-caught finch-fish, and toast with slabs of melting butter. There was yellow cake, cut into cubes and mixed with jam and eaten with a spoon; it was superbly good. Mal scraped the jam pot clean, then stole some off Christopher's plate and claimed she hadn't.

Nighthand ate with both hands, chewing with his mouth open. Gelifen sat on the table, and ate the fish from a plate of his own. He ate carefully, as if minding his table manners. Ratwin glared at him.

'Is the lion-bird to sit in my place, Nighthand? And the miniatures to eats my fish?'

'It's not for long, Ratwin. We'll drop them off as soon as we see land, and never see them again.'

'You *says* that, but your face says you're getting involved. *Focus*: we go to Archos, sell the ormolu pearls, pick up the sail-cloth, and go on to Paraspara. I have laid outs the route!'

Mal put on her haughtiest face. 'We don't need your help.'

Christopher flicked a fish bone at her. 'We do, actually.'

'The last person who asked for help,' said Ratwin, 'we threw them to the kappas, and the kappas ate them, and then the kappas got eaten by the kraken. So they got eaten twice. So you should beware.'

'Really? Is that true?' said Christopher.

'No,' said the ratatoska. She fixed him with a steady, unembarrassed gaze. 'But it could be.'

At last, Nighthand finished eating, and pushed aside his mug. It crashed to the floor, but he seemed untroubled. He faced them, and his look was serious. 'So, little unvarnished idiots,' he said. 'Tell me your plan.'

'I told you last night,' said Mal, 'that there's someone trying to kill me.' She had jam on her chin, but it did not stop her jutting it.

'And it has something to do,' Christopher said, 'with the dying of the creatures.'

'The creatures ... I've also seen it,' said Nighthand. 'I've seen that there has been a sudden surge of death. The sea smells different – thinner, weaker.'

'We sailed past a hippocamp last month, dead in the water at the Lithian peninsula,' said Warren.

'But in what possible way could that be connected to you?' Nighthand looked at Mal, his mouth thin.

'I don't know. I don't know, I don't know! That's the whole point! He only said it was; he didn't say how.'

'Why didn't you make him?'

Mal's face was getting tighter and more exhausted, and Christopher bristled. 'Well, he was trying to kill her, so opportunities for conversation were probably a bit limited,' he said.

'And now I have nothing else, and nobody.' Her voice, attempting to sound businesslike, shook. 'So I need to find out why the creatures are dying, and then I'll know why there's a murderer after me.'

'But what is the humans' *plan*?' said Ratwin. 'None of this is plan-shaped.'

'We'll go to the Azurial Senate,' said Mal.

'Why?' said Nighthand.

'Because they'll know what to do.'

'You think they know everything?'

'Not everything,' said Mal. 'But if anyone knows, they will.'

'What's the Senate?' said Christopher. 'Is it far?'

She looked startled that he didn't know. 'Well, it moves, of course.'

Warren, wiping his mouth on his scarf, grunted assent. 'Each island is ruled in its own way, by its own populations – creatures, humans, both. But the Azurial Senate travels across the islands. It's a court of law; one that all human Archipelagians acknowledge. It hears disputes, settles arguments, passes laws. It's been that way for hundreds of years.'

'And when he says it travels,' said Nighthand, 'he means the building itself moves. It flies through the sky, carried by harnessed longmas. It sets down in each town in turn. There is a square, built in each town, for the purpose.'

'Wouldn't it be easier for the people to travel, rather than the building?'

'It's always been that way,' said Warren. 'It's tradition. It says: the truth is always journeying, always ready to be summoned.'

'The bricks themselves were forged by the sphinxes from their own mountains. They have the heat of wisdom in them,' said Nighthand.

'So,' said Mal, 'I'll tell the Senate, if you'll take me there. And they'll know what to do.'

'I,' said Nighthand, 'am not going near that Senate.'

'There may have been a few irregularities,' said Warren, 'with some of Nighthand's trading in the past.'

'Smuggling?' said Christopher.

'Of course not!' said Nighthand. 'Don't be disgusting! Buying and selling without troubling to notify the authorities.'

'Smuggling,' said Ratwin, 'is a word we doesn't deign to use on this boat, please to remember.'

'Then Christopher and I will go,' said Mal.

'You will, will you? And what have you, boy from the Otherlands, got to do with it?'

'He's my friend, isn't he.' Mal didn't look at Christopher, but he could see the tops of her ears turning red. 'And he's a guardian,' said Mal. 'He protects the waybetween.'

Gelifen created a diversion at that moment, by peeing exuberantly all over the floor. Mal leaped up – 'You can't be angry with him, he's still very small!' – and carried him off to the deck. Ratwin stalked out in disgust.

In the silence that followed, Nighthand said to Warren: 'There's something about that child ... I don't know what. Not just that she survived a murderer – something else. There's a strange feeling she brings with her. It's like ...' There was an expression in his face that Christopher couldn't place. 'Do you feel it?'

Warren looked blank. 'I just tend the boat, Nighthand. I've no idea what you're talking about.'

Nighthand turned to Christopher. 'She's a stranger to you? You didn't know her before yesterday?'

Christopher shook his head.

'And yet she said you are her friend?'

'I saved her life. Sort of.'

'I have saved the lives of many people and not one is my friend. If anything, many of them seemed keen to avoid me later.'

Christopher took a gulp of his coffee, so that he did not

have to look at Nighthand's face. It was exactly as disgusting as his grandfather's coffee. 'She brought me here, to the Archipelago. And ...'

But Christopher didn't have the words, then, to explain what, nonetheless, he knew: that sometimes, if you are among the very lucky, a spark of understanding cuts like lightning across the space between two people. 'It's a defibrillator for the heart. And it toughens you. It nourishes you. And the word we've chosen for it (which is an insufficient word for being so abruptly upended in a new and finer place) is friendship.'

(He would never find it again, that kind of friendship. But once is enough. You need it only once – so that you may know what your human heart is capable of.)

So he said: 'Yeah. She's my friend.' He looked very stubborn, and very upright, with mud and the blood of the kludde still on his clothes, and Nighthand smiled half a smile, and felt old, and poured most of a bottle of brandy into his coffee.

'What's your plan then, Christopher?'

'I'll go with Mal. I'll go to this Senate.'

'And how,' said Nighthand, as he drank the brandied coffee in one gulp, 'do you plan to get inside, what with her being five foot tall and you never having set foot on the islands before?'

'We'll have to work it out, I guess, won't we. Unless you'll help us.'

Nighthand sighed. 'I'll drop you at the port town in Lithia, Bryn Tor, where the Senate is next to land. It's not on my way, but it's not too much of a detour. And then that's it for me, do you understand? I have business to do, and people to see, and you impose over-much already.'

But though his voice was gruff, there was a light in his bloodshot eyes.

THE FLYING SENATE

They docked at Bryn Tor the next day, in the late afternoon. Christopher stood on deck as they came into the port, leaning out to watch, Gelifen on his shoulder. Warren stayed on the boat, with a tin of tar paint and an enormous brush and Ratwin for company, and Nighthand led them into the city. They strode through densely packed cobbled streets, with sea-stained buildings rising alongside, glimmering in the fading light. It was alive with voices.

'It's a busy place', said Nighthand, 'there's hundreds of traders passing through each day. Raw silk from Ceretos, gold and voulay-drops from Antiok.' They passed stalls, small shops, clusters of children playing on the street. One small boy was absorbed in a ball game with a cat with luminescent fur. The cat shone as bright as a street lamp, despite its dusty paws. 'Atidina trades its crabs here, frozen on ice', said Nighthand,

'Doushian traders bring pegasan sails.' Christopher stared as a phoenix came to roost atop a lamp post; nobody looked twice.

Mal was on edge, looking around her shoulder at every step. It was difficult to blend in. Christopher was conscious of his jeans – but largely it was Nighthand's size and musculature, which attracted looks from both men and women, and his strategy for moving through crowds. The words 'Excuse me' didn't seem part of his vocabulary. He was his own battering ram: he put his head down and strode.

'Stand clear!' he called, as he rhinocerosed his way through a crowd of young men. 'We'll cut through the old fountain square to the market.'

The square was shady, surrounded by trees and small, brightly painted cafes, but Nighthand would not pause to allow Gelifen to eat the scraps left on the tables. As Mal and Christopher jogged to keep up with him, a herd of hares, all with shining gold horns, came lolloping up to them. They clustered around Christopher and Mal, and he bent down to admire them.

'What are they?' The creatures' enthusiasm was dangerous; there were golden horns against his legs, jabbing at his hands.

'Al-mirajes,' said Mal. 'I've never seen them act like this in my life. They're usually very shy.'

'Leave them, Christopher,' said Nighthand. One approached him, and he nudged it away with his toe. 'The Senate will be landing.'

Reluctantly, he did. The al-mirajes followed in a long line, single file, the tip of one al-miraj's horn just touching the white tail of the one in front. Grass shoots sprouted behind them, leaving a trail, to show where they had been. A young ratatoska crouched on a cafe windowsill saw it, and took note.

They dodged around a group of sailors into a marketplace. The al-mirajes still trailed Christopher. He looked around the market in wonder: there were dozens of fruit stalls, with barrows piled with giant plums the size of watermelons and tiny oranges the size of his thumbnail.

'Through that street to the Senate. I'll be off before I'm seen by any of those official bill-waving types', said Nighthand. 'I would wish you luck with telling the Senate your story, but it would be wasted. You, Mal, look like you cut your fringe with a rusty fish knife, and the griffin, Christopher, has eaten part of your jumper. Plus, you have a train of golden bunnies. Neither of you inspire confidence.' He nodded, a brusque up-down of the huge head. 'Goodbye then.'

He left before they could reply, crashing into a stall of oranges. Christopher winced, watching him go.

'What are you going to tell them?' said Christopher to Mal. 'At the Senate?'

'I'll tell the truth: that I've been going to the forest, right, for months now – and the soil and the creatures are dying. It's not just the murderer – it's something bigger and worse than him. I found the body of a seabull on the shore. It was a baby. They shouldn't die until they're at least a hundred years old. It was bloated with the water, as if it had drowned – but how could a seabull drown, when they're *born* in the water? I told my great-aunt, and she said I should leave things like that to the adults.'

As she spoke the clock began to strike.

'Come on!' said Mal. 'It'll be arriving.'

They ran into the square. The al-mirajes followed. The square was encircled with elegant metal lamp posts, their tops made to resemble apples, and spotted with a few ancient-looking trees. Stewards in suits were holding the crowds back from where the building would land. Christopher peered up, shading his eyes against the late-afternoon sun.

'There it is!' cried a voice in the crowd.

The building was a dot in the sky. It was circular, built in yellow sphinx-mined stone with a great domed roof, and with bright painted shutters battened safely closed over the windows.

Above it flew twenty winged and scaled horses, each wearing a harness and beating its wings against the sky. The al-mirajes saw them, took fright, and vanished into the crowd.

The building swung in the air. The longmas held it steady, until it was quite still, thirty feet above the square. Then, as carefully as if laying a baby to rest, they lowered the great stone building into place. It landed with such perfect precision that the branches of one of the trees came to a stop half an inch from a window, as if reaching out to stroke the glass.

Immediately a shout went up, and some of the crowd approached, briskly workmanlike. A man and a young woman climbed a ladder set into the wall, careless of the dizzying height, to the roof, where they began untying the longmas from their harnesses. They tossed meat into the air and the longmas swooped to snatch it from the sky, circled once, and disappeared.

'The longmas'll come back, when it's time to move on again', said Mal.

The shutters of the Senate building were being thrown open, and a host of men and women in overalls moved to attend to it, checking for damage from the journey.

Christopher peered inside the tallest of the windows. He saw a large, high-ceilinged room, lined with oil paintings – some of humans, some of creatures, some of both, side by side. He could just glimpse, at the far end, a row of six men and six women, some cloaked, some bare-headed, one with a tattooed line down her chin, sitting on twelve vast chairs. The largest chair was occupied by a man in his fifties, with dark brown skin, a scholar's gown and a formidable look of power. Most were grey-haired, faces lined with time and learning: they looked stately, implacable.

From the side of the building, a bell began to toll, and the great crush of people surged forwards and into the Senate.

Mal and Christopher tried to surge with the crowd – heads down, Gelifen hiding inside Mal's coat, as inconspicuous as they knew how to be – but were stopped by a senatorial guard in a dark jacket with golden braiding.

'No children.'

'But we need to come in!' said Mal.

'You see the sign?'

Painted above the door, in five different languages, were the words: *Due to the nature of the Senate's work, minors of any species are not permitted.*

Mal jutted her chin at the man so hard it looked as though she would surely dislocate her jaw. 'We're not minors, neither of us. We're just shorter than average adults. And we moisturise our faces every hour on the hour, so we don't wrinkle.'

The guard was neither convinced nor amused. He only signalled to another guard – this one taller, and older, who said, 'Step aside, please, or we'll have to arrest you. This is not a place to frivol with.'

They backed away, and made their way round the side of the curved building, coming to rest outside one of the windows. Mal had to stand on tiptoe and hold on to the windowsill to see. Inside, the rows of seats were filled, and the first session of the court had already begun.

A young woman was approaching the senators. She wore heavy, careful clothing: lace-up shoes, a pilling woollen skirt in dark grey. Her skin was brown, with a rich sheen to it. She wore her dark hair short, and that too gleamed in the light. She had a look of great seriousness as she stepped on to the wooden podium to speak.

If they strained, they could hear her voice, echoing through the room. 'Senators, my name is Irian Guinne.' Her voice was deep and musical. 'I'm a marine scientist – a scholar of the oceans, stationed at the University of Alquon in the west of Antiok.'

Christopher edged further round, to the window next to

the tree. This one was smaller, higher, positioned at the very back of the room and partially obscured by a green velvet curtain. To his surprise, it opened a few inches when he pushed it upwards.

Inside, the woman was still speaking. 'The waters are suffering. All those of us who study the ocean have seen it, but few people have believed us. The last year has been the worst. The life of the waters is dying: the nereids, the naiads, the mermaids. They're suffocating in the water. Whole families of mermaids in the northern regions, up near Tār, have been found dead. We believe it's a weakening in the glimourie. Northern creatures which don't migrate are coming south and west and east: krakens, and seabulls. An entire ecosystem is ruptured.'

'Mal!' hissed Christopher. 'Listen to this!'

Mal came running. Inside, Irian Guinne went on: 'We need manpower, to monitor what has been lost, across the whole Archipelago. We need the Senate to provide funding to send an expedition to the site of the griffin colony, to discover what it was that killed them.'

The Senator General spoke. 'Thank you for your testimony.' His voice was precise and sharp. 'We will take six months to consult with the relevant authorities, as is procedure, and let you know what is decided.'

They prised open the window further. It opened sound-lessly. A man in a cape glanced towards them from the benches inside, and they ducked down out of sight.

From inside, voices were rising. 'Six months will be too late!' said Irian Guinne.

Christopher mouthed to Mal, '*We could climb in.*'

'Madam, control yourself! We cannot strike terror into the Archipelagic population on the basis of one preliminary hearing. There would be chaos.'

Mal nodded. '*You first.*'

'There is already chaos! It is just that it's currently a chaos that humans are able to ignore. The creatures – creatures who rely on the glimourie – they are not afforded that luxury!'

The tree, he hoped, protected him from view. Christopher clambered up on to the sill, and, inch by inch, pulled the window higher. From here he could see the faces of the senators. There was true learning there, and a great sweep of understanding. But there was also a love of procedure, and resistance to change. There was arrogance etched on some of those mouths.

'Please!' Irian Guinne jumped down from the podium and pushed past the usher, striding towards the chairs. 'Let me show you! Let me show you what I have – this! Here!' She pulled something from her satchel. 'A dead starfish – a Karkaran starfish: they shine like stars for a hundred years! Dead, half-grown! The bone of a newborn hippocamp!'

'Madam! Do not approach the senators!'

Irian dropped to her knees. 'What if I knelt to you? If I begged you?'

Christopher manoeuvred himself, carefully, staying behind the curtain, readying himself to drop down into the room.

'Please remove this woman,' said another senator, a man with broad, bullish shoulders and a speckle of sweat on his pale skin.

'I can't go!' said Irian. 'Please – you're the last resort.'

'You'll be charged with contempt of justice.'

A guard approached her – but before Christopher could see more, he felt a hand close over his ankle, and a man's voice behind him said: 'Breaking and entering a law court, boy, is about as bad an idea as they come.'

Five minutes later, Mal and Christopher stood at the front of the Senate building, each in the grip of a senatorial guard. The guard's fingers dug deeply into Christopher's shoulder. A third man, his jacket pulled taut across his chest, had introduced himself without warmth as Gardan Carr, head of the Senate's protection. 'Take them to the Pavilion Cells,' he said, 'until you can find one of their parents.'

'You'll be looking for a while,' muttered Mal.

Carr glared at Mal, all thin lips and flared nostrils, but before he could say anything there was a commotion to their left. The great doors to the Senate building burst open, and Christopher spun round to see Irian Guinne being half dragged, half marched from the building by a fourth guard.

'By the Immortal! Take her too,' said Carr. 'Charge her with disruption of the court – and send out an alert for the kids. There must be someone responsible for them.'

And then – just as the day looked desperate, and the

whole world began to feel like sinking sand – a sudden voice rang out.

'Gentlemen!' The call came from across the square, and it was loud enough to shake the birds from the trees. 'A moment of your time.'

Nighthand was striding in a rapid circle around the square, pausing at each lamp post. Christopher's heart swept upwards, and he heard Mal gasp as she realised what he was doing, saw her face break into a sudden, scrunch-faced smile.

He came to rest at the lamp post closest to the guards. A small dagger, the blade barely six inches, was in his hand. With one easy swipe, he cut the lamp post nine-tenths of the way through.

He put out a single finger the size of a gun barrel, and flicked it. It keeled over with a shriek of metal and hit the next lamp post, which collapsed sideways into the next. Like dominos, one by one, the great circle of lamp posts fell. The noise was sensational: as if a brass orchestra were being sawn in half.

The guards were slack-jawed with shock, tonsils on view to the world.

Nighthand turned to the guards. 'I seem to have discovered,' he said, 'a design fault in your lamp posts.'

Carr recovered first. 'Jerim! Get him!'

Nighthand turned to Christopher, to Mal. 'I suggest this is the moment that the rest of you run.' And then, as they stared at the ruin around them: 'I said *run!*'

FIDENS NIGHTHAND'S PREFERRED DRINKING ESTABLISHMENT

They ran. Leaving Nighthand and the four men, Christopher, Mal and Irian Guinne sprinted out of the square and down one of the side-streets. The cluster of al-mirajes emerged from behind a kiosk selling newspapers and followed, green shoots erupting behind them.

Within a minute, Nighthand was with them, breathing hard. 'Don't dawdle', he said. 'I slowed their progress, but I didn't want to hurt them too seriously. There may be more coming. Quickly. Down here.' He led them out on to a small, twisting road. He turned to Irian. 'Who's this, with the librarian's shoes?'

'I'm a scientist of the sea', said Irian.

She spoke quietly, but it was the kind of voice that people hushed themselves to hear. Nighthand blinked a little on hearing it.

'And why were they arresting you?'

Swiftly she explained, and Nighthand grunted.

'I told the child the Senate would be no help. Walk faster. And keep your eyes out. If your murderer saw you jump on to my boat, he'll know where it's docked by now.'

A flash of fear passed across Mal's face. 'But how?'

'Coastguard reports. You have to register, on arrival. I tried to avoid it, but it was impossible without causing more havoc and mayhem than I felt in the mood for.'

'Really?' said Irian. 'You didn't have to register private boats the last time I was here.'

'New law. There have been too many attacks at sea; they're trying to keep better records.' He glanced behind him, and led them down a dark side-street, cobbled and high-walled. 'Water-creatures attacking ships. Gargouilles, in some places, and a bridgi.' Then, seeing Christopher's face: 'It's a kind of shark; it sucks ships down beneath the water. There never used to be many – one or two a year, perhaps. But the numbers are growing. This way.'

Irian walked swiftly beside Christopher. She had a satchel slung over one shoulder, but she walked upright, and fast. Her eyes were very dark, with silver flecks in the brown irises.

'What will you do now?' he asked her.

'That's a fair question,' she said. 'I planned to go back to my research post this evening, by the night ferry. But that was only if I was successful. Now – I don't know. What good is the research, if no one will listen?'

Nighthand turned to look at her.

'Those shoes,' he said to the woman. He spoke entirely without malice. 'Explain them to me. Did you lose some kind of bet?'

She laughed. Christopher couldn't tell if she was hurt; and if she was, she hid it well. 'Ah! I tend to go barefoot at home,' she said. 'But these are comfortable enough, and cheap. And they stop people from looking at me, which I like.'

'Why?'

'It's easier to think when I'm not watched. And thinking's what I care about.'

The streets got narrower, and less well lit, the further Nighthand led them. He pushed open a door in a wall. 'In here. You too,' he said to Irian. 'The Naiad's Tail. My favourite sot.'

A sot, it seemed, was like a pub back home, Christopher thought. It was small, with warm wood-panelled walls and low lighting. There were clusters of drinkers, mostly older fish-ermen and -women, and a piano. A small man sat at it, playing something slow and low on the keys without looking at his hands. In place of sheet music, he had a novel propped up. Every now and then he licked a finger and turned the page.

Nighthand gestured to the barmaid, who cast him a nod. 'The usual, Felia, if you would.'

They found an empty table in the back of the room. People turned to stare as they made their way to it, and Christopher heard a murmur – 'Is that a *griffin*?' – but Mal kept her protective hand on Gelifen's claws, and the griffin kept his head buried in her armpit.

As they sat down, a small, sleek-furred, red-brown creature – something that looked like a fox the size of a small mouse, with a long tail that forked in two – came out from behind the bar and sniffed at Christopher's ankles.

'It's a kanko!' said Mal. Her face, tight since their encounter with the Senate, lightened, and she grinned at him. 'Lightfoxes! They're lucky – I can't remember how, exactly, but they are.'

'Take care, Christopher,' said Nighthand. 'They like to build their nest on living things: on the heads of the warrior boars, or in the hair of people.'

Irian smiled. 'My cousin woke up with kankos trying to crawl into her ears and make a nest there. So watch out for your earholes.'

The kanko rose on its hind legs, set its claws in Christopher's jeans, and ran up to the tabletop. It licked his wrist, and the saliva shone like a glow-worm on his skin. The presence of this tiny creature ran through Christopher like a shot of electricity.

'It's good,' was all Christopher said.

Nighthand's eyes swept the room. He took out his dagger, still in its sheath, and set it on the table, just in case.

'May I see?' said Irian. The soft music of her voice was even more remarkable, in the relative quiet of the bar. A cluster of drinkers twisted to listen, until Nighthand glared at them: the sound seemed to cause even the wind in the chimney to hush a little.

Nighthand nodded, and she lifted the knife in her hands. 'How did you do that, back there?' she said. 'The lamp-post cascade?'

'This is the glamry blade.' Nighthand said. 'The Sailsman sold it to me. It's supposed to cut through anything in the Archipelago. Be careful!' he said, as she unbuttoned the sheath. He held out his bandaged hand. 'I tapped it against my thumb to test it – it cut to the white of the bone.'

Christopher looked at the blade in the woman's hands. It was so sharp that it was impossible to focus his eyes on the tip: it seemed to vanish into nothingness.

'Did you need stitches?' he said.

'I did it myself,' said Nighthand. 'I carry a thread and needle.' The barmaid Felia brought a bottle of wine.

'Did it hurt?' said Mal with interest.

He shrugged. 'I'm a Berserker.' He spoke as if this were an answer.

Mal was agog. 'A *real* one? Really?'

Irian leaned forward. She had the stillness of someone accustomed to listening well, and hard. 'I've never met a Berserker. I was under the impression they were all dead.'

Nighthand frowned, and poured wine to the top of two glasses, slopping it over the rim. 'Well, clearly they're not.' He turned to Christopher. 'Berserkers are warriors: the finest warriors the world has ever seen.'

'They don't feel pain,' said Mal.

'No. Not that. We feel pain. But we don't feel *fear*. So the pain is not a problem, unless it grows so bad that the body refuses to cooperate.'

'When you say you don't feel fear,' said Christopher, 'do you mean you physically can't?'

'I don't know. I never have yet.'

'And that's why your boat is called the *Neverfear*?' said Mal.

He shrugged, and drank deeply. 'It is. I didn't name it – Ratwin did. I'd have called it *Boat*, but she disapproved.'

Irian gave him back the blade. 'That's quite a tool. You can feel the glimt in it. And it truly cuts anything?'

Nighthand refilled and downed the wine. He nodded at Irian; something in her face seemed to launch the recklessness in him. 'Want to see it in action?' He spun it in his fingers and with a single sweep sliced the top two inches off his wine glass. The wine poured out on to the wooden table. It made no noise, no screech of metal on glass: the cut was perfect.

'You'd better be paying for that, Nighthand,' the barmaid called out, 'or I'll kick your substantial arse out of here.'

Nighthand gave half a grin. 'I'd be politer, if I was you, to the man with the glamry blade.'

'Glamry or no glamry,' she said, approaching with a cloth, 'nobody trims my glassware without paying.'

'You know it's a Berserker you're talking to?'

'I do, yeah.' She spoke tartly, but not without affection. 'And it's all very well being fearless and that, but a little bit of anxiety about insulting everyone you speak to might make you look like less of a thug.'

'Berserkers have no need of manners.'

'I know all about Berserkers, thanks.' She mopped up the liquid, and thumped down a new glass on to the table, with a plate of cheese and a jar of something pickled. 'But there's been no Immortal for you to protect, has there, not for a hundred years, so what you are, *sir*, is an unemployed drunk who just so happens to be unusually large. An unemployed drunk, *specifically*, who had better have enough money to pay for that glass.'

The kanko sniffed at the plate. Christopher broke the largest piece of cheese in two, gave half to the creature, and ate the other half himself. It was firm and salty and delicious.

'Hey! Don't feed it all to the kanko,' said Mal. 'I want some too, and Gelifen.'

'There's plenty left!' said Christopher. 'Anyway, should a griffin have cheese?'

'If he wants it, he can have it,' she said. Gelifen did want the cheese – he clambered across the table, joyfully hungry, and devoured half the plateful, before Mal lifted his reluctant, flapping body away. There was a brief interlude, while Gelifen objected, and his feathers were smoothed, and Mal ate more than her fair share of the remaining cheese and raised her eyebrows at Christopher, daring him to object.

'What next?' said Nighthand. 'Now I've kept you all out of jail – what do you plan to do?'

'We're not giving up,' said Mal. 'We'll go somewhere else. We'll find someone who *does* know what's happening.'

'There's the sphinxes,' said Irian.

Mal frowned. 'But my great-aunt says – *said*, I mean ...' and she whispered, '*Said, said, said.*' She swallowed. 'She said that they're impossible to get to.'

'Not impossible,' said Irian. 'But it's dangerous water, and there's a cliff to climb to reach them. They're well protected.'

'And,' said Nighthand, draining his glass again and peering down the neck of the empty bottle, 'they eat their visitors.'

'They do it very rarely,' said Irian. 'We shouldn't exaggerate, Mr Nighthand.'

'How often?' said Mal.

'One in a hundred times,' said Irian.

'If every one in a hundred times you consulted a book,' said Nighthand, 'the book ate you, you would read fewer books. So the majority of people choose to stay away.'

'They won't attack on sight,' said Irian. 'They're not like that. They're never impulsive. They're ancient; they have rituals, and laws, and considerations that are beyond our reckoning. They always ask their riddle, first. If anyone would know what this sickness is that's taken hold of the glimourie, it would be them. Them, or the dragons, but dragons are not scholars.'

'Could we go there?' said Christopher. 'To the sphinxes?'

Nighthand belched. 'I have a hundred cases of fire-wine to take to the eastern reach, and ormolu pearls to take to Archos.'

'It could wait,' said Christopher, 'couldn't it? Wine and pearls don't go off.'

'It can't, no. I can't keep it on board for too long. I don't need someone coming sniffing round after paperwork.'

'If you're a trader,' said Mal, 'why did the barkeeper say you were unemployed?'

Before he could answer, Gelifen vomited the cheese over Nighthand's shoes. 'Ach, by the Immortal! This is why I dislike children. They're heralds of vomit and ask stupid questions!'

'What did she mean—' Mal began again, but Nighthand glanced at her with the full force of his violently forceful eyebrows, and she fell silent.

'She meant, I imagine,' said Irian softly, and sipped her wine, 'that historically a Berserker's job is to guard the Immortal. Anything else – working on the boats, or in ship-building, or as a soldier – is not true work, for a Berserker.'

Nighthand grunted, and signalled for another bottle of wine.

'Are you sure?' said Irian. 'Shouldn't we keep our wits about us?'

'I see no reason to. I prefer the world when drunk. It disappoints me less.'

Mal hauled the subject back round again. 'Christopher doesn't know about the Immortal,' said Mal. 'You're a scientist, Irian, right? You tell him.'

Irian nodded. 'The Immortal,' she said, 'was a soul born from the world's first apple, on the world's first tree: the Glimourie Tree – the tree from which all magic stems. And from the apple, the soul passed to a fish. When the fish died, the soul was reborn a hawk, a sparrow, a wolf, and a thousand other creatures, and at last a human. A woman.'

'And then,' said Mal, 'at every death, the Immortal is born

again. They can be born into any family – peasant, politician, prince, goatherd, warrior. They're the Immortal soul, in a human body.'

'Exactly so. They have lived,' said Irian, 'since the beginning of human life, and they will live until the end of human existence. Perhaps beyond. And they do not forget.'

'And the Berserkers have always guarded the Immortal,' said Nighthand. 'I am one of the last living Berserkers.' The barmaid put a new bottle on the table.

'I'm sorry ... An *apple*?' said Christopher.

'Look, I didn't make it up,' said Nighthand. 'Take it up with infinity.'

'And this is *real*?' said Christopher. 'Or a metaphor?'

'Real,' said Mal.

'The Immortal remembers everything they have seen, in every life: they are the living memory, and the living knowledge,' said Irian. 'They have seen all the possible ways of us. It means they can predict a disaster before it begins; they can halt a wrong before it's committed. They remember what has been done to save life, what has been done to destroy it. They advise regents and ministers and scholars.'

'And –' Nighthand took a gulp of wine straight from the bottle and held it in his mouth, thinking – 'they *know* us. They hold us. They know things from so deep and far that we have forgotten that we have forgotten that we have forgotten them. People in the Otherlands – your world – have known of it too. One of your old poets, John Dun, John something, wrote of it –

and it's in some of your old songs too. It's truth, boy.'

It sounded profoundly unlikely to Christopher. An apple; a wolf, a bird: an immortal soul. 'But if you're the Immortal's guard, why aren't you with them?' Nighthand did not have the relaxed look of a man on holiday.

'Because the Immortal vanished,' he said heavily. 'There has been no Immortal for a hundred years. It was when my great-great-great—' And then suddenly every inch of his massive body stiffened.

His eyes had followed the kanko's. The tiny creature had risen up, and was facing the door. Its hackles were raised along its tiny fox-coloured back. This was the luck it bestowed: the luck of attention.

The alcohol slur left Nighthand's voice.

'Mal. Christopher. Irian. There's an exit at the back, on to the side-street. Come. Now.'

'Why?'

'Blond hair, you said, didn't you? Cut on his cheek?'

All the blood in Christopher's body lurched downwards.

A shadow passed by outside the window, and the door began to swing open.

'Adam Kavil. Your murderer. He's outside the door.'

FIRE IN THE SKY

Nighthand slammed down coins on the table and they ran, in a flurry of griffin feathers and spilt wine, out of the back door into the street. Nighthand glanced behind him.

'To the boat. Fast.'

'But why are we running away?' said Mal. 'You could kill him, with the glamry blade!'

'I could kill him without the blade too.' He led them down an alley, past a corrugated iron lean-to, towards the dock. 'But in a town, unprovoked, with a dozen witnesses? I would end up in jail, and you two in an orphanage. And if he's been ordered to kill you, what is to stop whoever's commanding him from using someone else? No. Killing him isn't the answer.'

'How ... did he find us?' panted Mal.

A thought came to Christopher and he winced. 'I think

the al-mirajes left a trail,' he said. 'Green, in the pavement cracks. Like breadcrumbs.'

They reached a street populated with people in evening clothes, and they had to stop running for fear of attracting attention; instead they walked, the four of them, as fast as they could, through the dark streets.

Under the glow of the street lamps – real flame, Christopher saw, that burned steadily, without flickering – the *Neverfear* waited. The quay was largely deserted, boats stowed for the night, except for a cluster of men on the quayside, drinking coffee from a thermos.

Warren was sitting on a box with his pocketknife and a whetstone and looked up, startled, as they came.

'What's going on?' he asked. 'I thought we sailed tomorrow? And what are *they* doing back here?'

'A change of plan,' said Nighthand. He turned to the children. 'Up you go.'

Mal ran up the gangplank, followed by Christopher. Nighthand turned to Irian. 'Come with us?'

'To the sphinxes? So you're taking them? I don't think—'

'A scholar would be a useful thing to have,' said Nighthand. 'To answer the riddles. I'm no philosopher, and I prefer, in an ideal world, to go uneaten. And you do owe me: for the business with the lamp posts.'

'But ... I'm totally unprepared! I have no luggage with me, no nothing.'

'None of us do. We none of us expected this. That is, in

general, the nature of adventures. Adventurers tend to smell. The great epic tales stank, I think, more than the historians give them credit for.'

She hesitated only for a moment – a moment in which risk and reason, fear and a kind of buoyant, eager curiosity collided visibly across her face. Then she nodded. 'That sounds all right to me,' she said, and ran aboard, sure-footed.

Nighthand followed; anyone looking closely might have seen a pink tint passing, sunrise-like, over the skin of his neck and cheeks. He called to Warren: 'Where's Ratwin?'

'She should be back at any moment,' he said.

'We can't sail without her,' said Nighthand. 'Make ready, and we'll go as soon as she comes.'

Suddenly Christopher's stomach lurched. He grabbed hold of Mal's wrist, and pushed her down to the deck.

'Ow! What d'you do that for?'

'He's there!' he whispered. 'The man. Kavil.' He peered over the edge of the boat. Kavil stood at the mouth of one of the streets off the quay, looking left and right. His skin in the lamplight looked grey, and his eyes had purple smudges beneath them.

'Nighthand!' he hissed. 'We have to go.'

'Not without Ratwin,' said Nighthand. 'She's the finest navigator I've had.'

'There she is!' called Warren. 'Ratwin! Quick! No, don't stop to clean your whiskers!'

The ratatoska bounded up the gangplank, a map in her mouth,

and Nighthand hauled it up after her. 'Casting off!' called Nighthand.

The boat sailed out of the quay and on to the great dark of the bay beyond.

Ratwin spat out the map on the deck. She looked Christopher up and down and sniffed.

'Yous still here?'

'Yes,' he said. 'Clearly I am. What's it a map of?'

'The whole Archipelago. But this one has corals marked – corals that grow tall as trees beneaths the water, as'll tear a boat to shreds if it tries to sail up and over.'

'Is that true?' said Christopher. 'Coral forests?'

'I never tells the ratatoskan long-tall-tales,' said Ratwin, 'about navigation.'

Christopher opened his eyes the next morning to pure blackness. He coughed, and jerked upright in a scramble of feathers: Gelifen had fallen asleep stretched over his face. Mal lay next to him, just beginning to stir in the dawn.

Gelifen nibbled Christopher's fingers in greeting, plucked a feather from his own wings with his beak, and offered it to him.

'He means it for a toothpick,' said Mal, brushing her fringe from her eyes and sitting up. She grinned, and began to re-plait her hair, working the long gold thread through it. 'Since we don't have toothbrushes.'

A few paces away, Ratwin was perched on the side of the boat, talking to Nighthand.

'Warren and I didn't have time to load supplies at Bryn

Tor,' he said. 'So we'll have to stop at the next port, to take on water and food. What's nearest?'

She peered out to sea, and down at her map, and her squirrel face considered it. 'With these winds, and weathers? The Island of Vistaia is the best.'

'Good enough.' Nighthand nodded. 'I haven't been there for years, but I had a good friend in the town – a trader in sala-mandric fire.' And, seeing Christopher listening, he added: 'The fire breathed in a salamander's final breath. If you catch it with a scrap of wood or paper or straw, it never goes out. The lamps in the dock use it.'

Mal brushed her fringe from her eyes, and sat up. 'Is there breakfast?' she asked.

There was. They ate it – the five humans, the griffin and the ratatoska – sitting on the deck in the rising sun. There was a dark flat bread, which they ate dipped in olive oil. There was a slab of cream-coloured dried fish, delicious and so salty it was like eating the sea itself. Gelifen was given the lion's share – 'the griffin's share', according to Mal. He thanked them courteously, tapping each with the tip of his beak.

'Am I imagining it, or is he ... getting bigger?' asked Christopher. The griffin, clambering over his lap, felt heavier.

'You're not imagining it,' she said. 'They grow fast, in sudden spurts. He's six months old now – he'll be bigger than me when he's an adult.'

Christopher fed Gelifen the last of his fish, just to see him vibrate with pleasure. A large butterfly, grey and blue, landed on the deck, and Gelifen launched himself after it.

'They're joy-birds, griffins,' said Irian. 'Cornucopial life-admirers.'

Ratwin sat perched on a stack of ropes, cleaning her small green ears. 'Strong wings, griffins. I once knew a griffin,' she said, 'fly all the way to the moon, and eat a chunk of it for breakfast, and be back for dinner.'

'Is that true?' said Christopher.

She flicked a piece of wax from her ear with her claw. 'No.'

Mal's face was tight, watching Gelifen. 'I think –' the words sounded hard-formed, and painful in her throat – 'he's the last.' Christopher realised, looking at her, that she had never said it aloud. It cuffed them all into silence, and they watched the griffin pounce upon the butterfly, and miss.

Ratwin broke the silence. 'A little more to the wests,' she said, and Irian took the tiller. Her hand on it was light as she steered them across the blue sheet of ocean. Nighthand looked surprised.

'This is a stubborn boat,' he said. 'She doesn't usually bend to anyone's hand but mine.'

'I spend a lot of time at sea – studying the glimourie for my work,' she said quietly. 'Sail-ships, fishing boats, coracles. I'm happiest in boats or in libraries – those are my places.'

Warren watched her, open admiration in his rheumy eyes. 'And what are *not* your places?'

Irian looked, Christopher thought, as though she were about to say something serious – but then she shook her head. 'Parties,' she said, and smiled. 'I speak four languages fairly well, but put me in a room full of strangers and I can't think of a single word to say.' She spun the tiller. 'I once panicked and asked a man if he had a preferred type of badger.'

Nighthand looked bemused. 'I have never in my life been at a loss for words.'

'We knows', said Ratwin. 'The fearlessness makes the man a conversationalist', she said to Irian. 'And he fights like a light-ning storm in a hat, but he's also gots us fired from eight different jobs, any of which would have done us well enough.'

'Last February he rode a seabull across the straits of Semper, in a storm, to rescue a unicorn foal who had been swept out to sea', said Warren. 'Which sounds all very big and noble, except the man was drunk, and he abandoned the ship he was supposed to be steering without warning and it ran aground, and they lost a thousand gold pieces' worth of stock.'

Nighthand glared, and made an imperious gesture into a pile of stacked boxes, which overturned with a clatter. 'Would you have let the unicorn drown?'

Ratwin snorted, and returned to her lookout post, halfway up the mast. 'A little more eastward', she called, 'and we'll come in at Fishhook Bay.' Her eyes were stronger than human eyes; Christopher could see only a green blur amid the shining blue of the sea.

'It's one of the most beautiful islands', said Irian to Mal and Christopher. 'They have a rare species of sea-urchin that you find nowhere else in the Archipelago. The spines are a foot long, and they turn red in the presence of predators.' Her eyes were warming as she spoke. 'But what's really fascinating is the excreta they produce. It smells of cat urine, and it's used by some centaurs in their oldest and wildest potion-work, but its chemical components suggest ...' She stopped, as Mal's face took on a schoolroom look, and laughed. 'Forgive me. I forget, sometimes, that urchin talk isn't universally fascinating.'

Nighthand was watching her from across the boat. He did not complain about the urchin talk.

The boat passed swiftly over the waves, and Christopher crossed to get a better view of the island. Warren strode past, a roll of rope over his arm. 'Sweet people, round here,' he said. 'You know what they say: soft water, soft souls.'

Christopher turned, keen to hear more. 'What else do they say?'

Warren looked taken aback at his interest. 'Oh ... well – you get a very specific kind of person, from the dragon isles. They grow up round fire, and chaos. The children there don't go to school; some of them live alongside dragons, in the mountains, until they reach adulthood. And then in the north they're hardier, less talkative. And in the western central seas, the water's gentle, and people speak slower. There we are now – we'll be docked in a minute or two.'

They were close enough now to make out shapes. There was, at the water's edge, a cluster of square stone buildings. None had their complete allocation of walls and ceiling. They were charred black. A small number of goats tried to graze on burned grass. Their long brown coats were grey with charcoal dust. There were no other sounds of life; no music, no children yelling, none of the shouts and jostling of humanity. Just the goats.

There was a moment when no one fully took in the importance of what they saw; and then Mal understood. 'Quick!' she cried. 'Turn around! It'll be coming back!'

'What? *What* will be coming back?' said Warren.

There was a rumbling overhead. Christopher's jaw dropped open.

'Get down! You two! Get down in the boat!' cried Nighthand, and he heaved on the sails as Irian spun the tiller under fast, urgent hands.

Christopher crouched, but he would not look away. A great figure was gliding in over the sky, its wings moving in lazy flaps. It was deep black, and its wings were blood red on the underside. It was – exactly as the Bestiary had said – as large as a cathedral.

'Don't look it in the eye, Christopher!' said Mal, tugging at him, so that he dropped to his knees.

'I've got to see!' he said. He stomach-crawled the length of the boat, and pressed himself against the side closest to the island: just his eyes and the top of his head showing. Mal hesitated – then crawled after him.

They watched the dragon swoop low over the herd of goats. Its hind legs stretched out. The goats scattered, bleating wildly, and it dropped, lower, until it was almost skimming the ground, and snatched one in its claws.

With a flick it tossed the goat into the air, blew a great burst of fire over it, and swallowed it whole while it was still alight.

They sailed on in silence. It was a long time before anyone spoke.

Irian swallowed. 'Dragons don't travel this far from their mountains, as far as I know.'

'No,' said Nighthand. 'But we have moved far beyond what we know.'

REPAIR

Later that day, Christopher went to find Mal. She sat in the prow of the boat, ducked low enough to be protected from the wind by its high sides. The material on her lap, he saw, as he came closer, was her coat.

'What are you doing?' he asked.

'Sewing, of course. What does it look like?' The dragon had left her quaking, and even now she still shook with the adrenalin, though her expression dared him to mention it.

Her hands were small, and lacked the strength to push the needle through the thickness of the cloth, and her fingers were spotted with blood where the needle had slipped.

'I dunno. I think it looks –' and Christopher grinned – 'like you're trying to donate blood very, very slowly?'

'Are you good at sewing?'

'I've not tried before – but it's just stabbing, with added precision.'

'Then why don't you do it?' And she handed it to him, her chin in the air.

He threaded the needle – difficult, with the rocking of the boat – and began to sew the tear in tight, overlapping stitches. Mal leaned forward to watch, breathing hard.

'The bits need to overlap,' she said. 'No, more than that. So no wind at all can get through.' Her brow creased. 'I don't know if it will ever work again.'

'Of course it'll work,' said Christopher. 'Unless you're going somewhere incredibly cold.'

'The coat's nothing to do with cold. It's a flying coat.'

'Flying!' A thrill went through him. 'What kind of flying?'

'I'll show you when it's done. The man who gave it to me told them I must never let down the extra material in the hem – look, see, here – or the coat will fly me too high. I'd die, he said. I wish he'd told them more about it, but my Great-Aunt Leonor didn't like his face, or his smell, or any of it, so she threw him out.'

'What man gave it to you?'

'A traveller, on the ocean-boats – when I was born. He was my namer. You know, the person who gave me my name.' He shook his head, and she said, 'Well, how do *you* choose names?'

'Your parents just choose whatever they like the sound of. Or, sometimes it's in the family – your grandfather, or great-aunt. Someone safely dead, usually.' Christopher was named after his Scottish great-great-grandfather: an old eccentric, who was said to have spent all his time outside, atop a hill. A man who must, he realised with a jolt, have been a guardian of the waybetween.

Mal's eyebrows expressed an unfavourable opinion of this method of naming. 'Well, in the Archipelago you take the baby to the namer, and they go into a trance and name the child. It's a very old tradition – but it's dying out. Most of the namers are lovely old frauds, and you could slip them two bits of silver and they'd say whatever you want. Not my namer though. He was a seer. Great-Aunt Leonor said she could tell, because he was poor.'

'Is Mal your whole name then? Or is it short for, I don't know ... Mallory? Malinda?'

She laughed. 'No! Is Mallory a name? It's short for Malum. My great-aunt used to say it was prophetic. Because it means "mischief".' She grinned at him. 'You know: Latin. Most names have a meaning, in one of the old languages. Latin, Old Norse, Old Centaur, Old Arabian. Old Manticore, if your parents take you to a namer who's a bit pretentious.'

Christopher had, grudgingly, learned a small amount of Latin at school, and he had a feeling that *malum* meant something else entirely. But he couldn't remember what.

'How's my coat?'

'Nearly there.'

'Come on then!' She grinned at him. 'You said you were faster than me.'

The sewing took effort – the cloth was tough, stiff with age, and several times he jabbed the needle up into the space under his fingernails – but he found it unexpectedly satisfying. Ratwin watched from a distance, seemingly approving.

When it was finished Mal smiled as she took it from him, and thanked him, but she had bitten her lip so hard there was blood. 'If I end up in the sea, it's your job to rescue me, yes?'

'Yeah, all right.'

'Swear? Swear on the Immortal you won't let me drown!'

He laughed. 'I'll swear on anything you like. Go on! We're waiting!'

She put on the coat, handed Gelifen to Christopher, and clambered up on to the prow of the boat, standing atop the carved figurehead, which was shaped like an apple. The wind whipped her fringe across her face.

She gripped the edges of the coat, spread her arms – and leaped into the sky.

Christopher gave a yell, which made Nighthand turn to stare as Mal, arms outstretched, soared suddenly as high as the mast, her coat's woollen cloth flapping in the wind.

Christopher heard a laugh of pure delight, and Mal swept west, out over the chopping waves, dipped down to six feet above the water, the salt spray wetting her clothes, and then rose up again almost vertically, up into the cloud-white sky.

'Crazy girl!' shouted Warren, and something else unfamiliar, which was certainly swearing.

Christopher had never seen anything like it – part of him

wanted to shout at her to come back – but she had absolute control. So instead he gave a great whoop of encouragement, loud enough to drown out Warren.

'Yes, Mal! Higher!'

She swept in one wide, swift circle around the whole of the boat, hovered for a moment at the top of the mast, and then spiralled down, looping the mast like a maypole, with such ease that even Warren let out a roar of pleasure.

She landed with a thump of boots against wood in front of Christopher, steadying herself on his elbow.

Warren shook his head. 'I've been forty-eight years at sea,' he said. 'I'd have said that I'd seen everything I was going to see – most of it a few hundred times over. All my surprises used up and paid out, you know? But I've never seen nobody who flew like that.'

She was sky-suited, Christopher saw that now: her slight bones and sharp elbows had a bird-quality to them. In the sky, she looked free in a way she didn't on earth.

'Like I said, the coat is nothing to do with the cold,' she said. 'Entirely to do with the sky.' And her eyes were brighter than he'd yet seen them, and she looked ready, in a way that she had not before, to face the world.

KRAKEN

'North-west, up ahead!' Nighthand's voice was loud and sharp, and Irian looked up from her papers to stare. 'Something in the water! A reef?'

It was late afternoon now. Warren was staring into the water. 'Don't be insane,' he said. 'It's clear for miles.'

Mal and Christopher ran to the front of the boat. Nighthand appeared behind them, shading his eyes with his huge hand. It was Ratwin who spotted it again.

'There! Nor'-nor'-west, fifty feet. A creature. As that wave rises – there.'

'What is it?' They could see only the blur of an advancing shadow beneath the waves.

'Behemoth?' said Ratwin.

'By the Immortal, I hope not,' said Warren.

'It can't be. We're too far from the shore,' said Irian. 'Hippocamp?'

'Could it be a makara?' said Mal.

'It's ten times the size of a makara,' said Nighthand.

'Cetus monster?' said Irian.

And then it reared up out of the water, as if gaining height to look across the horizon, and they all saw what it was.

'*Kraken*,' breathed Mal.

It was as large as the boat itself, grey and octopus-like and terrifyingly fast. Christopher had seen one in a medieval drawing, once, in which it seemed sweet and comical: two great eyes, the black tentacles waving in the sweep of blue that represented the sea. It did not look remotely funny now.

Warren stumbled backwards, his old cheeks quivering. 'There are no krakens in these waters!'

Nighthand looked out across the water. 'And yet there do seem to be,' he said. 'This isn't what I had planned.' He might have been discussing a rain shower at a picnic.

Mal gripped the rail at the bow of the boat. Her knuckles were white. 'Can we outrun it?'

'I doubt it,' said Nighthand. 'On the sail, Warren. Irian, the tiller. Ratwin, mount the mast – look out for others. Get down inside the cabin, both of you, Mal, Christopher.' He took the glamry blade from his belt.

'You can't knife-fight a kraken!' said Mal.

'That may possibly be true. I've never tried. But I am about to.'

The kraken's grey shape approached beneath the waves.

Mal turned, eyes wild. 'Where's Gelifen? Christopher! Do you have him?'

'No!' Christopher ran the length of the boat, calling the griffin's name. 'Gelifen!'

'Children!' called Irian. 'Get into the cabin! Now!'

Irian and Warren pulled at the sail ropes. The boat gave a kick of speed, and leaped forwards in the water – but it was not enough.

With a shriek like a gull's, the kraken rose up, breaking the surface twenty feet from the boat. Ten black tentacles swung through the air towards them, dripping water. They gripped the side of the boat, and it lurched sideways, so that the port-side was almost in the water. Christopher grabbed the mast, and felt terror rise in his body.

A tentacle as wide as a tree trunk swept over the back half of the boat. Nighthand ducked underneath it, and jabbed with the glamry blade. The kraken screamed, and its tentacles retreated. The boat righted itself, rocking wildly.

Gelifen came staggering up the steps from the cabin, peeping in terror.

As he did so, the kraken rose again; a tentacle flicked across the deck. It caught Gelifen behind the back and swept him against the mast. Christopher sprinted to the side.

'Leave him!' said Warren.

'I won't!' cried Mal. 'I can't!' She lunged for the mast. Three thick, grey, dripping tentacles came groping, sweeping towards them – Christopher slammed himself against the deck, pulling Mal with him.

'Gelifen!' she screamed again. She ran across the boat and snatched up the griffin, stuffing him down the inside of her sweater.

The water heaved and the kraken's head reared up in front of them in the water. They could see its face, beaked like an octopus's. Its eyes raked the boat; they were hungry eyes, globular and bulging. They looked straight at Mal. Its mouth gaped, wide as an opening door – and Warren was snatched from the deck and cast inside.

Nighthand roared, a bellow of fury which reached the horizon in every direction. He tore a piece of wood from the splintering cabin wall, and hurled it at the kraken. Its sharp edge struck the creature in the eye.

The kraken gave a shriek of rage like a cat on fire. Then it seized the boat, and the entire structure was flung up into the air, cracking and splintering as it landed again on the waves. Ratwin was hurled into the water; Mal and Christopher were thrown sideways, to left and right; he hit the cabin wall, and she struck her head as she landed on the deck, and lay unconscious.

The kraken twisted its great head to look: for one beat, it hung there in the water, blinking its huge grey eyes. And then the kraken reached out, and plucked Mal bodily from the boat. Nighthand lunged after her, knife in hand.

'No!' he roared.

'Mal!' Christopher yelled.

The kraken laid her on a piece of driftwood, as carefully as a child laying down a doll. And then, before Christopher could understand what had happened, its ten tentacles fired towards them, and the whole boat was crushed and pulled beneath the surface. The suction dragged Christopher down into black whirling chaos.

For what felt like minutes he spun, over and over in the churning sea. He fought, his lungs shrieking, back to the surface. A piece of wood, part of a table, rocked on the waves; he hauled himself on to it. There was sea-foam everywhere, he could see nothing; but there, suddenly, was Mal. As he watched, the driftwood bucked and she slipped from it; her eyes were closed, and she was falling.

His heart lurched. It was not bravery, but something wilder and more urgent that spurred Christopher off the table. He dived down, kicking, staring in the deep dark roiling blue – when a hand grabbed him, and pulled him up and away from the swirling wreckage. It was not a human hand.

Underwater, he screamed; and then he was above the surface, and choking, and calling Mal's name.

'No need to scream,' said the creature. Her hair was longer than her body, and it was silver; the colour of the sea in moonlight. Her face was the wildest thing he had ever seen, and she had Mal in her arms. Gelifen was tight inside Mal's jersey, snorting the water from his beak.

His first thought was: a *mermaid*. But she had legs, not a tail. Spray was all around them; while he trod water, ragged-breathed with the effort, she hung effortlessly in the water, only her feet kicking from the ankle. He thought of his grand-father's book of creatures. A *nereid*.

The creature spoke. 'Lóclóca! *Su ārstafasa? Su andgietu glimt?*' And she grabbed him by the wrist, and hauled him through the water.

'That's my friend!' He struggled against her, until he real-ised she was pulling him away from the froth the kraken had left behind. The tabletop spun past, and he grabbed it. 'Give her to me.'

The creature spoke again, this time in English. 'I will not hurt her.' The creature's voice was very low and very beautiful; it sounded like the wash of the sea. It was familiar, but he could not begin to say why. 'My name is Galatia; these waters are mine, and my clan's. I smelt the glimourie on her. U *gehygd*. I knew her for what she is. *Sáwoll*. And so I came.'

The nereid made no move to hand Mal over. The girl's eyes were closed and her head rested on the nereid's shoulder; she breathed softly.

'Why are you out in my ocean?' said Galatia. 'It is dangerous, these new days. The smell of my waters is different.'

'Different how?' He swam closer, pulling the piece of wood with him. He was looking for signs of the ship, of Nighthand or Irian, but could see only waves. He wondered if he could try to snatch Mal.

'Hollow. *Leasunga*. The glamry is being lost. Or ... no, wrong word: taken. *Blómaan*. Taken, if such a thing can be taken. Can it, human?'

'It looks like it can, yeah.' He kicked nearer, one hand still on the tabletop.

'We sea creatures that breathe in the glamry with their water, to survive. Seabulls, kappa, makaras—'

'What's a makara?' Nearer; almost close enough to make a grab for her.

'A makara. Crocodile jaw. Elephant trunk. Scales of fish. More generous than her face would suggest. The kappas, the makaras, the hippocamps – they are all starve-panicking. *Krakens.* There should be no krakens in these waters.'

'Oh yeah? Why are there then?' He braced himself to launch at her.

'The glimourie of their northern seas has gone, so they move. When the krakens panic, then we all have cause to fear. And now: her. The one they look for. In my ocean.'

Without warning, the nereid thrust Mal at him and vanished underwater. There was a call, long and low, from beneath the waves. When Galatia resurfaced there were eight other heads around her, all silver-haired. From the depths too rose a herd of eight water-horses, gold and green. The nereid reached out and pulled Mal on to the back of the hippocamp.

'Get on. Behind her,' she said.

'No! I can't leave my friends.'

The nereid smiled a sudden sharp-toothed smile, and whistled – and from the waves emerged Nighthand, and Irian, each riding a hippocamp. Nighthand held a wet and furious Ratwin.

'We need to go. It may return. Ready?' said the nereid. 'We go under. *Brimum*, yes?'

'I can't breathe underwater!'

'You will breathe while on the hippocamp. His skin against your skin. It will be enough.'

And they ducked beneath the water, and took off.

THE CITY OF SCHOLARS

The rush of water was ferocious against Christopher's face. He tried to keep his eyes open, but the sting of the salt and the speed meant that he saw only the other nereids around him, charging like stampeding buffalo.

They carried the shipwrecked crew through the ocean towards a city that rose in yellow stone out of the water of a lagoon. As the hippocamps navigated boats and punts, Christopher expected any moment to be tipped off into the water. But they were carried down a canal, passers-by turning to stare as they were borne through the water. Then there was a great heaving, and the humans were deposited on a wide piazza, surrounded on two sides by the wings of what looked to be an ancient stone library.

'Here', said the nereid. 'This is the Lithian second capital – the City of Scholars. We have dropped you at the edge of it. We can take you no further; nereids do not walk, except in great and urgent emergencies.'

'Why here?'

'You could use some knowledge, boy. *Andgietu*, no? There are things to discover.'

Christopher looked around. Nighthand was kneeling over Mal, who was spitting water and sitting up. Irian, though, had turned from the nereids, and walked away from the canal into the square. A nereid called after her in Nerish, something high and strangely pleading, but she did not turn. She glanced down at her hands, and thrust them deep into her pockets.

'Keep your eyes out from now on,' said Galatia to Christopher. 'These are dangerous days, and not to be trodden lightly.'

'Wait! Before you go – I need to ask – the kraken! Why didn't the kraken eat Mal? It had her there, but—'

But she had already gone, vanishing beneath the water in the canal.

In the square, they wrung out their clothes and assessed each other for bruises, and for a moment, the giddy pleasure of not being dead transcended everything.

But then Mal said, 'Warren. Is there any way he survived? He's definitely … ?'

'Gone,' Nighthand said. His voice was dry as sand, and rasping.

She looked up into Nighthand's face. 'Why aren't you sadder? He was your second-mate!'

But Nighthand turned away, so that no one could see his

face. 'Berserkers do not weep', he said. 'And they do not love. How could they, when they mustn't fear? Love has fear baked into it.' He pointed to a street ahead of them, with eyes that were red and so fixed that they looked blind. 'Come. We'll go to the dock and see about a new boat.'

Irian bent to Ratwin. 'We must tell Warren's kin. Can you get a message to them?'

The ratatoska nodded, her face set with sadness, and made off at a run.

Nighthand walked at double his usual speed. He led them on a march through the beautiful city on the water, over bridges, through squares, pushing through crowds who turned to stare at their wet clothes and Nighthand's scowl.

'Irian', said Christopher, after they had been walking for half an hour. 'What was that nereid trying to say to you?'

Irian hesitated. 'It's not important.'

'But she seemed to know you. And she said something, about Mal ... "I know her for what she is."' And he told Irian what had happened.

'Nereids follow their own laws, Christopher. They're profoundly rational, but in the same way that the sea is rational. Much of their language, Nerish, has no translation at all into any human tongue.' She shook her head. 'They're very proud. Largely they keep to themselves. I don't know why they saved Mal.'

But it had been more than that, he thought. The kraken too: even amid all the terror, he was sure he had seen the kraken lift Mal to safety.

They were passing through a particularly fine square, with a fountain in the form of a mermaid in the centre, when there was a noise overhead, of beating wings, and the sky called Nighthand's name.

'Nighthand! Fidens Nighthand, how dare you come to my city without informing me! I would have laid on a feast!'

Over the rooftops flew a now familiar horse-like creature, its wings beating in the air. Its body was covered in grey-green iridescent scales, and it shone. Its wings too were scaled; scales so fine that delicate pink membranes shone through on the underside. Its mane, though, was horse-like, and wild.

Nighthand gave a roar of pleasure so loud it caused the longma to shy and buck in the air.

'Anja!'

The longma swooped low. The woman who stepped down from the creature's back, holding its neck for support, was, Christopher thought, an astonishment.

She looked eighty or more, and she moved with stiff, arthritic caution. Her grey hair was wrapped in a great plait at the base of her neck. Her riding clothes were blue, shot through with ruby-coloured silk, and she wore rubies on bracelets all the way up her arms and in studs in her ears. Her look was daunting; wry and flinty and knowing. It was unreadable: not an easy face to be in company with.

'Nighthand!' Her accent was that of the city. 'Come here and let me look at you.' She studied him. 'You don't look a day older.'

Nighthand kissed the hand she offered. 'You do.'

'Such charm, as always. What happened to you? You look atrocious.'

'The *Neverfear* was shipwrecked,' said Nighthand. 'A kraken.'

'In these waters?'

The woman took from her pocket a small jewelled figure of a bird, cast in gold and emeralds, with a ruby-studded crest of feathers atop its head. She unscrewed the head feathers, and poured some liquid into her palm. It smelt of something rich and woody and slightly overpowering: like money, distilled. She dabbed it on her wrists, and upper lip. 'Forgive me, but you all smell unpleasantly hippocampy. Who are these people? Is that a *griffin*?'

Nighthand introduced them. 'And this,' he said, 'is Anja Trevasse. She owns the palazzo you can see, there, overlooking the Great Canal. And indeed much of the city.'

'And the palazzo is where I will take you now,' said the old woman. She beckoned the longma, spoke to it, and offered it some meat from a bag she wore on her hip. 'I shall fly there,' she said. 'My legs will no longer carry me. You may follow below.'

She took off into the air. Irian and Nighthand exchanged looks.

'Should we go?' said Irian quietly.

Nighthand shrugged. 'The food will be worth eating. And she'll know all the boat merchants in the city. I've lost my cargo, so I'll be in the market for more.'

'Oh Nighthand! Will you owe money for the goods?'

He pursed his lips: he looked, for a moment, exactly like Ratwin. 'Only if they can find me. We'll go with her.' He nodded at the woman above them. 'Just be careful what you say to her.'

He strode ahead, shouting conversation up at Anja as she circled above him. Ratwin returned, panting for breath, and leaped on to Irian's shoulder, and together they told Christopher and Mal what they knew of the grey-haired woman.

'Anja Trevasse is one of the richest women in the Archipelago,' Irian said. She spoke so softly that they had to crane to hear. 'I studied here in the City of Scholars, years ago, and she was famous. Every day she flies to the Gem Palace, the largest jeweller's in the city.'

'Every day she sits there, amid the jewels, dragon-style,' said Ratwin. 'Most days she buys something – for herself, or for people she wants to have in her debt. She knows everyone rich or important or high-stepping in the city. She likes every single one of thems to owe her something.'

They crossed an arched bridge over the Great Canal, and Christopher and Mal paused to stare. Boats passed underneath them, full of scholars and tradesmen and children. One boat, he saw, had a woman with a kanko on each shoulder, and another burrowing in her hair.

'How does she know Nighthand?' Christopher asked Ratwin. It didn't seem an obvious pairing.

'The Trevasses knows everybody; everybody who mights be useful to them. Her great-grandfather was governor of the city; he was so rich he had coins for teeths', said Ratwin.

'He had a powerful business partner, I believe, who died and left him everything: so he essentially inherited the city wholesale. Anja has a network of people who report to her', said Irian. 'News of the city, news of the Archipelago.'

'And two dozen ratatoskas', said Ratwin. 'They reports too.'

'She hoards secrets. She says it's the most powerful kind of treasure', said Irian.

Mal shivered. She was still wet, and her lips were blue at the edges. Gelifen fluttered his wings, and warmth began to radiate from him. She held him close, and steam rose from her wet clothing, and she smiled, for the first time since the kraken, into his feathers.

'They met when Nighthand was working on a boat she was travelling on', Ratwin went on. 'He was thrown out in the end, smash-bang-inevitable. But before that there was a greatsome accident, and he saved her life. He fought off a hundred makaras, all with teeth as long as swords.'

'Really?'

Ratwin sighed. 'Always with this *reallys*! No. But he did save her life. She fell in, he fished her out.'

Christopher turned his ear to Nighthand and Anja. They had been talking in low voices. The old woman was almost kittenish around him.

'Still wearing your coffin fund?' She gestured to Nighthand's earrings.

'Of course.'

'It's morbid – carrying your death in your ears.'

'Practical, I call it,' he said. 'It's a Berserker tradition,' he said to Christopher, in answer to his look. 'The earrings are worth enough to buy me a coffin and a burial, wherever I die.'

'I've always liked Berserskers,' Anja said. 'I like those born well, or born strong. It's unfashionable to say it, but birth is important.'

Christopher looked at Mal, his eyebrows high behind the woman's back, and they exchanged grimaces.

The longma banked, and Anja called down, 'Here! My palazzo. My great-grandfather built it. He was not a man who did things by halves.'

She swooped over the wall, and they followed, through an enormous double wooden door. Inside was a courtyard, and a vast, sun-warmed building, eighteen windows across and five high. There was heavy golden leaf on the windowpanes, and two carved dragons guarding the door.

The longma landed in front of it, and Anja dismounted with Nighthand's help. 'I've heard from Nighthand what you are doing, and why.' Slow, catlike eyes ranged over Christopher, Irian, Mal: and there they lingered. 'I'm wondering if I will lend you my ship.'

'The *Shadow Dancer*?' Nighthand said. 'You still have it? I never saw a boat move so fast and so silent.'

'I do. It could be ready in less time than it will take to find you fresh clothes. But there's a condition. I want to speak to the girl. Leave her here with me. The rest of you, go in. My seamstress is waiting.'

They exchanged glances; then Mal shrugged, and put on her haughtiest, most unflinching face.

'Fine,' she said. 'I'll stay.' Christopher hesitated, and Mal scowled at him, a sure sign she was afraid. 'Go on. Take Gelifen.'

Four hours later, washed and spruced and fed, Mal and Christopher, Ratwin, Irian and Nighthand walked through the city towards the dock where Anja's boat was moored. Christopher was self-conscious in his new clothes – black trousers, a wine-coloured jumper and new boots that came up past his ankles – but they were finer than any he'd had before. The map was safely stowed in his pocket, wet and bedraggled but still readable.

Nighthand was resplendent in a thick dark-blue jacket. Clothing him had been a difficulty – he was so broad at the shoulder and bicep that he had split the seams in three consecutive coats each time he flexed his arms.

'He erupts like a kraken out of all my clothes! Bah! I think what am I supposed to do with a man like this?' the seamstress had said. In the end, she had sent for her whole couture studio, and they had sewn him a jacket on the spot. Christopher saw Irian watching, the hint of a smile at her mouth, as six stern seamstresses circled the Berserker with pins.

Irian wore exquisitely made leather boots and high-waisted trousers. She had rejected the extravagantly frilled silver blouse they tried to put her in, and selected a thin, emerald-green jersey, tucked into the trousers. The clothes removed some of her careful, standing-in-corners look; the green made her skin glow. 'Good,' said the chief seamstress, and the other five had nodded, a synchronised swimming team of flinty approval. 'Throw away that skirt. It is a talent, to learn to dress like yourself. Beauty is overrated, but it is not a sin.' She replaced her pincushion on a hook on her belt. 'It's just one of a thousand pieces of possible luck, and you were lucky.'

Irian laughed and looked at the floor, and so did not see Nighthand turn to look, nor the expression on his face.

Only Mal had refused to change. 'Leonor made it,' she said of her jersey. It had been dried, with her coat, in front of a sala-mandric flame, but it still smelt of its many and various adventures. 'I'm not taking it off until it falls apart.' And nobody, seeing her face, had even tried to argue.

She had told Christopher, as they walked, what Anja had wanted. Mal sounded baffled. 'She just asked me loads of questions about the coat. About the seer who gave it to me, and a bit about when I was younger. And then she said she wished us luck with the sphinxes.'

They were less noticeable now than they had been, but still a scraggy young ratatoska watched them from the bridge. Its eyes were careful and watchful. Christopher was about to point it out to Mal, when a woman sidled up to them.

She spoke, first in the fast and lilting language they had heard across the city, and then, seeing their uncomprehending faces, in English.

'Tell your fortune?' Her long blonde hair reached her waist, and she wore a dress and coat in matching red velvet. Both had once been exquisite, but now the plush had worn away at the elbow and hip. She looked, Christopher thought, like someone who had known richer and easier days. Two boys – tall, thickset teens – trailed behind her, clad in threadbare suits, looking bored and sullen. Both had their arms crossed. One had a tattoo of a knife on the back of his wrist. It looked like he had done it himself, possibly in the dark, possibly with a blunt needle.

'One bronze piece. You won't regret it – and money's hard for a fortune teller, these days, with everyone anxious and nobody clear why.'

'OK,' said Christopher, eyeing the tattoo. 'Mal, can I borrow a coin?'

'It's a con, you know,' said Mal, but she handed over a bronze piece anyway.

The woman took his palm, spat on it – he flinched, but she hung on to it – rubbed it with her thumb, and began to croon.

'You have a noble hand, boy! I see danger, and love, and wonders. Dark places, and great glories.' There was a pause.

'Is that it?' said Christopher.

'Yes.' She sounded peevish. 'What more did you want? I said love and wonders, didn't I?'

Mal snorted. 'You sound like the back pages of a cheap newspaper. That's not worth a full bronze piece,' she said. 'Come on, Christopher.'

But the woman stood in their way. Before Mal could snatch her hand away, the fortune teller had seized it.

'And you. I see a tall blond stranger, great adventures.'

'You can tell that from my palm?' Mal ran her hand through her wonky fringe and smiled her finest sceptical smile. 'Amazing. We're going.'

'Wait then.' The woman scowled at Mal. Her eyes, for the first time, took on the look of actual looking. 'There are strange days ahead. The most dangerous human talent is forgetting.'

And then she looked again. 'Your lifeline: it's ...'

Then, still holding Mal's hand, she reached into her pocket, and handed back the bronze coin. She dropped Mal's palm, and walked swiftly in the other direction.

Mal watched her go with her eyebrows raised.

'What was that about?'

The woman reached the corner of the road, followed by her sons. She glanced back once over her shoulder. Her face had fear in it, and hunger. It made Christopher shiver. It made him think of the murderer, and his knife.

THE SPHINX PENINSULA

The boat Anja lent them was, the men on the dock said, 'the finest small ship we've seen this decade'. She was named the *Shadow Dancer* – Ratwin wrinkled her nose at the name: 'pretentiousnesses' – and she was in perfect condition. She was white, with billowing sails glowing against the evening sky, a neat foredeck and six portholes. It was large enough to sleep twelve, two to a cabin. There was a tiny galley kitchen for cooking, twin tanks of drinking water, and a general sense of cleanness and completeness and purpose.

The sails looked different from the canvas of Nighthand's *Neverfear*. Ratwin moved across the ship, sniffing in corners, flicking out a small light-green tongue to taste the paint. She saw Christopher reach up to touch the cloth of them. 'You can feel it?' she said to him.

'They're so light,' he said.

'Pegasan sails.'

Irian came up behind them. 'Sails that catch the slightest wind, made from the wings of the pegasus.'

'The winged horse?'

'White-winged, and fast as the wind. They migrate, each summer, to the south. I saw them flying overhead once – enough of them to carpet the sky.'

'How do they make the sails?'

'I've seen it done, years ago, on a research trip to the east. They strip the feathery material – the vane, they call it – off the shaft of the feather, and make it into a ball. I saw a woman weigh a ball as large as my body, and it tipped the scale at a single ounce. Then they spin it into thread, and weave the thread into sails.'

'But that's incredible!'

She smiled wryly. 'It's also extraordinarily expensive, because you can only use the naturally shed feathers of the pegasus – otherwise they'd have died out long ago. A single sail's worth might take a weaver two years to collect.'

She took the rudder, Ratwin called out directions, and they moved fast across the water; Christopher leaned over the ship's sides, and within minutes the City of Scholars was out of sight. They passed ships large enough for two hundred sailors, and darting one-person craft. Within an hour, though, the cities gave way to much smaller towns and villages, and they saw more creatures, fewer people. Mal and Christopher found bunks below deck – his had a deep red counterpane, embroidered with a dragon, hers a yellow one embossed with a griffin – and slept.

They woke to find the sun high, and a salt sweetness to the air. As they drank hot milk and honey from white enamel mugs for breakfast, they passed close to a tiny village. It was built right against the shore, the houses low wooden cabins, painted in faded colours. A crowd of children saw them pass, and ran down to the sea-edge to wave and shout. Christopher waved back, and then gave a yell: 'Mal! Come and see this, quick!'

There was a boy in the crowd, his curly-black hair wild in the wind, riding on the back of a boar the size of a cart horse. Mal gave a yelp of delight. 'A twrch tryth!' She pronounced it *twoork troeeth*.

The boar's tusks were as long as baseball bats, and its fur an iridescent blue-black.

'They're very hard to tame', she said, and there was warm envy in her voice. 'But if they adopt you, they'll fight to the death for you.'

As they watched, two more great boars came clumping down to the seashore, each ridden by a child of about ten. One stood up on the tryth's back, and did a pirouette, her hair whipping around her head. Mal and Christopher applauded, and the girl laughed and bowed.

Mal swung hungrily over the edge of the boat. 'I'd never seen one. We don't have them in Atidina. There's so much I've never seen!'

'Yeah, well. There's even more that I haven't.'

147

She was in a voluble, exclamatory mood. 'We'll see it together!'

The tryth with the girl waded into the deep blue water, the girl still standing on its back, and swam towards the boat. The girl dropped to kneel, unworried about the water staining her cotton trousers. Mal took a dried fish from a case and threw it to the tryth. It fell just short, so she gave one to Christopher, who pulled back his arm and threw it as hard as he could. The tryth caught it in its jaws and gave a grunt of pleasure. The girl beamed, touched her two fingers to her heart, and held them out to Mal, then Christopher. Mal returned the gesture.

'It's better than anything I've ever imagined,' said Christopher. He felt it getting into his skin, into his lungs: a kind of wonder. He felt taller, and tougher, and he gripped the side of the boat. It was of this, he thought, that his grandfather was guardian; it was this he himself was supposed to guard.

Soon the wooden cabins were in the distance, and then there were no more humans. The landscape began to shift. In the morning, they passed meadows spotted with purple and red flowers; he saw a group of human-sized creatures, their skin mottled like bark, dancing to a song he could not hear. But as they sailed north, it grew harsher. As the day went on, the land grew rocky.

Ratwin launched herself overboard to catch fish, eventually filling a bucket, each fish bearing a small set of tooth marks. Christopher and Mal found knives and began to gut them. He rubbed the seawater between his fingers. 'It's changing, I think,' he said. 'The water feels colder.'

'The sphinxes are hardy,' said Irian. She scraped the scales from a fish with long, elegant fingers. 'And the cold keeps away predators. Dragons prefer warmer breezes.'

Christopher stared. 'You're not seriously telling me that dragons don't like the cold?'

'They're cold-blooded – they feel the chill. In your world, you tell stories of dragons living in damp caves; that's nonsense. They crave sunlight. More cold equals fewer dragons, generally speaking – and it's colder the further north you go.'

'Except at the farthest north though,' said Mal. She gave the guts to Gelifen, who took them daintily from her hand. 'On Arkhe. That's hot – because of the Somnulum, obviously.'

'The Som-what?'

'The low-slung sun.' She looked astonished. 'You know! Where Icarus flew.'

'Icarus flew into the sun.'

She snorted, and grinned at him. 'Not the actual sun.'

'Yes! The actual, literal sun. His father made him wings out of feathers and wax, and he flew into the sun, and the wings melted and he died.' His knife was blunt. He held the fish out to Gelifen. 'Geli – can you slice along here?' And he took the griffin's claw in his hand, and helped him run his talon along the fish's belly. 'And he's a Greek myth, so he didn't *actually* do anything.'

'Christopher.' Her voice was full of sardonic faux-pity. 'You are aware the sun is very, very far away?'

'I am, thank you! I'm not an idiot.' He hooked the guts out, and put them in a pile for the griffin.

She tucked her chin into her neck and raised her eyebrows.

'Icarus didn't fly anywhere because Icarus is a metaphor!' said Christopher.

'Icarus was not a *metaphor*! He was a person. He was on the island of Arkhe and he flew too close to the Somnulum.'

Christopher held out another fish to Gelifen; the griffin sliced it down the front.

'She's right,' said Irian. 'There are good historical records of Icarus's life. And the Somnulum isn't really a sun – it's the purest form of heat, in the sky above the first tree, above the maze.'

'It burns pure glimourie. We learned it at school,' said Mal. She cut herself on her gutting knife, and sucked her thumb, and then winced at the taste. '*Ugh*! Fish guts.'

'It formed when the ring of protection around the Archipelago was put in place by the Immortal,' said Irian. She worked twice the speed of any of them. Her fingers were rather longer and slimmer, he realised, than those of any woman he'd known; and faster too. 'The Somnulum's gravitational pull holds the protection steady,' she went on, 'in the same way that the moon pulls the tides. Your waters, of course, have some glimourie to them too; a trace amount, across the oceans.' She dropped the last of the fish in the earthenware dish. 'There. Nighthand can cook these. Haul up some water, and wash your hands in it.'

Christopher leaned out over the edge of the boat, hauling the bucket. He stared out at the sea. He'd been taught the science of the moon at school. If you thought about it clearly – thought hard and sharp and sideways – it was fully as astonishing as the glimourie: that the moon could move the waters of the Earth. If the glimourie protected the Archipelago, what protected the rest of the Earth?

A wave cracked against the side of the boat, and he shook himself. There were no boats now for miles, and no people; only the mountains. The landscape had a bleak splendour – rocky cliffs, spotted with hardy-looking trees which grew, windswept, amid the stone. Some of the rocks were black, and some slate, but many were silverish, shimmering with what looked like malachite. It glittered. It was a fierce and dauntless beauty, but it was not welcoming.

Ratwin appeared, Nighthand with her. Nighthand had been drinking the night before, hunched over a bottle of whisky and two glasses. One of the glasses, set out opposite him, where Warren should have been, remained empty. His face now was the same green as the ratatoska's fur.

'We're very close,' Ratwin said, assessing the mountains on the coast. 'It's impossiblated to moor at the foot of their mountain, so you'll have to drop anchor further out. You can row-boat in. I shall guard the ship. If marauders come, I shall eat them.'

Christopher looked out at the rocky waters. 'It looks – that bay, there – quite sheltered?'

Nighthand smiled. 'It does. But when Ratwin says it's not possible, she means that the waters will not allow it. The sea in the Archipelago is opinionated. Only small boats can moor at the foot of the sphinxes' mountain.'

'Some islands make it impossible to land at all,' said Irian, joining them. 'You would simply sail and sail and never reach the shore.'

'On the Island of Murderers,' said Ratwin, 'it's the opposite-face. Any boat can approach and land, but nobody – no boat, no mans, no ratatoska, no flying or swimming creature – can ever make it out again. The reef would suck you into the seabed and keep you there forevers. And that,' she said to Christopher, 'before you go asking with your *but-what* face and your *no-really* eyes, is purest fact.'

'Except dryad-wood,' said Irian. 'I once read an old text that said a dryad-wood ship can sail in and out, being wood with a heart of its own.'

'That's a children's tale.' Nighthand gave a snort. 'And I thought you were a scholar? There's no such thing. Let's go, before my hangover gets worse. I feel like a lavellan is eating my eyeballs from the inside.'

Nighthand rowed, clutching oars which looked like cutlery in his huge hands, Gelifen perched in the bow. The closer they got, the more wild and forbidding the mountain looked. A short beach of grey-white sand led to the cliff edge, which rose, a great face of variegated rock, for fifty feet. There were shrubs clinging to the surface, and birds perched on occasional outcrops – crows, a nest of sand-martins and a flock of four silver-grey hawk-like birds Christopher had never seen before.

Nighthand leaped out into thigh-deep water and dragged the boat up on to the shore. Irian approached the rock face, and ran careful fingers along it.

'We'll have to climb.' A heavy brown vine wound over the rock, and she snapped a piece of it off. 'This is greensword. It shouldn't be brown: it's evergreen. Alive all year round.'

'Which means?'

Irian shook her head. She put the piece of vine in her pocket. 'I've never seen it dead, like this. It worries me.'

Christopher approached the rock face. It had good hand-holds, but they were far apart. He was nearly as tall as Irian, but both would have to stretch. For Mal it would be impossible. And the fall – if they fell – would be deadly.

'Mal will ride on my back,' said Nighthand. He turned to the wall with a face impassive as granite. 'Unless you can fly?'

Mal licked a finger and held it to the air, her face careful: a connoisseur of wind. 'I don't think I can,' she said. 'Not for more than maybe a few seconds. It's too erratic.'

'Then climb on. The sphinxes await!'

He bent for Mal to climb on to his massive back. He was so tall and so broad that it was a scramble for her.

She held on gingerly to his shoulders, Gelifen clinging to her. Nighthand shook himself impatiently. 'Hold me round the neck – you won't hurt me.'

'We need to move fast,' said Irian. 'The sphinxes will know we landed. It's best not to keep them waiting. An impatient sphinx is a dangerous thing.'

Nighthand climbed first. He climbed with the confidence and speed of what he was: a person who has never once in his life contemplated the idea of falling. He appeared not to feel Mal's weight.

Irian went next: Christopher followed. It was painful, difficult work. The grips were often jagged-edged, and cut at his fingers. But he made progress – slowly he ascended, breathing hard. Ten feet, fifteen, twenty, thirty.

Then, just as he was nearing the top, a piece of rock he had gripped in his left hand began to crumble in his fingers. He twisted to the left to look; the greensword had burrowed into it, through the cracks, and now the rock was disintegrating into pieces. He had just time to register that the rock was coming away in his hand when his foot slipped from under him.

He fell.

THE OPPOSITE OF FALLING

The thought went through his head, far faster than speech: *This can't be happening.* And: *I'm going to die.* And: *Dad will never know. He'll have to wait, forever, not knowing if I'm coming back.*

And then he jerked, suddenly, to a hard and painful stop.

He had landed on a shrub, growing from the rock; he caught hold of it with one hand, snatched at it with the other, and held there. His lungs were in his throat, his stomach somewhere near his knees. The shrub – which was, up close, a stunted little tree, smaller than him – grew from a ledge: four foot across, and ten inches deep. He scrambled for a foothold and stood, waiting for his breath to return, both arms embracing the tree.

He forced himself to steady; worked his way up from toes to knees to elbows, willing each joint and muscle to stop shaking.

'I'm *alive*,' he breathed.

He looked down, which was a mistake. The drop was forty feet. But before terror could take full hold of him again, he heard shouts from above, where the others had completed the climb.

'Christopher! Are you hurt?' called Irian.

Only Nighthand sounded untroubled: 'That seems an eccentric place for a rest stop.'

Mal's face appeared; she crouched right at the edge of the cliff, holding on to the rock. 'Don't *do* that! I thought I was going to be sick: I turned round and you were falling,' she said. Under her imperious tone he could hear a tremble. There were frightened tears in her eyes.

'I'm not hurt,' he said. It wasn't true – he was bleeding from both knees and would have a bruise that would purple his whole shin – but he was alive.

Nighthand's low voice came on the wind: 'Can you see a handhold? Can you get up?'

Christopher looked. All the handholds in reach above and below had collapsed with the rock; the only grips looked like they would crumble if he touched them.

'The stone's unstable,' said Christopher. 'It won't hold.' He reached out one hand, and gripped at the rock face. He tugged it, hard, and it came away in his fingers.

'Then I'll have to come down,' said Nighthand.

'Don't!' said Irian. Her usual calm was shattered. 'The rock won't take you both – you'll both fall!'

Then there was a hiss, and an 'Oh!' – the sound of an idea taking shape – and Mal called down. 'Christopher! I'm going to throw down my coat. Are you ready?'

She lay on her stomach, her head and shoulders hanging out over the drop. She bundled the coat into a ball.

'Wait!' he called, as the wind gusted, blowing dust from the rock into his eyes and mouth – but it was too late. She dropped it.

The wind caught at the coat and pulled it sideways. He let go of the shrub with one hand, lunged, and snatched at the sleeve as it fell.

He heard Mal gasp and hiss in fear, and then in approval: 'Now put it on, but don't button it.'

One hand at a time, he did as she said. He tried not to look down.

'Then you take hold of the edges – where it would button – and you spread your arms – and the wind will lift you. It's not a good wind, but it's better than falling.'

'Are you sure this works for other people? Not just you?'

'Of course I'm sure.' This, although he did not know it until later, was a lie. Mal had never shared the coat before. There hadn't been anyone worthy of sharing it with; nobody she had cared about enough, until now.

The worst moment was when he had to let go of the tree, to take hold of the insides of the cloth.

He opened his arms and felt the wind catch at the coat. Then there was a tug, a sudden pull at his whole body, and he felt his feet leave the ledge. He shot upwards, lurching sideways, first away from the cliff and then – astonishingly fast – towards it. He dipped his left arm down and spun away, sideways, down low, and then up again.

He could feel, suddenly, how it worked – how to angle the way the air hit the shape of the coat. He swooped upwards, and Mal gave a great whoop of triumph, as he soared past her, past Irian's smile and Nighthand's crooked eyebrow.

'Come down!' called Irian. 'Before the wind drops!'

But there was nothing in the world he wanted to do less than come down. He soared up, and the wind was whipping his hair into his eyes, and it felt like pure glory – his legs out behind him, his whole body as light as air. He angled higher, up towards the birds, which flew with a cacophony of squawks to greet him.

'*Christopher!*' called Irian.

He pretended not to hear. Glee tore through him. He whooped.

'Christopher, the wind is falling!'

'Get down!' called Mal. 'She's right!'

Regretfully, he angled downward and landed on his feet. It jarred one ankle, but he stayed standing. He took off the coat, and handed it to Mal.

'That was incredible,' said Mal. 'I didn't think you'd be able to do it.'

Nighthand nodded at him. There was admiration in his face, an expression it was patently unused to. 'I congratulate you on not dying,' he said.

THE WRITTEN MOUNTAIN

What Christopher might have said in reply will never be known, because there was a noise among the small, wind-stunted trees on the clifftop, and out on to the rocky stretch of ground came a creature that silenced him completely.

It was vast. Its body was leonine, deep yellow, with paws as large as Christopher's torso. Its face was as if a human consciousness and human eyes had been laid upon a lion. Folded along its back were wings, vast and feathered and sand-coloured. Its tail was long, and lay behind it on the ground. He knew at once what it was.

Next to him, Mal hurriedly wiped her hands in her heavy black fringe, and stood as straight as if in the presence of royalty. She smoothed Gelifen's feathers, and stepped closer to Christopher.

It came nearer. A thrill of adrenalin went through him. Nighthand put his hand to the glamry blade at his belt and stepped in front of Mal. He sniffed. 'Smells like a cat,' he said.

'Strangers,' said the sphinx. Its voice was low and rough. 'What have you come for?'

'For information,' said Mal. And then she added, in the face of so many teeth, '*Please*.'

'Then you have come to solve a riddle? We do not give information without trial.'

'But why not?' said Irian. Christopher was startled to see how unafraid she seemed of the sphinx. 'Isn't that the point of knowledge – to pass it on?'

'We ask riddles for two reasons.' The sphinx's voice was strangely staccato, as if human language were not the tongue it was used to, but its English was perfect. 'We would be swamped by visitors – inundated with seekers after trivial knowledge that they could have found for themselves. The risk of death –' and its long tongue came out, and licked the top of its nose – 'whittles down the numbers.'

'Yes,' said Irian. Her tone was bone-dry. 'I can imagine it would have that effect.'

'And second, why tell truth to those not yet prepared to receive it? The riddles ensure that we tell our secrets to those who have already *learned how to think*.' Its yellow eyes grazed over Christopher, over Mal. 'And thirdly—'

'You said two reasons,' said Nighthand.

'Third', the sphinx said, louder, and its wings opened for just one moment, a great sweep of feather and threat, and the air shook, 'because it is a way of attracting food.'

'We'll answer the riddle', said Christopher. 'That's why we've come.'

The sphinx bowed his head. 'And if you get it wrong, perhaps we will eat you.'

'Perhaps?' said Mal.

'It is not my choice. If it were, there would be no perhaps. But it will be the choice of Naravirala, my mother, leader of our clan. My name is Belhib; I am her fourth son.'

'Would you eat all of us?' said Nighthand. He sounded interested. 'Or just the one who gets it wrong? It's important to be precise about these things, I think.'

'All of you', said Belhib. 'And the griffin. My mother will be interested in the griffin. Follow me.' And he set off at a swift lope across the rocks.

The cliff was part, Christopher could see now, of a huge mountain range. There was one great peak ahead of them; the incline was steady at first – rock and grass and lichen – and then steep, in sharp jags.

'Quicker', said Belhib.

Christopher and Mal climbed side by side, both breathing hard, talking – when they spoke – in whispers, heads close together, so that the sphinx could not hear. Gelifen curled around Christopher's neck. Christopher could feel his beak vibrating against his ear. Untroubled by the sphinx, the griffin, one of life's great anticipators, quivered with hope at what might come.

Irian followed, scrambling up scree fast, but rendered clumsy by the newness of her boots. Once, she slipped, both feet giving way at once, and Mal and Christopher twisted to help, but Nighthand, seemingly without looking, shot his left hand out and caught her round her upper arm.

He let go of her very swiftly, once she was back on her feet. 'You hurt?'

She had scree cut into her palms, but she shook her head. 'Just a little grated.'

'Keep steady,' he said, his voice gruff. 'Those shoes need treading in. Your feet are used to libraries.' And she laughed, and determinedly did not look round again. Only Christopher saw Nighthand glance down at his left hand, and touch his right thumb to the palm, before he began the climb.

They had been clambering upwards for at least an hour, perhaps two, when Christopher first noticed the marks cut into the rock. They came where the stone was smoothest: scratches, lines, curves and strikes. They looked like they had been gouged into the grey stone by a strong and confident claw. There could be no doubt about what it was.

'*Writing*,' he said to Mal.

She ran her fingers over it. 'I wish they'd taught me something useful at school, like Sphinx, instead of all that algebra.'

At that moment, the first noise came on the wind. It was soft, barely audible, but it was there: the thrum of voices.

'Do you hear that?' said Christopher, and she turned to it, her mouth slightly open to hear better, and nodded.

'It's coming from round the side of the mountain,' she said.

'Follow!' called Belhib. 'Faster!' They rounded an outcrop, moving on hands and feet – and stopped short.

The mountain was alive with movement. Over the surface of the rock face, dropping between ridges, prowling up and down the slope with the effortless ease of vast ballerinas, lying with their faces turned to the sun and wind, were what looked, at a distance, like yellow-gold winged cats: cats that stood ten feet high.

They walked closer, Belhib calling out in his own language as they came.

'Are you telling them not to fear us?' said Nighthand.

'I am telling them not to *eat* you. It's impossible for a human to hurt a sphinx.'

Nighthand looked like he might be about to debate that, but Irian raised her eyebrows, and he fell silent.

The sphinxes' strength, Christopher saw, was dizzying: they leaped like coiled springs upwards over the rock, covering twenty feet at a bound. In the lee of a boulder, a circle of sphinxes was eating something meaty and unidentifiable, tearing at it with teeth as long as his fingers and twice as thick. They spoke to each other, in a brief guttural language. There was no sweetness in their faces. Christopher felt fear rise in him, and pushed it back.

The peak came in sight; it formed the wide, blunt top of a ridge, huge and broad and windswept. Two of the largest and oldest sphinxes were at the summit, scratching with their vast forepaws into the rock face, writing.

Christopher nudged Mal. 'Look', he said. 'The whole mountainside!'

Above their heads, as far as he could see, nearly every surface of glittering stone was written upon. Some of it was in the alphabet he knew, some of it in alphabets he had never seen, with pictures, or great hashed strokes of geometry.

Irian too had seen. 'I'd heard about this', she said. There was awe in her voice. 'They move from mountain to mountain, etching their knowledge into the rock: histories, philosophies, songs, mathematics.' She ran her hand along a diagram gouged into the stone: a planet, bifurcated. 'They cut deep, so it will last a thousand years. When, after years, the whole mountain is written, they move to the next.'

Christopher watched the two sphinxes carving into the mountain as they approached; the rock gave way to their claws with a high, grating sound. Both had tails that ended in a ball of thorns, and expressions of deepest concentration. Belhib, who was the size of a car, was clearly small, by the standards of sphinxes.

With a final scramble, they reached the ridge. Birds circled overhead; the late-afternoon sun shone sideways into Christopher's eyes. It was beautiful and strange enough to make you shake.

'This is Naravirala', said Belhib. 'She will give you your riddles.'

And over the edge of the ridge, her fur rippling in the wind, came the largest sphinx they had yet seen.

She was old; the fur around her mouth and ears was white. Her back was densely muscled, and her claws long and sharply pointed, and with her came a sense of overwhelming power. Her face was neither kind nor unkind; if a face could look like distilled knowledge, it would be this. She looked them over. The scrutiny was like being bitten: it made Christopher feel something had got into his skin.

'I welcome you as guests,' she said. Her voice, like Belhib's, was tight, as if she prized words too much to waste any. 'But you are also trespassers, until we know your purpose.'

Irian stepped forward. She bowed, and touched two fingers to her heart. She introduced each person by name. 'Our purpose, my lady, is that which you believe it to be.'

Naravirala nodded. 'Good. You know the old customs.' Nighthand glanced towards Irian, surprised. 'Always assume the sphinx knows. And in this case, I believe that I do. But first, the riddles.'

FOUR RIDDLES

Naravirala roared. The sound carried down the mountainside, and there was a rustling, a hiss and bubble of conversation, as two dozen sphinxes came loping back up it. They prowled around them, seemingly uninterested in the adult humans – their eyes were on Christopher and Mal. An unreadable expression came over the sphinx's face as she prepared to ask the riddles.

Naravirala turned to Nighthand.

'First, the Berserker, with the strength of ten men and the courage of ten thousand. *I am light as a feather, yet the strongest person can't hold me for five minutes. What am I?*'

'I can think of nothing I could not hold for five minutes. A dragon, perhaps.'

'Answer the question.'

Nighthand looked across at Irian, who stood with her eyes on him, and then at Mal.

He scowled. There was a tinge of red to his cheek. 'I don't know! I said, I can think of nothing. Tell me, if I forfeit, will *all* of you try to eat me, or just one?'

Mal focused her eyes on him. She sucked her lips in, and puffed out her cheeks; she was turning red, her hands twisted together, her eyes wide.

'Oh!' and Nighthand gave a snort of angry relief. 'I understand. Your breath.'

Naravirala's eyes flickered, but she only nodded. 'Next, the scholar. *What has words, but never speaks?*'

Irian looked straight at Naravirala. Barely above a whisper, she said, 'A book.'

Under his breath, Belhib muttered something that was not celebratory.

Naravirala turned again. 'Now the girl. For you, I ask the oldest of riddles. *What walks on four legs in the morning, two legs in the afternoon and three legs in the evening?*'

Mal looked briefly panicked; and then a great relief crossed her face. 'I know this! A person. Four legs is crawling, two legs is walking, and three legs is an old lady with a stick.'

Belhib could be heard cracking his jaw in disgust.

'And finally, boy from the Otherlands. You have been brave in a strange place; but you will have to be braver, before the end. Here is your riddle. *There are two sisters. The first gives birth to the second, which in turn gives birth to the first. What are they?*'

Christopher wondered for one mad moment if the answer could be eyebrows. 'Think,' he whispered.

Belhib smiled.

'Is it ... the sea and the land? No – that doesn't work – wait! That's not my answer!'

The smile grew. Belhib was one hundred per cent dentistry. His teeth shone like daggers in the sloping sunlight.

Sunlight. A thought kicked another thought into being. 'I think ... Is it the day and the night?'

'It is.' Naravirala dipped her head in salute, and around her all the other sphinxes followed suit. 'You have passed our test. We will answer your question.'

She straightened up. At her nose and mouth there was the hint of pleasure. 'I will confess something to you. I hate riddles.'

'Mother!' said Belhib. An uneasy murmur reverberated around the mountain.

'It is the truth. They bore me. I hate questions with just one answer.'

'I feel the same,' said Irian. 'I hadn't expected to find so much in common with a sphinx.'

'For instance: consider the greatest riddle of all – what you should do with your one brief life? The answer is different for each person. There is no neat answer, though many have tried to offer one. There are no answers to being alive. There are only strong pieces of advice.'

'Such as?' said Irian. 'The wisdom of a sphinx would be worth hearing.'

The sphinx swept her eyes over them. 'For example –' and she looked at Christopher, at Mal – 'stop expecting life to get easier. It never does; that is not where its goodness lies. Or –' and she looked at Irian, at Nighthand – 'do not wait for people to be faultless before you allow yourself to adore them. Adore them anyway. Such things are worth more than riddles.' There was a murmur of dissent from the sphinxes behind her, and she flicked her tail in a quick whip of frustration, and they quietened. 'But it is a sphinx's duty and pact to ask riddles, so I keep the tradition.'

'And too often, the riddles are solved. We have not eaten human for several years,' said Belhib.

'Enough.' Naravirala turned a cutting look on her child; she whipped up her wings in warning, and beat them, huge feathered sails above her head. 'Come. Humans. Let us dine.'

'But we need to ask our question!' said Mal. 'It's urgent! Eating will take forever.'

'Are you not hungry?'

Gelifen nipped Mal's hand, and she said, 'Yes, starving, but—'

'I know what you've come to ask. It is the same question we have been asking ourselves. An hour will make no difference.'

They dined in the lee of a standing stone on the mountain top, on hard little apples, and bird meat, with the most senior sphinxes. There were nine of them, varying in size from rhinoceros to elephant. The sphinxes' table manners were non-existent. Christopher and Mal exchanged glances, and then followed suit, tearing with their hands and teeth at the meat. It was charred black in places, and tasted faintly of leather, but the day had left him ravenous; juice rolled down his chin.

One of the sphinxes brought, in her mouth, a large stone bowl, and in it a heaping of purple, pear-shaped gourds; Gelifen made straight for them.

'Pantherfruit!' cried Mal. She threw one to Christopher. 'I love these', she said. 'But they go rotten very quickly once you pick them, so people make them into wine, or jam. I've never had them fresh.'

The outer skin was tough – Mal spat hers out – but biting through to the flesh of it was astonishing. It was translucent, and tasted like red grape, only sweeter and deeper. He ate two so fast that juice ran down his wrists all the way to his elbows. Mal was similarly covered.

'Why is it called pantherfruit?' he asked.

'Because it looks like a panther's head. You know – they're mythical – black, with claws – they run as fast as the wind? You must have heard of them.'

'Panthers aren't mythical.'

She stared at him. 'Yes they are! Huge cats, that outrun horses?'

'They're real! I've seen one, in a zoo. And they didn't look particularly like fruit.'

Naravirala spoke to them. 'It's true, Malum, that panthers exist.'

Mal looked at her; but she did not argue with so many teeth.

'Humans have always travelled between the Archipelago and the Continents', said Naravirala, 'but still there is ignorance on both sides. People have always disbelieved travellers – particularly when they return, windswept and wild-eyed, and not quite in control of their tongues.'

She flicked her gaze at Christopher. 'There are many here in the Archipelago who believe that your story of Henry VIII is a metaphor, or a parable: a warning to little girls, not to get involved with kings. And your panthers, your hedgehogs, your giraffes, your swifts: they all sound just as improbable and mythic to Archipelagians as unicorns do to you.' She rolled back her gums and bared her teeth. 'You humans must take care that they do not become so in reality.'

THE MAN WHO SAID NO

At last, though, as the sun began to dip behind the mountain range to their left, Naravirala turned to the humans.

'Tell me now. Tell me what you have come to ask.'

Nighthand looked at Irian, but it was Mal who spoke. She did so carefully, and honestly. She told the sphinx the whole story, ending, 'So we want to know – what has happened to the glimourie? Why are dragons attacking, and krakens leaving their waters?'

The sphinx's great eyes swept over the company.

'The story is a hard one. It starts long ago.'

Mal and Christopher sat next to each other, waiting. Gelifen stretched himself in Mal's lap.

'Do you know how the protection around the Archipelago was made?'

Mal nodded, but Christopher shook his head.

'It was three thousand years ago. The Immortal – a brave woman, known as Heletha of Antiok, made the decision to protect us from the relentless destruction caused by human-kind. She chose to cut off the Archipelago from the rest of the world. She used the Glimourie Tree, from which the first magic grew – the strongest power there is, greater than that of any human or magical creature, power beyond all power – to place a barrier between the islands and the rest of the world. It allowed the magic to be concentrated here. Here it is thick enough in the soil and air for the creatures to thrive and live long, noble lives. We ourselves, we sphinxes, depend on it.

'But, as the millennia passed by, it became clear there was a risk. Every few centuries, some charlatan, some crawling, vicious soul, would try to get close to the Glimourie Tree – to steal it, to take it for their own. To conjure the greatest magic, to command a power beyond human power.

'It was a constant battle, to keep it safe.

'So, many hundreds of years later, the Immortal – by that time, a man named Ahmed Telos, a slow-voiced, gentle man of great tenacity and care – built a maze around the tree. He went into the non-magical world – the Immortal has often travelled, to learn about the world in its entirety, and spent whole lives in the non-magical Continents – and found a single man of genius. He was a man of many parts: a scholar, an artist, an engineer, an architect, a man of peace and a man of war. His name was Leonardo da Vinci. Leonardo, together with his cousin Enzo da Vinci, the finest stonemason in the world, were hailed as the greatest architects of their day; experts in the building of the most sophisticated fortifications and city walls. Leonardo drew up a master plan. He would, he said, build an impossible maze, a maze so complex that it could never be solved by those who did not know the way. The Glimourie Tree grows in a cavern, deep in the warmth of the earth; he cut the maze into the rock. He set it with traps, and tricks, and hidden perils. And safe at the heart of its deep mystery, the tree would flourish, forever safe and secure.

'It was vital, therefore, that only the Immortal knew the way through the maze. So once it was built, the two men agreed to take a potion that would make them forget. It was made by a centaur – the centaurs alone know how to make potions of such power – and the two men took it, and forgot. Leonardo and Enzo returned to their homes, infinitely richer, remembering nothing of what they had done.

'Since then, once in each lifetime, the Immortal enters the maze. They go to the tree. They tend to its roots. They make sure that it still thrives. And they take one infinitesimally small piece of bark, and eat it. Their skin will smell, very faintly, of the glimourie.'

'Which is all very well,' Nighthand burst in, 'but this tells us nothing new! There *is* no Immortal. There hasn't been for a hundred years. Nobody knows why.'

Naravirala inclined her great, white-freckled head. 'Perhaps very few humans know why. But some creatures do. We sphinxes take in news from everything – the ratatoskas, the

174

stars, the naiads and dryads and nereids. Even the manticores.'

Mal made a face of fear and disgust.

'The manticores know a great deal,' said Naravirala, 'though they rarely choose to do anything helpful with their knowledge. And from these sources we have pieced together what happened, a hundred years ago. We have written it in the stone.

'What happened was this:

'At every death, the Immortal is reborn within moments. The baby is exhausting for its parents. All human babies are, of course, but the Immortal, as a baby, is exceptionally so: they say it laughs and weeps without pause, for the first three years.

'One hundred years ago, the Immortal was born male, in the north of Lithia – he was a young man named Marik.'

The wind was picking up. The sun had dropped below the mountain range, and it was growing suddenly, fiercely cold. Mal took off her coat, and draped it over both their laps. Christopher nodded in thanks.

Naravirala went on, slow and clear and heavy-voiced: 'As Marik grew to be an adult, he grew more and more furious at his fate; at what he was. He loathed the Immortal knowledge that had been laid on him. He loathed that he could forget nothing.

'At last he reached a point when he could no longer bear it. He looked at the world. He saw its cruelty, and its sorrow, its bloodshed. He asked: Is it all, the Archipelago and the world beyond it – is it, the angry thing of the world, worth its own pain? Is humanity worth the pain it inflicts upon itself? His

175

whole body revolted; his whole heart told him, No. He said: No. No to his memories, no to knowledge, no to the terrible responsibility that comes with knowledge.

'So that was his great cry: No, to the world.

'He told his family that he was renouncing his gift.

'Everyone, of course, said that was not just mad but impossible. You *cannot* cease to be the Immortal.

'But Marik was determined. He remembered the potion of forgetting that Leonardo and Enzo da Vinci had taken. He went to the centaurs – there is a herd on the Island of Antiok who pass the secret of the potion from son to daughter to son.

'He paid them untold amounts of gold to make the potion: a potion stronger than any they had ever made. He put everything in order. There is a palace that an Immortal built six hundred years ago – the finest building in the Archipelago. Marik closed it up, locked the doors, and sent away the people. There was a boat – a dryad-wood schooner – and he hauled it out of the water and put it away.'

Another, older male sphinx broke in. 'It was so. He put it in the dining room, for Time to eat it.'

'And then he took the potion. And he forgot.' Naravirala blinked, and there was a weight of misery in the blink. 'It was a great, determined forgetting. He knew, when he drank it, that not only he, *but all the Immortals who came after him*, would not know they were Immortal.

'Do you understand? There have been at least two or three Immortals since then – perhaps more – who were born and died, unknowing. They did not know who and what they were. They lived as ordinary babies, ordinary children, ordinary adults.'

'Can it be undone?' said Christopher.

'It is possible. There is an antidote to the potion, as there is to all potions. None has ever taken it, but it could be made. And without the protection, the knowledge, the watchful and iron-willed care of the Immortal, the Archipelago is vulnerable. There is nobody who can enter the maze, to see that all is well with the Glimourie Tree. There is nobody whose sole job is the protection of what we cherish.

'And we have come to believe that the worst has happened. We have come to believe – through the stars, and the waters, and through messages that reach us – that something has made its way into the maze. The tree is dying; or being consumed.'

'But that's impossible!' said Nighthand.

'It should be. No one had knowledge of the maze but the Immortal. But it has happened.'

'What will happen?' asked Mal, at the same time as Christopher said, 'What if the Glimourie Tree is destroyed?'

'The protection for the islands will vanish. The creatures will not live for long, without the glimt. Everything that you have seen and loved will die. The griffins are, as you know, already nearly lost.' She bowed her head to Gelifen. 'The unicorns, the dragons, the ratatoskas.' She paused, and added, 'The sphinxes. We too. And the Outerlands: they would be at the mercy of such power.'

177

Belhib, behind her, made a tight, miserable noise in his throat. He moved to be close to his mother.

'What happened to the Immortal man – to Marik?' asked Christopher.

'He woke the next day, blank with forgetting. It took him some time to recover from the potion. For a month, he could not walk. And then he made himself a life, of sorts. He remained a wary kind of person. Afraid of curiosity. He died young, in an accident at sea. And after that ... We simply do not know who the Immortal is. We do not know in whose body the soul of all eternity resides.

'So if you want to find what is at the heart of the maze – if you wish to know what has happened to make the glimourie fail – first you must find the Immortal. Find the soul who was born of the first apple of the first tree, and who has known humanity since the beginning.'

AN ERUPTION OF VIOLENCE

They sailed back, largely in silence, to the City of Scholars, and docked the next morning at the quay. The first thing Irian did was make her way to the library, her face set with concentration. 'There must be something, somewhere, about the Immortal that we can use.'

'What about us?' said Mal. 'Where should we go?' She picked her nose, and inspected the snot on her finger, and ate it.

'Mal, that's disgusting', said Christopher.

'I saw you pick your nose yesterday.'

'I didn't eat it!'

'Then you're just disgusting *and* wasteful. At least I'm only disgusting.'

Nighthand was watching them, eyebrows high. 'Don't move from the boat', he said. 'I have some old contacts, who hear gossip other people don't. I'll seek them out, see if they've heard anything about the Immortal. Ratwin'll do the same.'

'We're coming too,' said Mal.

'No you're not! These contacts are not people you'd enjoy having tea with.'

They waited until the Berserker was out of sight, then exchanged a glance.

'Do you think ... ?'

'If we're quick ...'

'We didn't actually *say* we would stay ...'

Christopher grinned, and jumped down on to the quay.

'Let's find something to eat,' he said. 'Can't live on snot.'

They bought three huge slices of pillowy white sponge cake – one for Gelifen – and ate them walking through the streets, past shops selling bread and fruit and fish, and then down a silent side-street next to a canal. The cake was soft as velvet, but Christopher's mind wasn't fully on it.

'Mal,' he said. 'If the sphinxes can't tell us where to go, what are the other ancient creatures who could remember something? You said dragons are thousands of years old. Is there any way we could speak with a dragon?'

'I don't think dragons have much to do with humans,' said Mal. Gelifen took a mouthful of her cake. 'They're so old, and so wild, they barely think about humans. I think we're like ants to them.'

'But, the glimourie affects them too,' he said. He hesitated. 'The nereids – they said something about you. About you, and the glimourie.'

She was instantly alert. 'What?'

'It was difficult – there was so much sea, and only parts were in English—'

'Come on! Tell me, Christopher!'

'She said—'

But he was interrupted by a terrible scream. He turned to see a boy grabbing at Mal's arm, hauling her sideways. It was one of the two boys who had been waiting with the fortune teller.

She lashed out, and the boy swung at her, full in the mouth. Gelifen launched himself into the boy's face, and she smashed the heel of her palm into his nose. As he reeled back Christopher tackled him around the chest and the boy dropped, roaring, to the ground.

They barely had time to breathe, before the second boy came out of nowhere. He grabbed Christopher's hair, and, holding it, used the grip to punch him in the head. The shock took the breath out of Christopher, and he went limp, but the boy held him up and punched again, in the neck.

Mal stood with her back against a wall, winded, trying to catch her breath, staring down at the first boy. There was red on the pavement, and it seemed to have come from her lip. Christopher saw it, and his whole body turned hot.

He reached up and embraced the second boy, hugging him hard, so that the blows were smothered between their chests. Then he bit down, hard, on the boy's nose. The boy roared, and tried to pull away, and as he did, Christopher kicked his ankles so hard they slipped from under him. Mal moved away, Gelifen in her arms, making retching noises.

'I'll jump on your ribs next time until they break and stick into your lungs.' He felt his own face. He would have a black eye. 'What do you want her for?'

The boy spat, but said nothing.

Christopher's body was no longer red hot, and he no longer wanted to inflict pain. His head was buzzing, and there was blood in his mouth. But he lifted a foot back, as if about to kick again.

'No!' The boy muttered something that sounded like 's'ortal'.

'What?'

The first boy tried to get up. 'Don't tell him!'

Christopher was breathing hard through his nose. He felt sick rising in his throat. 'Tell me, or I'll make it so much worse.'

The boy groaned. 'She's the forgotten one, an't she. Our mother – she saw it in her palm, didn't she.'

Christopher remembered the fortune teller and looked at Mal, who was vomiting on the pavement several feet away, scowling.

'Forgotten what?' And a thought – a pin-sharp, unacknowledged thought that had dogged him since the kraken had lifted Mal on to a piece of driftwood – made him say: 'The Immortal? The lost Immortal?'

'There's a man – Kavil, he's called, this big blond one, with that bruise on his face – looking for her, and he's offering money. Real money – change-everything money. He says she's the Immortal. Our mam says it too.'

'But how does Kavil know?'

'That's not our business, is it. Said he was working for someone.'

Before he could ask more, the other boy had dragged his brother up. They ran for it, and Christopher didn't have the strength to stop them going.

He reached Mal just as she finished vomiting. 'I hit him in the nose,' she said by way of greeting. 'I think it broke.'

'How did you know to do that?'

'I don't know. It just came to me. And he – I don't know – he was scared to touch me. He had to force himself.'

Christopher opened his mouth to tell her what the boy had said – and then shut it again. Not here, not now. 'Can you walk?'

'Yes.' She stood up, wincing, and dusted the dirt from her hair, and tried to smile. 'Can you, more's the point?'

Christopher ran his tongue along his back teeth. Nothing was broken. 'Yeah. Let's go back to the *Shadow Dancer*. Fast.'

He didn't tell her what the boy had said until they were back at the boat, safe on board, sitting on camp chairs and feeding Gelifen a handful of prawns.

'The Immortal!' Mal said. She spoke lightly, but the strain in her voice made it sound high and thin. 'Everyone's obsessed with the Immortal! Immortal this, Immortal that. Believe me, I would know if I was immortal.'

'But that's the point – you wouldn't!' said Christopher. A great ball of tension – of the mad possibility of it – was rising in his chest. He thought of what the nereid had said; of the way that Gelifen breathed in her scent; of how the waybetween had opened exactly when she needed it. The thought filled his chest with chaos: something like panic, burgeoning into something like hope. 'That's what the sphinx said.'

'Saying it's me, it's like saying I'm a *centaur*. Knowing the secrets of all humanity isn't something that you can miss about yourself.'

'But you *wouldn't* know! And those boys—'

He tried to say more, but she got up, scowling. 'Please, Christopher, don't tell me you'd believe a fortune teller over me! They make their money from stupid little lies, and from idiots who believe them. Thankfully, griffins are immune.' She picked up Gelifen in her arms. His growth was more obvious than ever, as his hindquarters overspilt her arms. 'I'm going to make Gelifen take a bath. You can help. He tries to eat the soap, and then he farts bubbles for days afterwards.'

'Fine.'

'But not if you're going to keep talking about ... that.'

'Oh. Then – no.'

She looked, fleetingly, so hurt that he thought she would weep.

'I can't! Mal, *listen*—'

'I don't want to, do I.' And she left, and he stayed, staring out at the dock. The thought of what had happened took up so much of his chest that he was barely able to breathe.

That night, in his cabin on the moored boat, Christopher fell asleep almost instantly; but around midnight he jerked awake with the force of falling.

For a moment, he did not know why his whole body was tingling with shock. And then the word that had risen in his sleep came to him: a word that had been hovering at the edge of his brain, just out of reach. The knowledge was like a siren, filling the room. It winded him, far harder than the boy had done.

He went to find Mal. She was sleeping in her tiny cabin under the griffin bedspread. The ceiling was painted with flying dragons.

'Mal!' He shook her. 'Wake up!'

She was, understandably, annoyed. 'What?' She sat bolt upright. 'Is it Gelifen?' But Gelifen was safe next to her. 'Go back to sleep, Christopher. It's the middle of the night!'

'It's important! Wake up, properly, before I tell you.'

She rubbed at her face. 'Fine. I'm awake. I'm up. What is it?'

'Your name. From your namer's trance. *Malum*. It's Latin.'

'I know! I told you that. It means "mischief".' She smiled a sleepy smile, her fringe plastered against her forehead. 'We've achieved that, haven't we?'

'The thing is, Mal, *malum* has two meanings.'

'So?'

'It also means – "apple".'

There was a silence: long, stunned. He watched as comprehension overtook her: it flooded her face, which grew pale and rigid. And then into the silence came a whirring sound.

'What's that noise?' Christopher said.

He moved towards Mal's coat – the whirring was coming from the pocket. She snatched it from him.

'Don't touch that!'

She held the casapasaran in her hand. It was spinning, faster and faster, rattling in her palm as if it might break, whirring loudly – and then, as Irian and Nighthand appeared at the door, faces anxious, it suddenly clicked and came to rest, pointing due north.

'It's pointing to the first tree,' said Christopher. 'It's pointing to the heart of the glimourie. I told you! To the Immortal's first home.'

MALUM, APPLE

She was furious. Christopher had expected her to be many things, but not so bitterly, wild-eyed angry.

'I'm not the Immortal! Those boys, and you, and the casapasaran, are wrong.'

They sat on the deck, by lamplight, with Irian and Nighthand and Ratwin, whose faces were wide with astonishment, and wonder, and something else: something Christopher could not name. Something like fear.

'But what if they weren't wrong?' said Christopher. 'What if it's true? That potion – you could take the antidote! You could know all the secrets of the universe! You could remember everything, forever!'

'And what if I don't want it to be true?'

'Does that mean that you think it *is*?'

She was silent.

'Mal!' His voice rose to a shout of awe. 'Think of what you could—'

'If that man – Marik – decided he didn't want to know, it must have been for a reason! I want to have a normal, proper, real life. *One* life. Mine.'

'But you could save—'

She rose to her feet. 'Listen to me! Right now, every time I close my eyes, I see my Great-Aunt Leonor dead on the ground. One day, maybe, I'll forget a little bit. But if I take it, then I won't just remember that death, but every death the Immortal ever saw, forever. An eternity of dying. And – and all the stupid and cruel and embarrassing things I've done, and thought, and imagined! I'd have to remember that, forever, every day! The Immortal doesn't forget!'

He saw, as she spoke, what she meant: that it was too great a burden, a weight that would crush your body and soul. It was a truth to be afraid of. And she was so small, this girl, for such a weight to be set on her shoulders – small and stubborn and breakable. But still: the vast, astonishing possibility of it kicked at him, and he said, 'Mal – but think of what else you'd know, what else you'd see. It wouldn't just be death – it would be so much more than that—'

'I don't want to hear it!'

'Mal,' said Irian very gently. 'If this is true ... if it is – if the casapasaran, and the palm reader, and your name-day seer: if they were right—'

There was a sudden noise; a stamp, as Nighthand rose to his

feet. 'It is true,' he said. 'The casapasaran has glimourie in its metal; it can't break, or misguide. And I know it. I feel it. I have felt it, from the start, I believe, though I did not know what it was. Remember: it is the Berserker's duty, to guard the Immortal.'

Mal gave a suppressed scream of fury. 'I don't *want* you to!'

'I know,' he said. 'I know.' He strode abruptly away.

'But – the responsibility is—' began Irian.

'Yeah, well, I don't want it to be my responsibility! Why should it be on me? I still don't have all my adult teeth!'

Irian tried again. 'It may be, Mal, that there is only you. Only you, to save not just the Archipelago, and our glimourie – but the entire living world.'

'The world is huge! I'm sure somebody else can sort it out! If I take the potion – I will never rest. Never, never, ever, for eternity. So I won't.'

'But you could know all the secrets of the world!' said Christopher.

'I *don't want to*! OK? Think about what you're actually asking.'

'Mal,' said Christopher. 'The boat – the maze – if you don't—'

'Look, *you* bloody take the potion if you like the idea so much!'

Ratwin raised a hand, as if in class. 'It would kill him instantly.'

'Mal,' said Irian. Her voice was very tender. 'If this is true, then it's your duty, your calling.'

189

'No,' Mal said. 'No, no, no!'

She had never looked so small. Her skin looked thin enough for the air to blow straight through.

Nighthand reappeared as abruptly as he had left. He had shaved – so fast there were cuts on his face – and dipped his head in a water butt. He stalked to the side of the boat, and threw his flask of wine over the side.

He knelt before Mal.

'I kneel before the Immortal: before the eternal human soul. I offer you my knife and my protection, until the day of my death.'

Mal was weeping now. 'I don't want it. I don't want it!' And she turned and ran back down into her cabin, down to her bunk.

Christopher stared after her. 'I don't understand. She could know everything! She would be the most important and powerful person in the world!'

Irian sighed. 'It's not that easy. She will be thrown out of childhood. She will be even more alone. That's what happens to people who see and know more than others. There are some knowledges which mean exile.'

'But she'll still be *her*,' said Christopher. 'She'll still be Mal.'

'Will she?' said Irian. 'How much of us is what we know and what we've seen?'

Christopher waited. When Irian said no more, he said: 'Well?'

'There's no answer, only the question.'

LEAVING

Mal was waiting for him when he returned to his cabin. She had her coat on, and Gelifen in her arms.

'We're going,' she said.

'Where?'

'Back to Atidina. I'm not staying here.'

'But—'

'You can let me go alone or you can come with me. As soon as they're asleep.'

'But, Mal – the potion—'

'I don't care what they think. If you mention the potion again, I'll tear your ear off with my fingers, all right? You know I can.'

He looked at her: she was still shaking, shivering with shock and fear. He could not let her go alone. Immortal she might be, but she was physically small, and frightened.

'We'll walk across the city to the western docks,' said Mal.

'And I'll hire a boat, and go home, and I'll lock the door, and I'll never open it again.'

'But, Mal, the glimourie! Everything depends on it! The whole Archipelago—'

'Someone else will have to deal with it.'

'What if there are creatures in the waters? The sphinxes said they're afraid, and angry, and hungry—'

Her face was set: she looked seventy per cent jaw. 'Then we'll meet them, won't we? And we'll see who's angrier.'

The clocks were striking two when they crept off the boat. Gelifen sat on Mal's shoulder, his head resting against her cheek. They passed through the squares, crossing bridges over the moonlit canals in the dark. A ratatoska leaped from one lamp post to another. A bell chimed the quarter-hour.

'There'll be someone who will take us back to Atidina,' said Mal. 'For enough money. I still have quite a lot, in my coat. There are commercial sailors who will go anywhere, if you have the gold.'

They passed into a wide cobbled square, lined with shuttered stores. In the centre, a stone fountain in the shape of a mermaid sent water up into the lamplight. Heavy silver drinking cups hung by chains from its side, carved with unicorns.

'This way, I think,' said Christopher. 'This way is west.'

And then the whole night turned black, pitch and terrible black.

Adam Kavil stepped from behind the fountain.

Mal screamed, and Kavil ran at her. She was lifted off her feet, one hand on her mouth, the other on her flailing hands.

Christopher had no weapons: nothing. He looked wildly around the square. He seized one of the drinking cups and pulled; it came away with a great clattering screech.

He ran faster than he had ever run. He leaped on Kavil's back and set the chain against the man's neck, pulling backwards, backwards. Kavil gave a strangled roar and dropped Mal to face Christopher. His knife flashed in his hand.

Suddenly Gelifen was flying, furious, avenging, and his teeth and claws were among the darting, vicious blade.

Kavil turned, took aim with his knife and swiped at the griffin, who veered sideways with a long, high cry. Christopher swung the drinking cup on the chain and slung it with all his strength into the man's face. Kavil gave a yell, shock and pain together, and Mal seized the man's hand and sank her teeth into it, but the knife was rising again – she darted back, and it grazed at her skin – she twisted to spit in his face –

And then suddenly the terror was over: because Nighthand was there.

He came across the square like a one-man stampede, lifted Kavil bodily and hurled him against a wall.

Nighthand stood over him. Every line of his face was rage. 'You do not know how grotesquely stupid you have been. But you will. You will know.'

Kavil rolled away and up to his feet. His knife, and Nighthand's blade, flashed – a grunt – a stroke of blood – and then the top half of Kavil's knife, sliced in half, flew through the air. Christopher ducked and then hissed as it caught him on the shoulder.

The man pulled a second knife, longer, thinner, from his belt, and jabbed with it, his face lurid now with fear and hate; and Nighthand parried with the glamry blade as if he had all the time in the world, his face set and expressionless under the lamplight in the dark square.

And then Kavil twisted towards Mal again. He lunged at her, knife out, and Nighthand said, 'No. Enough,' and his knife-hand flashed, and the murderer dropped like a stone to the ground.

The Berserker bent over the murderer, and pressed his hand over a wound in Kavil's chest. Mal and Christopher ran to him.

Nighthand leaned close. 'Tell me why you are trying to kill her! Tell me! She is just a child.'

'She is not. She is the Immortal.'

Mal said: 'I'm not. I'm not!'

'She is. A namer – a seer – he told of a child whom he named Malum. He knew, or half knew, half hoped, what she was.'

'If you know that, what good is it to kill the Immortal?' said Nighthand.

'My master – he wishes the Immortal to be always a child.'

Nighthand's face was full of disgust. 'Why?'

Kavil shook his head, hair rubbing against the stone floor. 'I can't say. I am forbidden.'

Christopher said: 'Who is he? Your master, who is he?'

The murderer's voice was very thin. 'No,' he said again. 'He'll have me killed.'

Nighthand lifted his hand from the murderer's wound. 'You will bleed to death in three seconds unless I put my hand back. So tell me.'

'Stop! Stop! I do not know his name. He is the thing at the heart of the maze.'

'How did he get in?' said Nighthand. 'The maze is impassable!'

'Not to him. He is there, at the very centre – in the central chamber.' Kavil groaned, and his voice dropped lower. 'He got a message to me – he sent it on a breath of mist. He is gaining in his power.' He gasped. 'It grows daily. He will share it with the first who are loyal to him, and I will be first among the first.'

'You're a fool. He will not share.'

'He will,' breathed the man. 'When he controls it all.'

'All what? Tell me, man, or I'll remove my hand and leave you here to rot.'

'The glimourie. The world's glimourie. He devours it.'

'That's not possible.'

'It is. You're wrong.' Anger and hunger made his voice stronger. 'He did it. He went to the heart of the maze because he could see power awaiting him.' Kavil panted, and there was blood in his throat. 'He knew it was there for the taking. He risked death in the maze. And then he called to me, and told me what to do: to kill the girl. He told me it is wiser to side with power and darkness than with hope.' His voice rasped, and his face convulsed, a grunt of pain. 'Hope is a little lie that the powerless use to comfort themselves.'

'But no man can control the glimourie!'

'No! No man has ever done so *yet*. But he has found the way. And when he has consumed it all, he will have enough power in him to take not just the Archipelago, but the Otherlands.'

The whites of Kavil's eyes were red. But he looked at Christopher, and smiled a vaunting smile.

'The world entire. I know where you are from. I smell it. Don't think that you are safe. He will have all of it. He'll take hold of the world like a coin in the palm of his hand. He will make it his.'

Christopher couldn't breathe. He thought of his father, always so afraid, always anxiously holding the world at bay. It seemed in that moment that he had been right to be afraid, and Christopher had been wrong. Nothing in the world was safe – and for a moment, he pictured the Earth, spinning in starlit dark, and it felt to him as vulnerable as a newborn, and panic rose in him like a wild thing.

Kavil spoke again, barely a whisper. 'And he will give it to me. Nobody will be stronger, or more feared. Nobody will dare approach me.' The man's voice was growing weaker, and he began to mutter: half-words, none of them sense.

'What is he?' said Nighthand. 'Is he creature, human, what?' And then, as Kavil set his mouth in a tight line, 'How did you know how to find her? Tell me that!'

'Anja Trevasse,' he breathed. 'She told me.'

Nighthand let out a hiss of shock and horror, and Christopher stared, bewildered. 'Anja?'

But the man's lips convulsed, and his eyes closed. Nighthand rocked back, his head in his hands. Mal came to him, but he shook his head.

'Stay back, little Immortal.'

He bent, and lifted the man's body as lightly as if he were a doll, and carried him further into the alley, and laid him out, his hands across his chest. Christopher looked at the dead body, and then at Mal, who crouched down, with her back to a lamp post, rubbing at her bruised body.

A thought came to him with the force of a blow. 'Mal,' he said slowly. 'I know why he was hunting you. That thing in the maze – he wants you, and every Immortal, to be *young*. It's because he thinks children are helpless. He wants to make sure that the Immortal never grows to be an adult, so they can never be a threat.' It made a vicious kind of sense, and he felt it with a bitter certainty. 'Find the Immortal as a child, and kill them, and find them again, and kill them again, and again, and on like that, forever.'

She said: 'I'm not helpless.' But it was a mutter, low in her throat.

'I know that.' He reached out his hand to Mal and she took it, and rose. Together they watched Nighthand take the man's half-knife, and cut an X into his own palm. There were four there, Christopher saw, already; it made the fifth. His face had no satisfaction: only disgust. There was red on the cobbles of the square. Blood ran over stone.

And then a thin cry rent the air, and they turned, moving like twins.

What they saw was the worst thing of that terrible night.

It was Gelifen.

GELIFEN

They had not, in the dark, seen the blood in his feathers.

Mal ran to him where he lay on his side, on the broad rim of the fountain. 'Gelifen! Where are you hurt?' She lifted him, and cried out: suddenly blood was everywhere, on her hands and on his wings. She swung herself over the rim of the fountain and knelt in the shallow water, cupping the water over the griffin's body so that she could find the source of the blood. 'Don't panic. You'll be OK. You'll be all right.' But as Christopher leaped over the fountain edge, the creature's wings began to shake.

'Where's he hurt?' He gently parted the feathers: the knife had cut the little griffin across the torso. It was deep.

'Please don't,' Mal whispered to Gelifen. Her face – which could be so imperious, so miniature-queen – fell in on itself. 'Please don't die. I'll do anything. Please don't leave me here without you.'

199

Christopher knelt beside her and tore at his shirt with his teeth, wildly, like an animal, to make a bandage. A ragged piece ripped off.

'Here,' he said. 'This will help. It will. It just needs ...'

Together they fumbled with the cloth, and Christopher tied it tight. But it did not staunch the bleeding, and Gelifen's breath slowed and stuttered.

'Please no,' she whispered. Her hair fell over Gelifen's back as she bent over him. 'Please breathe.'

The griffin lifted his head, and laid it in the crook of Mal's elbow, and he inhaled her scent. Christopher bent his face to the griffin's face and whispered, very low, and Gelifen lifted one wing and fluttered it for him, but he did not give his familiar *burr*. His eyes closed.

Christopher was shivering. Tears ran down his face and lips and chin, and on to his hands, mixing with the blood. Gelifen was meant to grow large enough to shelter them under his wings, in the rain. They had talked about it, him and Mal.

His pulse was beating in his throat. A wave of despair and rage rolled over him.

Gelifen – the world's most magical creature, the joy-bird – gave a rasping breath. Christopher stifled a cry. He whispered, his mouth dry: 'No. He's the last.' It was so much beauty and intelligence, lost and not regained.

Mal held Gelifen to her chest. The scar he had left on her cheek showed red in the lamplight. The world contracted around them.

It was thus that Nighthand found them: Christopher kneeling next to Mal, the body of their most loved companion held between them. The fountain continued to play, and the water was red, and in the moonlight it looked as though the world itself were bleeding for them.

The last griffin died as the clocks struck the half-hour, and the noise rang out like a death toll through the sleeping city.

THE WORST QUESTION

They spent the rest of that night on the open deck of the boat, under the sky. Neither wanted to go to their bunk.

Sleep did not come. Christopher had never, until then, known what it was to break your heart. He had not realised it would feel so physical; that the place in his chest where his lungs should be would feel like broken glass. It hurt to breathe.

She spoke in the dark. 'I wish someone had told me.'

'What?'

'About the worst question.'

'What question?'

'The question, what if I had done it differently?'

There was a silence in the dark.

She said: 'Do you think – if I'd agreed to take the potion, right away – if I hadn't run away – if I'd known more – I wouldn't have lost him?'

He should have said: *Don't be ridiculous, don't be silly, you're just a kid, we both are. It wasn't your fault: it was only his, the murderer's.*

That is what he should have said. He knew it, even then.

But he didn't. There was a metal spike in his chest where his heart should be. He heard himself say: 'We'll never know now, will we.'

There was, on the outskirts of the City of Scholars, a forest. It had, once, been a royal cemetery. Here it was that, six hundred years ago, the last warrior queen was buried by her king. Now, with no queens or kings, it had grown wild, a forest of huge trees laced with dragonflowers and firelocks and bushes of orchids.

It was the night after Gelifen's death. Nighthand and Irian waited at the boat, talking in low voices, about Kavil, about Anja. Her betrayal had left Nighthand green and sick.

'I don't understand it,' he said. He said it over and over, as if the words would become a blade and cut through to an answer. 'I don't *understand*. She gave us the boat.'

'That was before she knew who Mal was.'

Mal and Christopher left Nighthand muttering vengeance, and stepped out alone into the city, on their way to the forest.

Mal had asked that only Christopher came with her. 'No adults. Nobody who will tell us what to do.'

They moved in the pitch-dark through the trees, guided

by torchlight. Shadows rose and fell around them in the forest, and they stumbled on branches, and creatures called in the night air, but neither was afraid. They had already lost.

They reached the great oak, at whose foot the warrior queen's stone showed where she had been laid to rest. A scrawny ratatoska sat in its branches. Gelifen lay in Mal's arms for one final time. She held him close to her chest.

Mal pointed out the spot. They took spades, and crouched and dug. They dug until their arms ached, and their hands were coated in soil. The bundle lay waiting.

At last Mal turned to lift Gelifen into his grave, but her hands were shaking. 'I'll drop him,' she said. 'I can't do it.'

So Christopher bent, and carried the griffin down into the earth.

'Wait! Don't fill it in. He needs something good, to go with him.'

Christopher looked around, up at the towering black trees, across to the flowers. Flowers he knew are thrown at the feet of dancers; at those who summon beauty. He crossed to a bush of white flowers, silver in the torchlight, and tugged at them, pulling and snapping. He took her an armful.

She nodded. She unwrapped the linen, and laid the blooms on Gelifen's wings, across his small, beautiful, unbreathing body.

She whispered to the griffin as she worked. Christopher could hear only snatches of words. 'When Leonor died ... you were the most living living thing ... it helped me live.' And more he could not hear, and then, so low it was barely a whisper: 'I'll remember forever.'

At last she stood back. Christopher, tears on his face, filled in the earth. He had promised, that first day in the lochan, to protect Gelifen. He should have talked her out of running away. He had failed.

A miracle had come to an end.

Mal took out Gelifen's grave marker. She had chiselled it with a penknife, in jerky capitals, working through the day, refusing to eat, or look up, or talk to Irian, who had come to coax her to drink a cup of cordial. She had hidden her face behind her hair, and her eyes had been walled by pain.

Christopher stepped back. Under the great canopy of the ancient forest, Mal cleared her throat. She read aloud what she had carved on the stone:

'With you so much is lost.
We won't forget.'

And beneath it:

'Here lies Gelifen
The Last and Best Griffin.'

Tears were running down her face and into her hair. Christopher moved so that their arms were touching, and she leaned into his side and sobbed like she would never stop. She wept in a way she had not wept before, for love torn away and protection failed and unbearable mistakes.

At last the two sat in the dirt, together. When she could speak, Mal gave a sigh that was as ancient as the forest. She said the only thing that could, at that moment, have restored hope.

'Gelifen, I'll make your death count. I swear it. Whatever it is, this thing in the maze, I will get to it.'

Her small muddy fists, clenched, were white at the knuckle.

'And I'll kill it.'

And though she was covered in earth and sweat and snot, Christopher's heart rose up and roared. His startled thought, as they turned to each other, was that she did, in that moment, look eternal.

They returned to the boat, through lamplit streets. It was 5 a.m., and the sun was just beginning to rise. He felt no surprise as Mal strode past the adults to the tiller. She pointed them towards the open water.

'Pull anchor,' she said. 'Cast off.'

'Mal,' said Irian. 'What are you doing?'

'We're going to Antiok – to the Island of Centaurs, to find one who can make the potion.'

'What?' said Nighthand.

'I'm going to remember.'

'But you said—'

'I know what I said. I'm not saying it any more.'

Nighthand strode closer to her, his huge bulk moving fast across the deck, his shoulder knocking a lamp off the wall. It shattered; nobody glanced at it. 'What do you mean?' He made no effort to try to keep the hot hope from his voice.

'I mean I'll take the potion, and I'll remember the way into the maze. I'll go to the centre, to the dark, and I'll find whatever evil creature it was that sent that man after me – and I'll destroy it.'

'Are you sure?'

She nodded, a jerk of her chin upwards, and the wind lifted her hair and made it nod too. 'If I don't, it won't just be Gelifen,' she said. 'It will be everything. I can't let any more be lost.'

There was the briefest silence, filled only by the noise of the sea – and then Nighthand gave a great roar.

'To battle then! To the unknown! To nobody-knows-what, together!'

And Irian pulled the map on to the deck and unrolled it, and Ratwin bent over it, and Nighthand put his hand to the glamry blade and moved to stand beside Mal, where every inch of his blood and bone had told him he belonged, and Christopher tried to smile at her.

And she smiled back. It was war, that smile. Her face as she turned to the horizon had the kind of look that ought to come with a warning sign: *Stand clear: danger.*

A PIECE OF COMPLICATING AND UNWELCOME NEWS

But it was not simple. Very little, after all, is ever simple.

For half a day, the voyage flew. The boat moved fast and sharp across the waves, skimming like a skipped stone. The water turned turquoise, and the weather was hot, of the kind that makes the skin between fingers and toes turn slippery with sweat. They paused, seven hours in, for Ratwin to fish, and Nighthand swung himself over the edge of the boat after her and into the water.

'Little dip?' he called up, and Christopher and Mal joined him in the ocean.

'I don't swim,' said Irian. She ran her hand through her close-cropped hair and looked away.

Ratwin watched her from the sea, her squirrel face sceptical. 'A sea-biologist who doesn't water themselves?'

'Somebody's got to stay on the boat,' Irian said.

The water was full of life – darting fish in blues and oranges, something flat and silver-grey moving along the bottom of the ocean bed beneath them – and Ratwin caught twelve large prawns, spitting them one by one on to the deck with a soft *pfft*, and then sitting back to wash her horn with her forepaws.

'Too much salt water makes it brittle,' she said. '*Dirt-horn* is a terrible insult to a ratatoska.'

They roasted the prawns on the deck, and Christopher and Mal were covered to the wrist in shreds of pink shell when a spot appeared in the sky.

'Look out above!' called Ratwin. 'Something incoming.'

The spot took on shape, and colour, and clarity: the long green wings of a longma. It circled lower and closer, and Christopher's whole body stiffened in shock.

It was Anja. She wore navy silk riding clothes, and sapphires, and an expression as inscrutable as the sea.

Nighthand's glamry blade was at once in his hand. '*Anja?* You dare show your face here?'

The old woman called down to them. 'Don't kill me, Nighthand. It would be a waste of good information.' She kicked the longma, and it dropped closer.

'Get out of my sight,' said Nighthand, 'or I swear I'll cut you down into the sea and leave you there to rot.'

Mal watched, her lips pressed together, and her eyes hot with rage.

'I warn you, I am going to fly closer,' said Anja. 'I can't shout across this distance.'

Irian breathed, 'You handed her to a murderer.'

The old woman did not apologise. Her heavy-lidded eyes blinked, once. 'I did not know he was a murderer. I heard – from the fortune teller, and a ratatoska – that the child was the missing Ever-Soul. I heard what you wanted her to do: to drink the potion, to remember all that the Immortal ever knew. I wished to stop it.'

'Why?' said Mal.

The old woman nudged the longma to move away: away from Mal, and her small, set face. There was a twitch in the woman's eyes; whether repulsion or fear or guilt, or some bleak mixture of the three, Christopher couldn't tell. 'I am the city's primary landowner; head of the guild—'

'We were told that. You own the city,' said Mal.

'And were you told that my great-grandfather was its governor? That he was elected in honour of the vast donation he made to the city?'

Mal didn't answer, so Christopher said, 'What's your point?' He saw no need at all to be polite.

The longma beat its wings, and Anja's voice grew flintier. 'My great-grandfather had a business partner – a man he'd known since they were young, working in selkie-rock mining. My great-grandfather had him killed, and took the profits of his work. I spent years hunting down and burning all written records of it. And everyone who knew him is long dead. But the Immortal knew.'

Ratwin's whiskers were quivering with anger. 'You said you likes the high-bloods, the ready-made-eliters, the born-on-tops. You told them so.'

'I did.'

'And you're not. You're the bloodline of a crook.'

'I –' and the woman's nostrils flared – 'chose to make an exception for myself. But I couldn't allow anyone to know. Not I wouldn't – I *couldn't*! It would end everything – not just for me, but for so many whose livelihoods rely on me—'

'Oh, you were being *charitable*, getting me killed?' said Mal.

'These are nuanced questions, far beyond your comprehension! My social position, my financial security ...' Her voice tailed off. 'So I took the necessary steps.'

Irian rose. 'You need to get yourself out of here, before I kill you myself.'

The longma dropped lower, hovering over the ocean, beating its wings in long slow beats.

'I didn't realise!' said Anja, and her voice quavered and cracked. 'I didn't understand his plan! I swear, in my heart—'

'Oh, please. You ate your own heart with a knife and fork long ago,' said Nighthand.

'I believed only that he would take her somewhere. He said she would be taken to one of the western islands, and kept there. He said he wouldn't harm her. And I believed him. Or ... I chose to believe I believed him.'

'Quite.'

'And so I owe you a debt. And I pay my debts!'

'Do you?' said Nighthand. 'Or do you pay what you choose to pretend is your debt? Who is your debt-accountant? Your own conscience? Because your conscience is a drunkard. What you have done is not a debt that's payable.'

'I don't want anything you can give me now,' said Mal. Her mouth was thin and sharp as a knife.

'Then listen, or don't listen! I know what you're seeking: the potion, made by centaurs. I heard it from a ratatoska.'

They waited, a row of upturned cold-cut faces. Nobody spoke.

'I flew to Antiok earlier today, to tell them to make ready. What the centaurs told me was bad news. There is only one centaur who knows the potion lore and has the skill to make it. His name is Petroc. He is no longer on their island. He has been banished.'

Nighthand bristled. 'So we'll go wherever he is. We have a boat.'

'My boat.'

He splendidly ignored her. 'We have our bodies and our knives and our wits.'

'He is on the Island of Murderers.'

There was a pause.

'That, yes, might be a problem,' said Nighthand.

'I flew to the Island of Murderers too – I cannot land there, of course, nor get close, but I was able to speak to him.

He says he'll make the potion, but there's one ingredient he doesn't have.'

'What is it?'

'He requires gold.'

'I have gold,' said Nighthand, and his hands went to his earrings.

'It must be plucked from the tree of living gold. The tree is on Areat, guarded by a jaculus dragon. There.' She cocked her chin. 'That is information worth having, no?' And before anyone could speak, she kicked the longma, and circled upwards into the sky.

They sat on the boat, mid-ocean, rising and falling on the waves. Ratwin sat at the tiller, but the boat drifted. They did not know where to steer.

'The Island of Living Gold is possible. It is guarded by a dragon, so it might involve being burned to death, but it is possible,' said Nighthand.

'The bigger problem is the Island of Murderers,' said Irian to Christopher. 'The island is impossible to leave. As Naravirala said, any boat can enter, but none has ever made its way out again.'

'Has anyone tried to swim?' said Christopher.

'They have, and they have died,' said Irian.

Nighthand's whole face lit up. 'That's an idea, boy. I could swim!'

'I just said, Nighthand. All who try it have died.'

'But with the glimourie fading, the waters are changing. The power of the waters around the island may have faded too. I say, I risk it.'

'And I say, I'd rather you didn't.'

'Why not?'

Her voice was quiet, but uncowed. 'It doesn't seem the most rational or reasonable route to take, Nighthand.'

'Rational be damned!'

'That's easy to say – but your strategy might leave everyone dead on the seabed. We will find another way. Let me think.'

Irian's eyebrows drew together, and her mouth tightened, and her whole face took on the look of an arrow pointed at a question.

At last, she spoke. She did no exclaiming; only a flicker in her eyes told that she had found her answer. 'The sphinxes,' she said, 'told us that the Immortal had a dryad-wood boat. The last Immortal put it in the dining room, for Time to eat it.'

'But Irian—'

'And a dryad-wood boat is the only thing that can break away from the Island of Murderers.'

'Irian, no matter what the sphinxes say, the boat *cannot exist*,' said Nighthand. 'I still vote for swimming.'

'Why can't it exist?' said Christopher. 'Until last week, I thought *none* of this could exist.'

'Irian knows why,' said Nighthand. 'It's because no dryad would give her tree for wood. It would be like giving your own skin.'

'But think,' said Irian, 'of what we know of the Immortal. Back at the beginning, when they were a fish, a wolf, an eagle – why shouldn't they have been a dryad?'

Nighthand's face was slowly shifting, from resentment to light. 'Irian ...'

'What if they made a boat from their own wood? That would explain its rarity, and its power.'

'Brilliant woman!' Nighthand clapped a hand on hers, registered the warmth and softness of her skin, and swiftly removed it.

'And dryad-wood doesn't age. So if we can find that boat—'

'Ratwin!' cried Nighthand. 'Mark out the way for the Island of the Immortal!'

Irian frowned at his departing back. 'It's not so simple as he seems to think,' she said. 'If the island has been abandoned for a hundred years, it could be overrun. And not only with plants. With creatures. Creatures that can kill with a single bite.'

'Well,' said Mal, 'so what. If I had to, so could I.'

THE ISLAND OF THE IMMORTAL

It took two days of harsh and violent storms to reach the island. At night, the stars were invisible beneath bulging thunderclouds, and there were moments when even Ratwin hesitated, unsure as to the way.

During the worst of it, Mal moved out of her room and into Christopher's, and they slept side by side, waking when they were tossed against the wooden walls. The side of the boat sprang a leak in the cold dawn, and as they came in sight of the island Irian bent over it, her eyes narrowed, hammering in nails. All five were hungry and tired and sea-stained, but Nighthand's face was alight with excitement.

'Welcome', he said, his voice deep and sonorous, 'to the Island of the Immortal.' He spoilt the effect by leaping into the water to haul the rowing boat on to the sand and misjudging the depth, disappearing up to his neck.

Nighthand – wet but untroubled – hauled the boat to shore, helped Mal down to the sand, and offered Christopher his hand.

Irian, they had agreed, would stay on the *Shadow Dancer*. 'If I don't get this mended, we don't sail', Irian had said. Ratwin stayed too, crouched beside Irian, her mouth full of nails.

They walked over soft, yielding white sand, which gave way to white pebbles and then to tall, silver-barked trees.

'Does it feel familiar?' Christopher asked Mal.

She shook her head. 'I hoped it would. But, no – nothing.'

They walked up the beach, into the trees. Christopher kept up a steady turn of his head, left to right. The woods were strange; although there were the calls of dozens of birds, nothing rustled or moved at ground level. It was eerie. At last the trees thinned, giving way to a sweep of meadow, and they stepped out of the wood into sunlight. Mal stopped. Her mouth formed an O of astonishment.

'And there's your house, little Immortal,' said Nighthand.

'It's a palace!'

The meadow led up to white stone steps, rising to an immense, flagstoned courtyard. From its centre the palace rose in deep yellow stone, crenellated and ornate, to the sky. Three towers, each topped with a dome in dusky pink, gave it a look of wit and knowing intelligence, and its vast arched windows with their broad sills gave it solidity and purpose. It had, clearly, once been lavished with time, and attention, and hope.

But time had taken it back. Its walls were barely visible for the sweep of red roses that climbed up its sides. The flowers, left untended for a hundred years, had rioted, and they were everywhere: white roses curling up window ledges and spreading across the domes, orange roses forming in bushes ten feet across, pink roses cascading across the huge slabs of creamy yellow flagstone towards them. Hundreds of birds nested across the domes, and as they approached took off into the sky, crying out in alarm.

As they moved across the meadow towards the palace, Christopher sniffed. The air smelt of sea and flowers, but as they grew closer there was another note to it – a scent of rot.

'Can you smell that?' said Christopher.

Mal nodded. They approached the palace, slowly, their nerves on guard. 'There's something wrong here,' she said.

'What?' said Nighthand. He stepped in front of her, one arm out to protect her. 'Point me to it!' He drew his knife.

'The grass on the meadow should be longer,' said Mal. Her face was tense.

Nighthand's face fell. 'Little Immortal, I cannot fight the grass.'

'She's right,' said Christopher. 'If the roses have gone so wild, why is the grass so trimmed?'

'Someone's been trimming it.'

'Or some*thing*.'

They were almost at the palace now; Christopher could see the windows, clouded with dust and thick with bird droppings; someone had painstakingly painted miniature images along the windowpanes: lemon trees, flowers, tiny mermaids, a stern and lovely adult griffin. His heart tightened.

Some of the windows were cracked, and in others the roses had broken clean through the glass, pouring into the palace. 'At least we won't have to break a window to get in,' said Christopher.

'Wait here,' said Nighthand. He clambered over the windowsill, looked left and right, and nodded, giving a hand to Mal and then to Christopher.

The window formed the end of a long, high-ceilinged corridor, marble floored, its ceiling studded with jewelled mosaics. The corridor was flanked on both sides by marble statues of creatures: nymphs and dryads, armed centaurs, a unicorn. In places, the statues were so over-twined with roses that only the heads or feet showed. Many of the faces were missing a nose or an ear, but the person who had carved them had cared about making something true and lasting. They seemed to breathe.

Their feet rang in the corridor. At the end, it formed a T, leading to left and right.

'Which way,' asked Christopher, 'to the dining room?'

'I don't know,' said Mal.

'No instinct?' said Nighthand.

'No! I *told* you.' She looked side to side and bit her lip. 'I don't like it here. That smell's stronger. We need to get out fast. Me and Christopher will go left,' she said, 'and Nighthand, you go right.'

Nighthand began to argue – but she turned, her chin high. 'That's an order,' she said, and strode around the bend.

Christopher caught up with Mal; they pushed open the door, and found themselves in a ballroom. The greenery of outside had come cascading in over the last hundred years, and there was a piano, entwined in ivy, and a cello, and some wooden instruments Christopher had never seen, covered in vines.

'Not here,' said Mal. 'Watch out! The sweet-suckle will give you a rash.'

It was then that they heard it. A ringing sound: of something hard and fast, clanging against the marble floor.

'It's up ahead!' she said.

'Quick! This way,' said Christopher. But as they stepped out into the hallway, he let out a hiss and pulled Mal down to crouch behind a statue of a centaur.

'Look,' he breathed.

The thing that came around the corner of the curving corridor had hard intelligence in its eyes. It was, at first sight, a horned horse: larger than a cart horse, but thinner, gaunt: its ribs were visible, and its skull was vivid beneath its skin. Its coat was darkest purple, and its hooves were yellow, stained and callused and cracking. Its hide hung loose upon its body, like that of an old man. Its horn was black, and pointed at the tip like a rapier. It stank of blood and rot and ruin.

The creature sniffed. It let its tongue loll out, and its nostrils widen. It was insolent.

'No,' breathed Mal. 'No.' And then, as much in anger as in fear: 'Not in *my* palace.' She moved as if to run at it.

'Don't be an idiot!' he hissed, and pulled her back.

The noise of slow hooves rang through the hall, and two other karkadanns joined it at the far end of the corridor. The karkadanns sniffed the air. They came closer. Their smell made Christopher want to retch: it was like meat left in the sun for too long.

The first was barely eight feet away now. Christopher could feel Mal shaking next to him. Her teeth were chattering; she clenched them. The karkadann bent its horned face towards the centaur. Mal gasped –

And then suddenly there was a great roar from the far end of the corridor.

'Horsies! Oh, little horsies!' Nighthand's voice was one of raw glee – and at it the three karkadanns wheeled round on their hind legs, turned and galloped away towards it.

Gratitude flooded over Christopher. 'Quick!' he said. 'While he's distracting them. We need to find the dining room.'

They burst into the next room – a gold-painted drawing room, with a hole in the ceiling, and chewed-looking curtains – and then into a room full of maps, with a collection of globes stained with dust.

'It has to be close,' said Christopher. They ran around a corner into a new corridor. Roses and bird droppings covered the floor, and they could see the imprints of hooves where they had crushed the flowers to mulch.

Mal moved on down the corridor, half running, but

Christopher paused. In among the thorns and flowers, he saw a rusted door handle.

'Wait! There's a door here!'

He pushed it open, and sudden relief flooded his whole body.

It was a dining room – vast, with a chandelier and moss-covered silver bowls – and in the centre, on top of the table built to seat a hundred people, there was a sailing boat. It looked just big enough to fit eight or nine people. On its side was chiselled its name: the *Ever Onward*.

Another roar came, from somewhere in the palace. They heard Nighthand's voice. 'Come closer, little karkadanns. I shall make your horns into attractive lamps, with a shade on top.'

'Shouldn't we help him?' said Mal.

'Boat first,' said Christopher. 'Or what's the point?'

Inside the boat there was a mast, collapsed into four pieces, and a set of sails, neatly folded. While the table was covered in roses and moss, and the wood had been pocked with woodworm, the boat looked as fresh as if it had been newly varnished. It was a deep, shining brown.

'Dryad-wood,' said Mal, her voice awed, 'really does last forever.'

They hauled it off the table with a great clang. It was too heavy to lift, but they could drag it along the floor.

Nighthand's voice came again, closer now. 'I don't know if you understand language, but if you do, may I say that you should rethink your attitude to dental hygiene?' And then they heard him grunt and gasp – and a thud.

They dragged the boat down the corridor, towards the double-wide window at its end. 'Faster,' said Mal.

There was a human roar, and then an animal cry of agony, and Nighthand backed into the far end of the hallway. He held a broken marble sword from one of the marble centaurs in one hand, the glamry blade in the other. Both were blood-coated.

'I killed all three,' he yelled. There was sweat running down his face, but he seemed unhurt. His eyes lit at the sight of the boat. 'You found it!'

'Christopher did.'

Nighthand gave him a rare flash of a true smile: it altered his face. 'Good.' He lifted the boat as if it were a wicker basket of fruit, and pushed it out through the glassless window, on to the paving outside. 'Come now.'

He turned back to the waiting two – but they had frozen on the spot.

'*Karkadanns*,' breathed Mal.

It was like a nightmare. Through the open door at the end of the corridor came karkadanns. Not one or two, but a herd of thirty, their bodies pressed together. Some had scabbed patches of missing fur. Saliva dripped from their mouths.

Christopher turned to the window, but more karkadanns were approaching over the flagstones – eighteen of them, their stink violent in the air.

Nighthand acted so swiftly that nobody had time even to scream. 'Get behind me,' he said. He took Mal's chin in his hand. 'Don't move until I say. And if I die, you will not weep, you hear me? This is what I was born to.' He pushed Mal backwards, into the corner, Christopher next to her. He drew the glamry blade. 'This is the thing my blood keens for – to protect something worth protecting.'

He let out one long, high whinny.

'Come on, ponies!'

And they charged at him, a sea of furious black, of yellow hooves and yellow teeth.

Nighthand catapulted forwards. He swept his knife-arm left, right, left, jabbing and spinning, so fast he was a blur. In his left hand, he swung the marble sword. As fast as they came, they fell – he cut at necks, horns, eyes, ears, flanks, ducking low to cut at one from below, slicing at the tail of another.

Ten, fifteen, twenty fell, crashing against the statues, toppling among the roses. Mal screamed and gripped Christopher's elbow; neither would look away from Nighthand.

The last karkadann came on, horn down. Nighthand swept it aside with a blow from the marble sword that sent it crumpling to the ground. He coughed, hands on his knees, breathing hard.

'Let's go,' he said. 'The gymkhana is over.'

'Nighthand!' Mal shrieked. 'Look out!'

There was a galloping of hooves. He turned, but it was too late – the horn of a karkadann tore into his arm, sinking deep into his flesh. Nighthand let out a roar of rage and agony, twisted in the air, and sliced the horn clean off. It hung there, impaled in his arm. He jabbed, and the karkadann dropped at his feet.

Nighthand staggered back against the wall. He pulled the horn from his arm, and blood poured from him. He looked stunned.

Christopher pulled off his coat and offered it to tie around the cut. 'Let us help.' He and Mal together wrapped it around the wound.

With a gargantuan effort, Nighthand smiled. 'Onwards,' he said. He brushed aside their questions, their further offers of help. 'Stop. You know I don't like that kind of noise. It is the only form of talk I find stressful.' With his unhurt arm, he lifted Mal over the windowsill. He took hold of the boat with one hand, hoisted it aloft, and led them back to the water.

Irian was waiting. Her face lit up like a sunrise when she saw them coming. They tied the boat to the *Shadow Dancer*, and Irian hauled up the anchor. The *Shadow Dancer* scudded out over the water, towards the Island of Living Gold.

Christopher, Mal and Nighthand lay panting on the deck of the boat. Ratwin perched at Nighthand's head, her nose pressed close to his.

'What happened?' asked Irian. She fumbled for bandages in the medicine chest, and bent to unwrap Christopher's coat. Nighthand did not brush her away.

'Horses,' he said. 'Angry, angry horses.'

'Yeah,' said Christopher. 'I wouldn't recommend entering them in any Pony Club competitions any time soon.'

He heard Mal laugh, properly, for the first time in days.

THE HEAT OF LIVING GOLD

Nobody was laughing a day later, as they sailed under a clear sky closer to the Island of Living Gold.

It was Irian who first noticed Nighthand's wound was getting worse. Christopher, wiping the salt from the boat's light-hatches with a rag, saw her turn suddenly to the Berserker. 'Nighthand – your arm!'

'What about it?'

'It's swollen. And it ... smells.'

It did. As Nighthand took off his jacket, the stench of something animal, left to rot, became unmissable.

Nighthand glanced down. His upper arm was a mess of blood and cloth and something worse – something sticky, a paste-like yellow pus at the edges of the wound. He peeled back the bandage, and then, with his fingertip, pulled away an entire strip of skin, as calmly as if flipping through a magazine.

'Ah. My arm does seem to have ... gone off, yes.'

'I am thinksing,' said Ratwin, 'that humans are not supposed to smells so much like a swamp, no?' Her small green face was anxious.

'Nighthand! You need to take this seriously,' said Irian. 'What did that? Karkadann teeth? Or horn? If it's teeth, it'll heal. But if it's horn—'

'Horn. Yes.'

'The horn has a poison that the karakadann secretes from a gland at the point.' She watched him and, as his expression didn't change, she added, 'It's bad, Nighthand.'

'I do remember hearing that it wasn't something doctors actively recommend,' said Nighthand. He looked as though they were discussing a misprint on a bus timetable. 'Is there a cure?'

'I don't know. But we need to get you treatment, fast,' said Irian. 'Ratwin! We'll need to re-route—'

'We will not!' The Berserker stared at her. He was suddenly, abruptly, coated in anger. 'We will go to find gold, and then to find murderers. Too much time has been spent already – we don't have more to waste.'

'Nighthand.' Irian stepped backwards but held his gaze. 'The poison intensifies over time. What good will you be to the Immortal if you are dead?'

He scowled at her, his hair more than usually unruly, his face strained. 'It's a micro-inscrutable skin-scrape from an ugly little pony. Irian –' and he put up a hand, as if to shield himself

from her look – 'do not waste your energy making that face.'
His own face, unsettled in a way it had not been amid a stampede of karkadanns, turned from her.

'Nighthand', she said again, and her voice rose, angry
now in her turn. 'I'm asking you to be reasonable. Do I have
to beg?'

But he walked, an uneasy storm of a man, away from her.
His voice was brusque. 'Christopher! Mal! Where are you?'

'Here', said Christopher – for they had not seen him.

'Wash yourself in the sea! We must make a powerful
impression on the dragon. Dragons notice appearances, and
you children look eighteen varieties of disgusting.'

Mal, coming across the deck, glanced at Christopher, who
could see she was thinking the same thing as he was:
Nighthand looked equal parts sea salt, blood and facial hair. He
looked like a crime scene on legs. But Nighthand was unpredictable, and angered, and six feet ten inches tall, so he did not
say it aloud.

The boat needed their full attention now; to keep its sails
taut, and to navigate the reefs and rocks that rose from the
water. Christopher found the place – *Areat; or, the Island of
Living Gold*, it read – on his map: it was barely larger than a
pinhead.

'Anja told us', said Mal, and her lip curled at the name, 'that
the dragon is a jaculus.' She was sitting on the deck of the boat,
her back against the side, her knees under her chin. She spent a

great deal of time like that: sitting, silent, watching the water. 'What species is that?'

Irian wrinkled her forehead, dredging through her stock of learning. 'I'm afraid I'm not good on dragons. I know the red-winged, the silver, the yellow, the starlit, the bearded and the orchard dragon. But the sea is my specialism, not the sky.'

'Well, we'll be able to see it,' said Mal. 'I mean, it's a dragon. They're hard to miss. So we'll just wait until it's not there, and then we'll leap on to the island.'

They stopped to refill with fresh water, dropping anchor in a cove on the Island of Karkara. It was uninhabited by humans, but teeming with wildlife – iron-beaked gaganas flew overhead, glinting in the sun, and as the boat drew in, a cluster of small wildcats with luminescent fur went sprinting away.

'Carbuncles!' said Mal. 'If you follow them, you can find where they've buried treasure!'

'Although,' said Irian, 'their definition of *treasure* varies. There's people who've hunted the carbuncles for months, and dug up a rat's tail and three fish heads.'

There was too a population of freshwater salamanders. The woods and hills were spotted with their pools, with soft steam rising over the water and across the grass around them in a mist.

Mal and Christopher bathed in the water of the pools – as hot as a bath, warmed by the salamanders' bodies – and scrubbed at themselves with sea-sponges they found on the shore. The scar left by Gelifen on Mal's cheek was still raised and red, and she touched it very gently with her fingertips.

They had competitions over who could hold their breath underwater longest (Mal won) and who could hold an underwater handstand (Christopher won; Mal collapsed immediately, spitting up water). They found sap on a slim, willowy tree. ('An aya, I think,' she said; 'I dunno, I'm not good at trees.' 'That's not a good sign, given the extremely tree-based quest we're on,' he replied, and she snorted with laughter.) Mal, her spirits rising with every moment they were on the island, showed him how to lift the sap off the bark in long, sticky tendrils ('No, idiot! Watch me – don't break it off. *Peel* it'): it tasted of charred honey, and was as chewy as liquorice.

When they were fully dressed, Mal fished in her pocket for her gold thread, to plait it back into her hair. Her hand, searching in her pocket, pulled out the casapasaran.

She frowned at it as the dial swept in a full circle, and came to rest. 'Something's wrong! It was pointing to Arkhe – now it's moved. What does that mean?'

He looked at it. 'It's pointing the way we're going. Towards the Island of Living Gold.' Worry was rising in her eyes, and he thought fast. 'Maybe,' he said, 'now you're the Immortal – I mean, now that you've agreed to it – if your home—'

But before he could finish she broke in. 'Oh! I know what you mean. Maybe, if it points the way home – and if I don't have a home in the Archipelago any more – maybe now it points the way to get one.'

A sudden thought clouted him, and before he could stop

himself he blurted out, 'But wait – does that mean it could point you through the maze? Without the potion?'

For a moment her face convulsed with shock, with hope, with something stranger and more complicated than both; and then she shook her head. 'The sphinxes said da Vinci set the maze with traps. Even if it could – I don't know if it would – it wouldn't be enough. It has to be me.' But she held the casapasaran tightly in her hand, and, when she thought he wasn't looking, he saw her press it to her cheek.

At last the wind picked up, and they swept over the water into sight of the rock. Even at a distance, it shone like a lighthouse.

The island was barely as large as a swimming pool, but the tree was a gargantuan thing, broad as an oak and three times as high. It gleamed yellow-gold, radiantly bright in the sunlight, reflecting the movement of the sea on its great trunk.

'There's no dragon,' said Christopher. 'We should go now!'

Nighthand got to his feet. He stumbled as he rose. 'Onwards! We go out golden harvesting.'

Irian hesitated. 'Nighthand ...' she began.

It was Mal, though, who spoke. They had agreed it, she and Christopher; they had seen that Nighthand would not be able to refuse her, not now he had vowed to serve her.

'No. You stay,' said Mal. 'Ratwin's planning the route, Irian's mending the boat.' This was a lie: the *Shadow Dancer* needed no mending – but somebody needed to stay with Nighthand. 'And

Nighthand: you need to keep watch for the dragon. Me and Christopher will go.'

There was an argument, of course, but Mal in these last few days had become difficult to gainsay. There was a rigid determination in her face; a fierce certainty had come to her since the night after Gelifen's death, and it made her formidable. She was more than a match for a Berserker.

And so it was Christopher and Mal who waded, together, through knee-deep water, up on to the island. They stood looking up at the tree. Up close, its gold nearly blinded them. The surface was textured, mottled like bark.

'I'll climb it,' Christopher said.

'Why you?' She looked prepared to fight him.

'Because if you fell and got hurt, or died, the next Immortal might never be found, or not for years. And then there would be nobody to go into the maze. That's why.'

She considered, pride and common sense battling across her face. 'Fine. Get on with it then!'

'I am! Give me a second to look at it.'

She grinned, despite everything, and circled the tree with him. It didn't look too hard, Christopher thought – he was a strong climber, had climbed all the trees on the heath at home when he was younger.

There were knots in the gold bark, some big enough for his foot. 'Right,' he said, and gripped a golden nodule that protruded from the trunk.

'*Ow!*' He swore. 'It's burning hot, from the sun.'

'Are your hands blistering? Dip them in seawater!'

'No time.' He again set his hand, wincing at the heat on the bark.

The tree was hard and unyielding, his fingernails bending and scratching against its surface, but it was possible to climb. He reached the first branch, and edged along it.

From it sprouted another, smaller branch, and from that a fan of thinner branches. He took hold of one, thin as his little finger and long as his forearm, and pulled. It snapped off, hot and brittle and radiantly shining.

'Look out! Catch!' and he dropped it down to Mal. He heard her give a small hiss of pleasure.

'How many branches do we need?' he called.

'I don't know. Better to have too many than too few.'

He shifted further along, dropping the thin gold twigs down to Mal's waiting hands. Some were harder to snap than others, and he wobbled, lying on his stomach, and wrapped his legs more firmly round the barrel of the branch.

Tiny buds had broken out along some, and gold leaves, hard as the bark, were forming.

He cleared one whole branch of its twigs, and moved higher. The leaves were bigger, up here, twice as large as his palm. He moved to snap one off.

'Stop!'

Christopher's heart gave a lurch. He nearly fell. The voice was high, and shrill, and commanding. The accent was not familiar; not, in fact, human. 'I am the Jaculus of Golden

Island, and I command you to stop!'

Christopher looked about him, but he could see nothing. He hung by his hands and dropped the eight feet to the ground, landing in an ankle-jarring crouch.

'Where are you?' he called.

'Here! Oh, by the name of the Immortal, down *here*!'

The dragon rose in front of him. It was bright shining silver, with green-golden wings. It was the size of a humming-bird, and it was vibrating with affront.

Mal snorted with laughter. The dragon turned to look at her.

'You find something amusing? My size, perhaps?'

'No,' said Mal. 'No! I wouldn't dare laugh at a dragon.'

'I am small but, mistress, I am not harmless.' The dragon turned aside its head and snorted, and a little fireball launched itself from his nostrils. Christopher flinched backwards.

'I am a jaculus. The tree-dragon. And it is my bounden right and duty now to eat you. It was courteous of you to come ready-washed.'

Christopher's eyes flickered to the boat. It was too far for anyone to hear them shout.

The jaculus was looking them up and down. 'You – boy – are not from the Enchanted Islands. Have not the tales of the mighty miniature dragon reached you in the Otherlands?'

Christopher shook his head. 'The dragons in our stories are all large, I think. I'm sorry,' he said.

'Your man – Pliny – he travelled here, through the

waybetween. He said he would tell people about me when he returned. You *should* know about me!' He snorted a spark of outraged fire, twelve inches from Christopher's elbow; he flinched sideways.

'Do you have a name?' asked Mal.

'I have just told you. I am a jaculus.'

'But I meant ... I'm called Malum. And he's Christopher. To tell you apart from the other jaculuses.'

'From whither do they come, these names?'

'I was given mine by my parents,' said Christopher.

The jaculus looked them up, down, up again. 'I hatched, alone, from an egg,' said the jaculus. 'No dragon has named me. I have travelled, but never further than I need to go for food.'

'It doesn't have to be your parents. A human could name you.'

'Most of the humans who have come to my island I have burned, as is my duty, at which point any kind of naming would have been impracticable. I have eaten them, very slowly, over time. The charcoal stops the flesh from rotting.'

'Why didn't you burn us?'

The jaculus sniffed. 'The boy. He has a scent. There is a pull in his blood, towards the living world; there is a *call* in him. I found myself curious. And you, girl: I know what you are. I can smell the glimt in you. Even a kraken would not devour you. It is ill luck to eat an Immortal.'

The wind was picking up. Clouds scudded over the sun, and the tree cast a long shadow on the water. Christopher gave a shiver. The island was a harsh place, for all its glorious shine.

'Is it just you here,' he said, 'guarding this tree, for a thousand years?' Despite himself, he felt a spark of sympathy for the minuscule, imperious dragon. 'Won't you start to hate it, eventually?'

It was a mistake. The dragon rose into the air, a flurry of anger in miniature. 'Upstart cur! You presume too far! I will not harm the Immortal, but I will eat you—'

'Wait! I only meant, don't you get lonely?'

The jaculus gave a low rumble in its throat; it sounded like a warning. 'Dragons do not feel loneliness. That is an emotion for humankind. And perhaps some of the weaker dryads.' It snorted fire.

'But why do you stay here?' said Mal. 'You could fly anywhere.'

'The jaculus must guard the tree of living gold.'

'How do you know, if you never had other dragons to tell you what to do?'

The jaculus's voice was querulous. 'How does a bird know which is the route to fly south, from Paraspara to Edem each year? I simply know it to be so. And I have learned a great deal from the humans who have come, before I ate them. I have learned language: Arabic, Sanskrit, Old French. Two hundred years ago, an explorer came and taught me English. I did not eat him until I had learned all the irregular verbs.'

'But you never learned your name.'

He hesitated, then nodded his dragon head. 'I did not.'

'If we gave you a name,' said Christopher, 'and if I swore,

when I get back to my world, to tell stories of the importance of the jaculus – would you let us go?'

'You? Write about me? A chronicler?'

'Yeah. Yes. Exactly.'

'It is true that dragons need those who sing of them, in the Outerlands. Without the songs, they are ... diminished.'

Christopher nodded, and Mal nodded beside him, fever-ishly up and down. 'I can do that,' he said. 'I can swear.'

The dragon hesitated. 'And it would have to be a good name,' he said. 'Or I would have to burn you, and feast upon your body.'

Christopher met Mal's eye. She looked, briefly, panicked. Her lips formed the word, 'Norman?'

'How about ... Jacques?' he said quickly.

The jaculus considered. 'Jacques the jaculus? Is it not ... too simple?'

'Neat, not simple,' said Mal. 'Smart. Elegant.'

'Spelled J-a-c-q-u-e-s,' said Christopher. There had been a boy at school called Jacques. 'But pronounced Jac. So you would have silent letters, which are just for you.'

'Jacques,' said the dragon. He looked again at Christopher, and at the gold. Then, without blinking, he took off into the air.

'I must tell someone,' he said. 'I must introduce myself. Jac. Jacques.'

THE ISLAND OF MURDERERS

The Murderers' Island was large, and harsh, and unwelcoming. The land rose in one slow-sloped mountain to the west, and other, smaller hills, rising and falling to the east. The mountainside was, from a distance, grey-brown, but as they came closer, Christopher could see it was varied: some terraced crops, wheat and another, stockier grain; some trees, some damp red dirt, across which ran goats.

Most of the houses, grey stone taken from the mountain itself, were clustered at the foot of the largest hill. It was an austere, desolate place. The sky above them was stormy, and as they sailed closer, rain began to speckle the surface of the sea.

'It was chosen, hundreds of years ago, for the way its waters hold its inhabitants tight against its bones,' said Irian.

'Do all murderers get sent there?' said Christopher.

'No,' said Irian. 'Only those judged to have done unspeak-able harm.'

'Don't they all murder each other, on the island?' said Mal. 'Aren't they afraid of each other?'

'I think some people – who murder once and find it not unpleasant – find it easier, each time, to do so again,' said Irian. 'But for most, the act of murder is born of dire panic, or blinding anger, or sickness, or terror. Not habit.'

Nighthand shot her a look. 'I don't know. I've known people sent there, and I would not care to meet them again. It's an ugly place, Mal. You stay close, you understand?'

Christopher had expected the sea around the island to be wild, perhaps with ten-foot waves, or some other ferocious way of holding people within, but the sea was only the sea: restless, grey, without malice. As they came closer, they saw, rising from the water on wooden posts, a series of wooden signs in fifteen languages.

Those Who Enter May Not Leave.

Those Who Can, Turn Back Now.

Nothing Good Awaits.

'The convicted are loaded on to small boats here,' said Irian, 'and sent on alone. This is where we switch boats.'

Nighthand dropped a bow and arrow he had found in Anja's cabin into the *Ever Onward*, along with a handful of kitchen knives – the others flinched as they clattered down – and all four clambered on to the dryad-wood boat.

Irian pasted a scrap of sail cloth over the boat's name. 'Just in case', she said.

Nighthand touched Ratwin's head with his large, gnarled hand. The skin on his fingertips was turning a little blue, but he held himself upright. 'Guard the ship for us', he said. 'Bite anyone who encroaches on the face.'

Mal turned to Christopher. She tried her best to grin; it was a failure. 'Let's hope the boat works', she said. 'Or we won't be coming back.'

Christopher felt the fear rise in him, but he nodded. 'It *will* work. We'll get the potion, and get out. I know we will.'

She looked at him, and he stared back, unflinching. He was a good liar. She smiled, more widely this time, and nodded. 'Good.'

The dock was built in the old-fashioned style, thick stone making three corners of a square, lined with buildings, the fourth side open to the sea. The moored boats were all very similar to one another, Christopher saw – smaller, even, than their own, and painted clinical green or black. The dock blew with cast-off bits of paper and water-slicked rubbish.

There were crowds too, grouped in clusters of threes and fours, to watch them come in. Most of the crowd were men, of every age and race and stature, but among them a few women, their faces deeply lined.

Nighthand leaped heavily on to the dock, and used his good arm to loop the boat's rope around a hoop set into the stone. Theirs looked very like all the other boats, rising and falling in the grey water of the port.

One of the men stepped forward. He wore a clean suit, tattered at the sleeve and lapel, and his voice had authority in it.

'New arrivals, is it?'

'Yes,' said Irian.

The crowd saw Mal, and Christopher, and reared back. One of the young women muttered, '*Children?*'

'As you see.' Nighthand drew himself up to his full height, his coat covering his ravaged arm. He kept his face dark and aggressive. Everything about him jutted outwards: jaw, elbows, brow. 'Nobody is to approach them. Nobody is to ask them questions.'

'It's been known, I suppose,' said the man grudgingly, 'that people have been given the right to bring their families. Is that what *you* would be then? Family?' He looked from Nighthand to Mal to Irian to Christopher. None of them looked remotely related.

'We are ...' said Irian, 'together.'

The man sniffed. 'My name is Guillaume Broch,' he said. 'I'm one of four wardens here – as much as there are wardens on an island where nobody, including me, can ever leave. There are procedures, you know, to process newcomers. Accommodation, work, food – we need to talk about that. You can't just–'

'In good time,' said Nighthand. 'We have an urgent request first – we must speak with the centaur, Petroc.'

A ripple of discontent and distrust ran through the crowd.

'Why?' said Broch.

'We have a message,' said Nighthand.

One of the men, small and old, and yellow in the teeth and fingers with tobacco, spat into the water. 'Dunno how anything can be urgent here,' he muttered.

But Broch rolled his lip at the man. 'I didn't ask you.' He turned back to Nighthand. 'The centaur is easy to find. He's in the forest,' and he pointed to a road that led down a street of houses and small, squat stone shops, towards the trees beyond. 'Just follow the noise of the forge.'

The forest was very different from the forest through which they had ridden on unicorns. It was darker, and many of the trees were thorned. The branches reached for them, as if trying to halt their progress and turn them back. The rain fell more heavily, and thunder rolled over them. Back in the town, dogs howled.

'Listen!' said Irian. 'Can you hear that?'

In the distance, very faintly, there was a clanging of metal on metal. The further they walked, the louder the sound grew. The woods opened abruptly into a clearing – one that had been hacked, not formed by time. There, in the centre of the trees, bending over a cauldron on a fire, was the centaur.

His horse's body and skin were both stark white, and his hair black, cut short, and his eyes green. His skin was rough, burned in places from standing over the fire. Nature had meant his face to be staggeringly handsome, but the cruelty of the lines etched around his eyes and mouth made it impossible.

'Oh', Mal whispered, and Christopher, following her gaze, realised with a jolt that the centaur was chained.

The chain was locked with cuffs to his two hind legs, and was just barely long enough to reach across the clearing. It was pure gold.

His voice was harsh, but he greeted them with some gesture towards courtesy.

'Sit, if you want', he said, and pointed to some rough-carved stools close by him. Mal made to sit, but Nighthand shook his head, and she doubled back. They remained standing, out of the reach of the golden chain.

'The old woman on the longma told me to expect you.' As he spoke, he added a handful of leaves to the cauldron, and a bitter, acrid scent rose from it. 'I didn't believe her. Who would come here to collect a potion that couldn't be transported off the island?' His voice had a guttural quality: it sounded rarely used. 'Do you have a way out of this place?'

Nighthand's face was flat and careful. 'It's no business of yours, Petroc.'

The centaur waited.

'We do', said Mal. 'Yes.'

'You brought the gold from the living tree? If you haven't, there's no point in being here.'

'We have', said Irian.

His eyes looked her up and down, impudent. 'Show me.'

Christopher took from his pocket the scrap of cloth they had wrapped around the golden branches. He crossed to the centaur, shivering in the rain, thrust them into his hands and half ran back, beyond the chain's reach. He could smell the sourness of the centaur's breath. Petroc unwrapped them, and there was a great leap of some fierce, wild satisfaction in his expression.

But he only said: 'I see.'

'So you will do it?' said Nighthand. 'Make the potion, to bring back the Immortal memory?'

'Perhaps.'

'*Perhaps?*' Nighthand pulled the glamry blade slowly from his belt. 'We have not come here for *perhaps*.'

The centaur only raised his eyebrows. 'Put away your little daggerette,' he said, 'or I won't speak to you. I don't like what blades do to a conversation, do I.'

Nighthand hesitated, then sheathed the blade. He was breathing heavily and his legs were not, Christopher saw, steady under him.

'Even if I make the potion,' Petroc said, 'I can't administer it. D'you understand me? It needs to be heated by dryad fire, and there are – you may have noticed – no dryads on this forsaken island.'

'But you can make it?' said Irian.

'I can, yes. I haven't said I will.'

Mal spoke as if she had been struggling to hold in the question, and couldn't: 'What have you done, to get chained? Nobody else we've seen is chained.'

He turned harsh eyes on her. 'Why ask, when you so clearly aren't ready to hear the answer?'

Mal glared at the centaur, flushing red, and Christopher glared too, in loyalty. 'Who says she isn't ready? Did you kill someone?'

Petroc lifted his eyebrows. 'Surely even a human could see that that's a stupid question. Yes, I did. And part of my punishment, my people decided, was to be chained. Chained in an alloy of living gold, which I cannot break. It's unusual for one centaur to murder another.'

The centaur turned back to Mal. The rain intensified, and gleamed on his horse's flank. 'So you're the one, are you? The long-hunted, ever-missing Immortal? Come closer, so I can see you. There are people out there would pay a million gold pieces to get their hands on you.'

But Mal jerked away. She crossed to a tree, sat down against it and put her chin on her knees. It was cold: there was emptiness in her arms, where the burning warmth of Gelifen should be. She breathed in the scent of her jumper, where the griffin once had lain against her skin.

'My people speak of her,' the centaur said. 'It's an obsession. They've been waiting for her for a hundred years.' He scraped the ground with a hoof. 'But I didn't know it would be a child. The stars didn't say so. My people put a lot of faith in the skies, but I've always been sceptical about what they tell us. Too vague, too high.' He looked balefully at them, and wiped the rain from his face. 'I only trust things that you can touch – blood and gold and fire and dirt.'

His eyes raked over Mal; he spoke lower.

'Is she up to the task? She's small. A little ant of a fly of a speck of a nothing much.'

Christopher did not like the way the centaur looked at Mal. He put his hand on the long-bladed kitchen knife he'd tucked into his belt as they'd left. 'She's brave.'

'Is that true? Or some of your baffling human politeness, where you say neat and tidy things about people you despise?'

'It's true. I've seen it.' He wanted to force the centaur to see it. The fumes from the cauldron were making him thick-headed and ill, but he shook himself. 'She can fly. She escaped a murderer. She won't give up. It's not something she knows how to do.'

Petroc still stared at Mal. 'They say, if the glimourie isn't saved now, it never will be saveable. It's a concept you humans have always struggled to grasp: that time might run out.' The fire behind him sparked, and he sniffed the air. 'It will be an ending: a dark, cold end. We centaurs understand that. I understand it, very well. I see the power and beauty of such an ending.'

There was a *chuh* of disgust. 'Enough.' It was Irian, louder than Christopher had ever heard her speak. She stepped close to Petroc, close within the circle of his chain. 'I don't care what you say or think.' The pressure, the strange, dark pull of the centaur's presence, snapped in the presence of her clear, steady look. 'Will you make the potion? Yes or no. If yes, do so. If no, tell us, and we'll leave you alone with your chain and your smoke and your miserable patch of mud. But we'll take the gold with us.'

Nighthand was watching her. His eyes, red and swollen at the lid, burned with admiration.

Petroc rolled his lip at Irian. 'Fine. But I won't work under surveillance. Go into the town. Return at dawn.'

'Dawn is too late. We haven't got that kind of time to waste,' said Nighthand. He winced with pain, and Irian moved closer to him, just in case.

'You'll have to waste it. I have in my stores the bones of the chimaera and the blood of the cetus, and the sap of the red urchin. But the blood needs six hours of steaming. And the forest has a bush of long-stemmed dew-wort, but it only flowers in the two hours before dawn. So you will wait.'

Back in the town, they looked in vain for somewhere to pass the night. There were a few cafes and bars, but they looked careless, dusty and joyless places.

They spoke to a woman standing at a stall on the corner, her hair pulled back under a scrap of cloth. 'Why would we have hotels, when we don't have visitors?' She stared at them, suspicious. 'But I can sell you some food.'

They bought tomatoes, small round flatbreads and some kind of dried squid. She offered a bottle of wine, stoppered with a screwed-up rag. 'Panther-wine? I make it myself. It'll burn the thoughts out of your head for a day and a night solid. Take your mind off that wound.' Her eyes travelled from

Nighthand's arm – which had swollen so badly he'd had to cut the sleeve from his shirt and jacket – to his face, which was greyish white.

Nighthand shook his head, then turned to Irian. 'Unless you want it?'

'I'll keep my thoughts unburned, thank you, for now,' she said.

They agreed, in the end, to sleep in the boat, taking turns to keep watch through the night. It was not a place to take chances.

Minutes passed, under the chill black sky. Stars shone down on the murderers' streets. Rocking on the water, Mal and Christopher lay side by side.

'Mal. Are you awake?'

'Of course.'

'Mal ... Have you thought about what it will be like? The potion, and afterwards?'

She gave him a look; a look that aimed for high scorn, but landed on fear.

'I don't want to talk about it.'

'Why not?'

'Have *you* thought about what it'll mean?'

'Yes.' He had: he had imagined it, over and over. Sometimes he felt a spark of jealousy burn in his chest. 'You'll know everything. You'll be asked by kings and dragons for your opinion.'

'But have you really imagined? Properly? Hard?' Her voice

was very small, under the vast sky. 'What I'll have to know, and see, and remember, forever?' She breathed out, a rough-edged tight little *burr* of breath. 'I'm scared. Sometimes I think about it and I can't breathe. I've never been so scared in my life. And what if I take the potion, and then I'm scared, like this, for eternity?'

In her sleep, later, she stirred. Her face, always so vivid in waking, was screwed tight in sleep. One of her wrists was flung out from under the blankets. It was scarred, where Gelifen had nibbled and scratched at it.

Christopher sat awake for several hours, watching over her, keeping guard.

Christopher woke an hour before dawn. The night was still grey-blue above, and something was wrong.

There was a clanking of hooves along the deserted water-front. Through the empty night walked Petroc, unchained. In one hand the centaur held a glass vial.

He stood, on the edge of the dock, and called to them.

'Humans! You will take me with you, in that boat, off this island.'

Nighthand rose up, looming at his full height. 'You are mistaken in that. Don't come any closer. You'll regret it.'

'Oh, I've no doubt you could kill me. But this, right here, is the potion. It needs one more ingredient.' He held out a palm, in which lay two leaves. 'It's either the heart of a viram flower, or a ferenleaf. You don't know which. But I do. So what's going to happen is this: you take me off this island, and when we reach your ship, moored out there by the barriers, we'll board it, and I'll add the final ingredient.'

Irian's gentle voice had a bite to it. 'How did you unchain yourself?'

A smile flicked at the corner of the centaur's mouth. 'The living gold is not an ingredient of the potion. You simply helped me forge the key to my chain.'

They had no choice.

Mal and Christopher pushed themselves against the sides of the boat to make room, and the centaur stood at the front, as Irian and Nighthand rowed. They reached the boundaries of the island's water, and the centaur stiffened, but the *Ever Onward* moved swiftly past, untrammelled by the island's enchantment.

They reached the *Shadow Dancer*. Ratwin was perched on the prow, and as they came in sight she let out a cry of pleasure. Then she saw the centaur, and called out, 'Nighthand? What's this? Why the horse-man?'

'Move aside, squirrel.' Petroc heaved himself, the muscles straining in his great back, up on to the boat. Irian made to follow, Nighthand holding the *Ever Onward* steady against the side of the *Shadow Dancer*.

Petroc unstoppered the vial. He added the heart of the viram flower, and carefully restoppered it, pushing hard with callused fingers. With what might have been a smile or might have been a grimace, he threw the vial into the water.

Mal screamed. Nighthand made to leap into the ocean, but standing struck him with a fit of dizziness and he collapsed against Irian. Christopher dived into the waves.

The water was ice-cold, unsoftened by the dawn sun. The glass vial tumbled downwards, and Christopher kicked desperately after it. He had only one chance – once it sank down where the water turned black and cold and unreachable, it was gone. The thought clawed at him, and he kicked harder, his muscles screaming with effort. *Faster.*

He shot to the surface, coughing, his throat burning with seawater. Ahead of him, the centaur had hauled the anchor of the *Shadow Dancer*, and taken hold of the tiller. Ratwin leaped at Petroc, but Christopher watched in horror as he kicked her aside with one strike of his hind leg.

'Bite him, Ratwin!' shouted Nighthand, heaving himself to his feet. He plunged into the water and swam towards the *Shadow Dancer*, but it spun in the wind and sailed away at a vicious speed, cutting head-on through the waves. Nighthand hung in the water and roared: a wordless bellow of fury that shook the air.

But Mal was not looking at the ship, or the Berserker. 'Did you get it?' she cried.

Christopher swung out a hand above the waves: in it, tightly clutched, was the vial.

THE STINK OF MANTICORE BREATH

Christopher clambered into the *Ever Onward*, his heart racing. The sun was rising, casting the water a hundred shades of vermilion and rose, but he could see only rage.

'He kicked Ratwin!' he said.

'I wouldn't underestimate a ratatoska,' said Nighthand. 'She'll get him in his sleep.'

The Berserker had seaweed strung through one of his golden earrings, and he was wheezing. He stripped off his shirt – Irian looked away, and up again, and away – and Christopher saw with dismay that his arm had turned a terrible purplish-grey. Nighthand saw Christopher looking, and shook his head, a single, tight No.

'Nighthand!' said Christopher. 'Your arm isn't supposed to be that colour.'

'Nonsense. My arm can be any colour it pleases.'

The Berserker coughed, and grimaced.

Mal turned the vial over in her hands.

'Did the seawater get in?' he asked.

'I don't think so.' It was unopened. 'No. Look, there.' She shook it upside down. 'You can see, it's watertight.'

They sat in the *Ever Onward*, looking back at the Island of Murderers.

'What now?' said Mal.

There was a pause. And then: 'He said we need dryad fire,' said Christopher. 'So – I vote we go to the dryads.'

'Onwards then,' said Nighthand. He rose to his feet, struck a valiant and determined attitude, all pointing hands and jutting hips – and collapsed with a hideous thump into the bottom of the boat.

They made a blanket from their warm clothes, and tried to make him comfortable. He half lay, with his back propped against the side of the boat, watching the horizon. He insisted they go on; and so, after much argument, they did.

Irian guided the *Ever Onward*, with one eye on the Berserker. Every time Christopher turned to her, her eyes were moving steadily between the sea and Nighthand, Nighthand and the sea.

They had been sailing in the Immortal's boat for half a day when Irian left Nighthand, edged round the sail and came to them.

'I've been looking at Christopher's map. The nearest place that I know for certain has dryads is the Island of Tār; there's a dryad queen there, Erato, who rules the forest. But the way to Tār is past the Island of Manticores.'

Mal looked sick with horror. Irian saw Christopher's blank face.

'The Island of Centaurs,' Irian said, 'Antiok it's called, doesn't *just* have centaurs, any more than your England only has Englishmen. I was born there. But the Island of Manticores is the exception. They're the only thing that lives on that island.'

'Why?' said Christopher.

'Because they eat everything they see,' said Mal.

'Oh,' said Christopher. 'Right. I can imagine that would do it.'

'Look.' Irian pointed on the map. 'They fly to nearby islands to get food. They lack stamina – they can't go far – but they're fast. We have to go past them, to get where we're going. But here –' she pointed to the sea – 'are coral reefs, growing thirty feet high under the water. The coral's as sharp as knives – nereids have died there – and the boat would run aground, dryad-wood or no dryad-wood. We could go the long way, back round the cape of Lithia, but it would take weeks.'

Christopher thought of Kavil, and the way he had spoken of the creature in the maze. He thought of his father and grandfather, waiting, perhaps angry, perhaps terrified and panicking, for his return. He thought of Gelifen; and he said, 'We don't have weeks. How close do we have to pass, to avoid the coral?'

'About a hundred feet. Less, if the depth gives out to the east.'

'Is that smelling distance?' said Christopher.

'Yes. And they have the eyesight of lions.'

'What's to stop them,' said Mal, 'flying over and landing in our boat and killing us?'

'Well, we have the kitchen knives, and the bow and arrow.'

'Anything else?'

'Our hands and teeth,' said Nighthand. He tried to smile, but his voice was a whisper. His skin had begun to blotch with a red raised rash across his face. The skin around his lips was vivid white.

'Nobody is to *bite* a manticore,' said Irian. 'And that's final.'

The island stank. They could smell it on the sea wind before they could see it. It smelt of what it was: not-quite-finished prey, left out by the manticores in the burning heat of the sun.

Nighthand said something – it sounded like '*teeters*'. Irian leaned down.

'He says they're messy eaters,' she said.

He tried to sit up. His voice was a ghost of itself: 'If they kill us, they will not eat us all: they will leave parts of our bodies strewn about. So somebody will probably be able to identify us – not Christopher, but the Archipelagians, at least.' He coughed, and when the cough had passed, he added: 'If we don't rot first.'

'Thank you, Nighthand. We'll bear it in mind,' said Irian. Her tone was far warmer than her words. She kept one hand on the tiller, the other on her bow. The island came into view – sandy at the shoreline, forested further back. The boat moved fast; the waves were choppy, but it rose and fell in rhythm with the water. They crouched low in the boat, peering over the sides.

They were halfway past it. Nothing on the island seemed to see them. They sailed beyond the island's northern-most point. They were safe.

Christopher's stomach, which had been iron-cold and hard with fear, relaxed. He grinned round at Mal.

The wind picked up, and a sudden wave lifted the boat. As the boat dropped again, it thumped against the water and Nighthand was jerked from his position, sideways, landing his full weight on his injured arm. He gave a single, loud, fevered cry, swiftly stifled. It rang through the sea-salt air. Irian cried out in turn. She crossed to him, crouching low.

'How bad is it?' she whispered.

'Not.' His voice was less than half what it should be.

'Did you open the wound?'

'No.'

'You did! I can see it, Nighthand.'

'Are you calling me a liar?'

'Yes! That's exactly what I'm doing. We have to get you help.'

And then his voice became suddenly sharp: 'Look out! Above!'

Something moved fast among the trees on the island behind them. Three dots rose and moved towards them, flapping in the air. They flew in a tight knot, their wings almost touching, and their speed was staggering.

Nighthand stood. He lurched across the deck, and pushed Mal behind him, his good arm holding her against the side of the boat.

She struggled. 'Don't! I need to see – I need to fight—'

But Nighthand held her back. 'It is my *work*,' he said. His voice had a slur of pain in it, but no inch of fear. 'They will have to eat me first.'

There was a lion's roar from the sky, and something like a thin javelin shot past Christopher and stuck into the side of the boat.

Nighthand grunted. 'The filth-cats come.'

Before Christopher had time to see more than a blur of tawny skin and yellow wings, Irian took aim and fired, again and again, sweat pricking along her forehead: the air was full of arrows – some went wide, but four found flesh or wings: two manticores fell.

'Christopher! To your left!'

He twisted; it was above him, diving low, wings outstretched, clawed feet extended, lion's mane matted with sea salt and blood.

He ducked and Irian sent another arrow, which missed by

a hair's breadth. The creature swerved in the air, twisted to lunge at Irian, and with a great roar Nighthand hefted himself to stand in the boat, and sent a kitchen knife spinning into its flank. The manticore dropped into the water.

'Thank you,' she said.

Mal was still pressed against the side of the boat. There was a fleck of manticore blood on her cheek.

'Anyone hurt?' called Irian.

'No,' whispered Mal. Her fists were balled, and her eyes wide.

'Are there any more?' said Irian.

'I can't see any,' said Christopher.

'Good. Because we have no arrows left.'

'Over there!' cried Mal.

It was the largest creature of the herd; it had come not from the island but from the sky over the water. It flew, straight and fast as a propelled stone, towards their boat.

Mal ran to the bow of the boat where Irian stood. She whispered to the wood, hands on its two sides, urging it on, but the boat could go no faster. They could do nothing: they could only watch the manticore come closer, and closer.

'Mal!' Nighthand crossed to her.

Christopher stood alone, watching at the port side of the boat. It was awe-inspiring. Its body was leonine, but its face, furred and matted with dirt, had human eyes and a human nose and mouth. Its teeth, though, were not human. They were huge, and grey, and sharp.

It hovered over their boat, looking down at them.

Nighthand took the glamry blade from his waist, holding it in his uninjured hand. But he did not dare throw it and lose it: it was not a thing that could be thrown.

'Humans!' said the manticore. Its voice was rusty, as if its tongue were unused to speech. 'You are not welcome here.'

'We're only passing through,' said Christopher. His voice shook.

'You! Your scent has the outside in it. From where have you come?'

'From outside the Archipelago. From the Outerlands.'

'So you have never yet seen a manticore?' Its wings beat above his head.

'No. Not until now.'

'A piteous and distressful thing, then, that you will not live to return home and tell what you have seen.' The creature swooped suddenly; Irian gave a cry, but it only landed on the deck of the boat. It turned to Nighthand, to Irian, to Mal.

'If you come a step closer, I consume the boy. Stay where you are.'

The manticore drew back its lips – pale, almost white – and bared its teeth. Its head was level with Christopher's as he stood with his back against the boat's mast.

'Handsome thing, you are,' said the manticore. 'Don't move – no – none of you – or I will bite out the boy's eyes. We will not eat the man. He would, I think, be poison. But you – you will be a piece of culinary delectation.'

The stink of the creature's breath was hot and vicious on Christopher's face.

'Do you find me frightening? Are you scared-chested?'

'Yes.' And then, because if he was going to be eaten, he did not want that to be the last thing he said, he added: 'It's not difficult to be frightening. It's not a talent. Any idiot with a knife could be frightening.'

The manticore moved a little closer, its claws biting into the wooden deck. 'You should have more respect for fear. It's the engine in all your human history, fear. Fear, married to greed, married to power.' The manticore licked his white lips. His tongue, pointed at the end, flicked upwards.

Christopher reached into his pocket, to see if there was anything he could use as a weapon. There was nothing. He tensed his muscles – he would try to blind it with his hands, when it came.

'Oh, yes. You are afraid of each other – oh, *deeply* afraid. Afraid of humiliations and laugh-and-points. Afraid of death, so you kill others before they can kill you.'

There was a noise behind him, a retching, breathless sound – it was Mal, trying to get to Christopher. Nighthand grabbed her by the shoulder, to stop her moving.

'A quivering, scratch-greed, terrified little race, humanity.'

'That's not true,' said Christopher. 'You're just a dirty cat with big teeth. You know nothing.'

'And what do *you* know? You are too young: you smell of your mother's milk. You have the bumptious, graceless confidence of the recently born.' The manticore padded closer, and his meat-thick breath was hot as an oven on Christopher. 'You will see. You will see it very soon. It is what will destroy you all: one man's fear. And then we'll feast, my people.'

'What man?'

He purred, a phlegmy rumble in his chest.

'I met him a hundred years ago. He was so afraid of being at the mercy of some other man's whims, so afraid of other people's power, boy – so afraid of being a little average nothing of a man – that he sought to control everything that lives. Not just here in the Archipelago. In the Otherlands. *Everywhere.*'

Christopher was hot with horror, but stayed where he was. He was equal to it. He had not expected to be, but he found himself able to stand, and to talk, and the terror in his blood, strong as it was, did not pull him to the floor.

The manticore gave a snort that might have been a laugh. 'The man who went into the maze, one hundred years, seven months and six days ago. I spoke with him, on his journey there. He was full of talk, talk-talk-sneer. He had seen there was power for the taking. He was going to make his way into the heart of the maze, he said; he was going to reach the glimourie tree.'

The manticore sniffed. 'I could smell it, that he was like you – from outside the Archipelago. A man from the Otherlands.'

'What did he say, when you spoke to him? Did he say how he was going to get through the maze?'

The manticore blinked – a long blink of pleasure. 'Oh, he knew how. He had the plans. He held them in his hand; ink and vellum.' The tongue came out again, and licked away a crumb of dead flesh from the upper lip. 'Enough. We shouldn't chatter for too long: it disgustulates you. It gives time for the adrenalin to flood your blood. It has a sour taste.' He exhaled as he came closer, his great lion feet heavy on the deck.

Christopher tried to back away, but there was nowhere to back. 'Wait – wait!' His only thought was to make the creature keep talking. 'You said *plans*? What plans?'

And then the air around him was on fire.

Christopher felt it before he heard it: a sudden searing, blinding heat, and then a roar, inches from his left shoulder. He dropped to the deck, instinct acting before he had understood.

The manticore screamed, high and terrible, a cat's screech more than a lion's roar. Its body was engulfed in flame. It stretched its burning wings, tried to fly, and failed.

The burst of fire came again, and a tiny voice roared, 'Get back, vermin! That is my biographer!'

The manticore dropped, charred, unmoving, to the deck of the boat. Great gouts of smoke filled the air, acrid and choking. Christopher could hear Mal coughing, gasping, but something else too – laughing, he thought. The fire did not burn the wood of the boat, though it smoked – but a rope, Christopher saw, had burned instantly to ashes.

Jacques, his tiny wings outspread, smoke still spiralling from his nostrils, turned to Christopher.

'I hope you don't object,' he said. 'I followed you. There were a few points I wished to make, for the account you will tell of my life.'

FIDENS NIGHTHAND

Nighthand's wound grew worse as the day went on. Every movement of the boat jarred him, and each time he moved he grew whiter and whiter.

'We will have to find an island,' said Irian. 'We have to get some help for him.'

But there was no land in sight for miles, and no wind; only the calm blue sweep of the sea.

'Is there any way to send a message to anyone?' said Christopher. 'Don't you have some kind of Air and Sea Rescue?'

Irian turned to him. 'Say that again.'

'What – Air and Sea Rescue?'

'Air and sea. Air and *sea*.'

She looked down at the soft afternoon sea. The water was still, and very clear.

Irian pulled off her jumper, her boots. She strode to the

prow of the boat. She glanced once backwards at Nighthand, who lay unconscious – stretched her arms to the horizon, and launched herself with a spring into a perfect swan dive. She hit the water without a ripple, and torpedoed down into the depths.

'Irian! *Irian!*' called Mal. She turned, panicked, to Christopher. 'She said she can't swim!'

Irian was different in the water. If Mal belonged in the sky, Irian belonged at sea. She moved faster than he had ever seen a human swim, her arms tearing through the blue. She did not move straight down, but twisted left and right as she went, rippling and winding with the current. It was as if the water had a mind of its own, and she alone knew how to read it; as if the ocean itself had birthed her.

'I think she said she *doesn't* swim,' said Christopher.

Irian did not come up for air. She swam down, down, feet tight together, until she was so deep he could see nothing but a dark shape.

And then from the water, he heard her call – a call that was not in English. It was the same high call he had heard, days before, from the nereids. A beat: he and Mal held their breath, pressed shoulder to shoulder at the edge of the boat. And then, far away, so faint it might have been the sea itself, an answering call.

Irian erupted to the surface, thirty feet from the boat. She swam to them with long, soft strokes, and hauled herself up. Jacques gave a huff of admiration into the sea, and the waves boiled.

'What did you do?' Mal asked.

'I sent for help,' said Irian.

Mal was looking at her with a new light in her face: it was awe. 'How do you speak Nerish?'

Irian looked down at the boat, hauling her clothes back on to her wet body. 'I'm part nereid; on my father's side, some generations back. The salt water does this: see. It only lasts a minute, but it shows.' She held out her hands, palms up. The tips of her fingers shimmered with a silver sheen.

'But that's incredible!' said Christopher.

She smiled ruefully. 'To you, maybe. It's not something I advertise. There's people who'd treat me as some oracular kind of mystic; and others would be afraid of what I might do, and their fear is dangerous to me. So I keep it quiet, and stay out of the water when people are around.'

'Now what happens?' said Mal.

'Now we keep travelling, and we wait.'

They waited several hours before there was a thrumming in the air, and a longma swept into view above the moving boat.

Anja Trevasse leaned down, and called to the boat. 'Irian Guinne! What is it? The nereids sent a message, via the rata-toskas. They said it was urgent: they said it was Nighthand.'

She was very different from the woman they had seen before. No jewels bedecked her arms. Her hair fell in a thin grey plait, and she wore a shift dress and a dressing gown. Mal flinched at the sight of her.

The longma dropped lower, so that its hooves almost touched water, and hovered there, beating its wings in long, slow flaps. Anja looked over at Nighthand, and her face grew stony and cold. The Berserker lay along the floor of the boat, draped in his own jacket. His eyes were closed, the lids fluttering with fever. Anja turned to Irian.

'Why did you let him reach this state? Why didn't you seek help sooner?'

'You, of all people, will refrain from lecturing me,' said Irian. 'I want to be clear, Madam Trevasse, that I called because I couldn't think of anybody else who might have the power to help. Otherwise I would strike you now, into the ocean.'

'And you think that saying this is going to help you, somehow? To charm me?'

'No,' said Irian to Anja. 'But you'll either help while knowing you're loathed, for Nighthand's sake, or not help at all. I won't pretend that you're forgiven. Your kind are excused so much, so often, so easily – a flash of money and all's well. I won't play that game. Nighthand wouldn't want it.'

Panic was rising in Mal's eyes. She whispered, '*Oh, don't.*'

Anja looked, nostrils flared very slightly, from Irian to the Beserker and back again. 'Tell me what happened to him.'

'It was a karkadann. Its horn caught him,' said Irian. 'You know of every healer in the Archipelago – can you get him to help?'

'I don't know.' Anja looked at Nighthand. There was a look in her eyes – dark, sharp, set under papery wrinkled lids –

that Christopher could not begin to decode. 'There's a centauride – a female centaur – on Antiok. But I can't take him there alone. I'm not strong enough to hold him on the longma's back. You'll need to come.'

Irian stared at her. 'I can't leave two children in a boat in the middle of the ocean!'

'Then you risk him falling into the sea. Which?'

Nighthand muttered in his delirium. Christopher struggled to hear: it sounded like '*rin*'. The man's lips were hot and dry and unnaturally white.

Irian looked from Christopher, to Nighthand, to Mal. Agony was riven across her fine-wrought face.

'Make your decision,' said Anja. 'Every minute you risk his life.'

'They're *children*.'

The old woman drew herself up on her longma. 'By the Immortal! You may think me whatever you wish – venal, weak, selfish, wicked, whatever you choose – I don't care. But I am not, I hope you'll agree, stupid. Children have been underestimated for hundreds of years. Why are you continuing the tedious tradition?'

Nighthand spoke again. This time they could all hear what he said. He spoke through fever, but the word rang clear as a clock striking. He said: '*Irian*.'

Anja flinched, but Irian didn't see. Irian looked only at Nighthand. Christopher felt suddenly he was intruding on something profoundly private.

She crouched down beside him. For the first time since they met, she touched him, carefully, deliberately, on the hand – and then on his face. His eyes were open. She rested two fingers on his cheekbone, on his brow, on his lips. She breathed harder, deeply, as if all the sky's oxygen had rushed over her at once.

There was a look in Irian's face of recognition: the joy of one at sea, who looks up and sees land ahead. It was the face of somebody who has suddenly felt, for the first time, the precise shape and weight of their own swiftly beating heart.

'Fidens Nighthand', she said.

DRYADS

Christopher and Mal sailed on to the dryads alone. If they were afraid, neither said so: it required both their full concentration to keep the sail steady and steer. They did not speak much. When they had time to rest, they sat shoulder to shoulder. When they slept, Jacques perched in the prow, watching them.

She had, at her belt, Nighthand's glamry blade in its scabbard. He had pressed it into her hand, delirious but insistent, as all four of them had lifted him on to the longma's back. His eyes hadn't focused.

'Yours,' he had said.

They followed now the arrow's point of the casapasaran. Occasionally, far below the waves, below the shadow of the boat, Christopher saw creatures moving; things too swift and fleeting to identify. Once, when the water was calmer, and they moved fast over it, he saw a mermaid, swimming deep below on her back, her tail fifteen feet long, looking up at them. He just barely glimpsed her beautiful, soft-featured face: but it was so full of fearful hope that it caught at him like a knife in the stomach. It was a demand, that look; a call to bravery. He shouted to Mal, but by the time she turned the mermaid was gone.

Christopher caught a crab and they ate it raw, slicing the shell with the glamry blade, the flesh sweet and cool from the sea. But Mal, who was always hungry, found she couldn't eat more than a few mouthfuls. 'It won't go down,' she said.

It was dusk when they reached the shore of Tār, the Island of Dryads. They tied up the *Ever Onward* at a small wooden dock at the edge of a small fishing town, and left Jacques to guard it.

People stared out of windows and shops as they passed, looking warily at them. They had shrewd, hard-worked hands and faces. Christopher did not know if they saw very few strangers, so far north, or if there was something in Mal that made them uneasy.

They would have been right to have found her frightening. She walked with the look of a moveable battleground. She was a one-girl army.

They followed the casapasaran through the streets. Her eyes were on it always: more, in fact, than they needed to be. It saved her from having to look up, or around.

The town had soon given way to a cluster of farm buildings, a barn of some kind where farm machinery was stacked, and then open land, and a forest.

'Mal', he said, when they had been walking half an hour. 'Are you hungry? Thirsty? Do you want to stop?' He was, and he did. But he didn't say so, because the time now belonged, he felt, to her.

She shook her head. 'If we stop, I'll refuse to get up again. Or I'll turn and run. So I guess we can't stop. We need to walk faster, actually, if anything.'

'You can drink as we go though.' And after a second's hesitation she nodded, and drank from their bottle, spilling a little down her front.

The forest was resistant to them at first, with thorn trees and brambles – but the further in they went, the taller and richer it became. The trees rose around them, some as high as electricity pylons, some no taller than Christopher. Many were flowered, with white or yellow or green blossoms.

'This is beautiful', he said, but she had that same fixed look, and only grunted.

It *was* beautiful, though, extraordinarily so; the trees were a thousand shades of brown and jade and silver-grey. The smell – the same smell he had found at the lochan – grew richer and wilder and kinder with every step. He paused to pull two apples from a tree, and though she wouldn't stop and he had to run to catch up with her, Mal agreed to eat one. The apple was sweet and sour at once, and the best he had ever tasted.

The casapasaran pointed them ahead to a space in the

wood where the trees seemed to thin, and they could see the setting sun in the sky. They stepped out into a clearing, circular, as perfect as if it had been made with mathematical precision.

'This must be the place,' said Christopher.

As they entered the clearing, the casapasaran swivelled, two degrees, to point at the tallest of the trees. It looked like an oak, it was so old that its bark seemed almost metallic, silver-brown in the fading light.

'What now?'

Mal did not allow herself to hesitate. 'Erato!' she called. 'Erato! We've come a long way to find you. Are you there?'

There was nothing except the birds, cawing overhead.

'Erato!' She sounded very childish, suddenly, her voice thin in the huge forest. 'Hello? You have to come out!'

There was nothing.

'Try again,' said Christopher.

'Erato!' and then, flushing, turning away from Christopher in embarrassment, she raised her voice and called, 'Erato, dryad of Tār, queen of the forest! The Immortal, born from the first apple of the first tree, calls out for you.'

The dryad who stepped from the tree was so beautiful that he forgot, for a moment, the logistics of how to breathe. She looked both very old and very young. Her skin and hair were brown, and her eyes the kind of green you see only in jewellers' windows.

More dryads emerged, from other trees; some were eight

273

feet tall, their skin the soft cream-brown of a sequoia, others the near-black of the alder tree. Some came from trees that were barely more than saplings, the girls smaller and younger than Mal, all long feet and hands and wide, excited eyes. All looked some form of female, and all had the same vivid, earth-rich, ever-growing look to them: rare and bold and wild.

Behind them, he glimpsed a girl-formed dryad step from the apple tree from which he had plucked the apples. She smiled at him with the barest glimmer of a smile, and winked.

They moved towards the children, clustering around Mal and Christopher, and for a moment they were engulfed in soft murmurs of wonder and the smell of sap, as the dryads reached out to touch them, their faces and hair and hands.

THE POTION

Erato held the potion in her strong, long-fingered hands. She had understood at once what they needed. 'Some of our mothers' stories,' she said, 'told that the Immortal would come again to the dryads. I did not imagine that Immortal would come to *me*.'

She sniffed the potion, but did not taste it. 'You know that it cannot be undone? Do you understand?'

Mal nodded. 'I know that. It has to be now.'

Erato called out; a cry that sounded like the moving of wood in storms. There was a murmuring of surprise – some in pleasure, some in unease – and then each dryad turned to her own tree, snapped off a large branch, and came forward, holding it in her arms.

'Now step back,' said Erato to Mal.

'I thought dryad-wood doesn't burn,' Christopher said.

'It doesn't, unless the fire is lit by a dryad. Then it burns as hot as the Somnulum. But it can be unpredictable.'

A dozen dryads stood at the edge of the clearing, watching, as Erato bent over the great pile of wood. She rubbed her fingers together, harder and faster until they were a blur, and flames sprung from them. The pile of wood roared into light.

'Return, sisters, to your trees – or if you stay, you must keep back. And children, stay silent. There can be no distractions,' she said.

Mal, though, could not sit. She walked around and around the clearing, her mouth in a line so tight no slither of red was visible.

Erato tipped the potion into a pot, and held the pot sideways over the fire, so the liquid flowed to its side, close to the lip but not overflowing. Some of the fire flickered against the liquid, hissing out when it met the potion.

After a few minutes, the potion turned from blue-black to a dark honey brown. Erato poured the liquid into a wooden cup.

'Are you sure?' said Christopher suddenly. It seemed too much: eternity. He found he wanted, desperately, to protect her; to protect the girl who was taking on all of time.

'Don't ask me that,' said Mal. 'I don't want that question.'

Erato gave her the cup. 'Here then. I wish you luck. For all our sakes, but most of all for your own, little Immortal. Drink it quickly, and in one.'

Mal took it with that same determined, inward, soul-gritted look she had had for all the days since they sat at Gelifen's grave.

She glanced at Christopher, and said, 'I suppose it's a kind of goodbye then.'

'It's not, Mal! You'll still be you – and I'll still be here. You said it yourself, didn't you? You said, *he's a guardian.*' He had not been clear, until this moment, what that meant: it meant this feeling. It meant burning to keep watch, for that which needed to be watched. It meant burning to keep it safe. It meant a ferocious and careful love.

She looked as if she would reply, but Erato said, 'Now, child, quick, before it cools.'

Her whole body shook, so that her hand could barely grip the cup. She tried, for one brief fleeting second, to smile at him.

She drank it down in one gulp – 'Ach! Too *hot!*'

There was a single moment, when Christopher did not breathe – and then she whispered, '*Dizzy,*' and crouched down on the cool of the moss-covered ground.

Her eyes rolled backwards, and he just caught her as she fell sideways. He laid her out on her back.

'No,' said Erato. 'Here.' And she moved Mal to lie on her side. Her breath became heavy, and laboured. Her eyes were closed. He waited. She began to shake, and then to retch. She coughed and vomited, copiously, but remained asleep.

'Help me clear her face, so she doesn't choke,' said Erato. She produced a bowl of rainwater, and a soft cloth, made from shredded and woven oak leaves.

The dryad's words were calm, but her face was not, and something in her expression made Christopher ask: 'Has anyone ever done this before?'

The dryad shook her head.

'So it could be killing her! It could be poison!'

'She's Immortal, Christopher.'

He glared at Erato, but she had turned her back, and was kneeling over the fire, extinguishing it. The forest suddenly felt very dark.

'Keep watch on her.' Erato's voice, soft, came from the dark. 'Wash her if she's sick again.'

Mal was sick, twice, and each time he wiped her face as best he could and lifted her to a spot of dry earth.

The moon rose. Mal began to shiver, and then to shake, and her lips went blue. Christopher rearranged her coat into a blanket, tucking it up around her chin.

It would have been quite something, to have had a sister, he thought. It would have been quite something, if she had been like Mal.

At last, he lay down next to her, in the centre of the circular clearing, under the moon-shadow of the trees, facing her.

He must have slept, though he hadn't meant to, because the next thing he knew she was moving, curling into a ball and uncurling. She was still asleep, but she was weeping. Tears poured down her cheeks. He moved his jumper to be a pillow under her head. He waited. Briefly, still asleep, the tears stopped, and her face creased and upturned itself into a sudden laugh – a choke of delight, her eyes screwed shut. Then she fell silent again, limp and still.

Then she began to speak – a stream of language – of English and Latin, Arabic and Russian, Cantonese, Pashto, Dragon, Sphinx. She spoke in voices not her own – old and young, rich and poor, ancient and modern.

Tell them there's fresh milk in the jar, and they can have it all –
Viṇi nāk!
It will heal, won't it?
Wouldn't trust his arse with a fart, but he's a sweet lad –
Non! Il a dit non!
It's a joy to see your face –
愛
I am sorry to tell you that he was killed on the last day –
Kultaseni, rakkaani
Love, my love –

And then she stopped, and fell silent, panting.

The sun rose on Christopher's still-waking waiting. A dryad brought him bread made from walnuts, and a bowl of crushed apricots stewed with honey. 'It is dryad fruit. It will do more for you than any other food.'

Mal coughed, and her eyes opened, then closed. 'Water,' she croaked.

Erato poured a little water into her mouth, and

Christopher dipped a piece of the bread in the apricot and put it between her lips.

'How are you?'

She struggled to sit up; she leaned the back of her head against a tree. She smiled, and he could see it was the most formidable effort he had yet seen her make. It was a smile with the world inside it.

'I'll tell you,' she said, 'but not today.' Her voice was different. It was rougher, as if the liquid had burned her throat.

She lay down again, but her eyes stayed open. He tried to offer her more water, but she brushed it away. 'Left,' she said. 'Left, and left ... right, and straight, and left again. Right ... and left, and three rights.' He could hear only half of what she said. 'Left, and ... left, and left, and over the chasm in the ground. And right, and left, and straight, and right ...'

'The maze?' he said.

She nodded, and pushed herself upright. 'We must go,' she said. She made to stand – and then collapsed before he could catch her, falling on to her side, scraping the left of her cheek and chin on the ground.

Her whole body was flushed red, then paled. She tried again; again, nothing.

'My legs,' she said. 'They won't.' She closed her eyes.

'If she can't walk,' said the dryad, 'how is she going to go through the maze?'

'That's easy,' said Christopher. 'That's the only easy question, really. I go with her.'

NO MORTAL MAN HAS EVER RETURNED

He carried her back to the boat, back through the wood and through the town. She was barely conscious, and though she wasn't heavy, he had to put her down often to shift her as his grip faltered.

He ate, when he paused, to give himself courage. He had been given a woven bag of apples, of plums and pears and apricots: dryad fruit, like nothing else on earth. They tasted still-living; fruits with opinions and jokes and laughter in them.

He laid her down in the boat. The skin around her eyes was purplish. It looked bad. Her eyes were brighter than they should be, and she shook without ceasing.

Jacques looked peevish, insofar as dragons are able to look anything.

'What have you done to her?'

'Nothing. She did it to herself.'

Aching, he hauled the sail of the boat, and told Jacques his plan. If Mal could not walk the maze alone, he would go with her.

'*She* is the Immortal one. You should not go in with her. You should wait for her to be ready to go in alone. No mortal man has ever returned from the maze.'

'And what if she's never ready?' He spat the words at the dragon: a little fleck of spit landed on its wings. 'The last Immortal – the man who said no – what's-his-name, Marik – he took months to be able to walk again. What if it's the same? We *can't wait*! The glimourie is going to be lost. It's not just the Archipelago. It's the whole of the world. It's everything. *Everything*. D'you understand that? It's *my* world, *my* home, *my* family.' He thought of his father, of his grandfather, whom he could not warn. He would not be there to comfort them if darkness came, and the thought cut through him. His hands, as he pulled a rope taut, shook.

Jacques turned away. 'You forget yourself, to speak in such tones to a dragon.' He waited another half-hour before he said: 'You know, the boat of the Immortal is dryad-wood.'

'I'm *extremely* aware of that, thank you.'

'So you don't need to row, or sail. You can just *tell* it where you want it to go.'

The look Christopher gave him made Jacques flinch, despite the dragon being so used to flames.

'The maze,' Christopher told the boat.

It took twenty-eight hours to reach the Island of Arkhe.

Mal slept much of the way. She spoke the directions of the maze, over and over. He fed her water, and fruit, and repeated the directions back to her. Jacques snatched a fish from the water, and burned it half-black, and she ate small flakes of that.

Jacques watched Christopher, as he recited the way through the maze back to her; back and forth they went, until he had it like a song, etched in his mind.

'No mortal man has ever returned,' said Jacques.

'You really are fantastic company, you know that?' said Christopher.

They spent the night half asleep, half waking, reciting. He found himself awakening with a jolt under the stars, roused by his own voice speaking aloud, 'Left, left, right ...' In the end, they stayed awake, staring up at the sky. It was alight with silver; it looked alive, an ancient breathing thing.

They had seen so much, he thought; and now everything else had fallen away. It was just him and Mal, and the future of everything. Oceans and tides and earth, in their hands. The thought was so vast it threatened to crush him, to stop the blood in his heart – and he moved so that his shoulder touched hers, and she moved at the same time, and they lay side by side, watching the splendour of the infinitely fragile night pass by overhead.

The island came in sight in the late morning. Christopher flinched as they approached: the water that rimmed it was angry and choppy, and waves spat seawater furiously into the air. He glanced at Mal, wrapped in her coat, and knelt beside her, as Nighthand had done, to anchor her in place.

But as they grew closer, the waves abruptly dropped, and Christopher could have steered the boat easily. He didn't though. He waited for it to beach itself, and then he dropped anchor, and stepped on to the island.

It was sandy, and hot, and so bright it dazzled him. Above them the Somnulum, hanging low in the sky, burned too brightly for him to look at.

He helped Mal out of the boat, and half carried her on to the shore. Ahead of them was a stretch of sand, and a great rising of rocks. Amid the rocks was a cave-like entrance, as wide as a double door. There was no doubt at all that this was the way in to the maze. Even before Mal pointed the way, he could feel it.

The opening was cold, despite the warmth of the island.

Mal sat in the shade of a rock, kneading at her legs with sharp little fingers. A tree would have been better, but there was only one tree in sight, a thorn tree, which could not be leaned against.

She bit her tongue between her teeth. 'We should go,' she said.

He slung a coil of boat rope, tied with a loop at one end, around his shoulder. Mal braced her arm inside his. It clearly hurt her to walk: he could hear her teeth grinding together.

'Are you OK?' he said.

She turned to him, and it was such an absurd question that both gave a snort of laughter.

Together, Christopher and Mal approached the mouth of the cave. Together, longing to turn back, knowing they must go forward, they stepped inside.

THE MAZE

The walls were stone, dry and rough, and the floor was smooth. The air smelt of a hundred years of undisturbed dust. Very swiftly, it became dark. The walls were lit with salamandric fire.

They came to a fork in the way. 'Left,' she said, though he didn't need her to say it. He knew. And at the next turning he spoke first – 'Left, again,' he said, and she smiled.

'It's familiar,' she said. 'I've been here hundreds of times before. I know it.' She tried to smile. 'I always had a terrible sense of direction, before. Not now.'

They walked deeper in, their steps and breath the only sound in the absolute silence of the dark stone. Her face was drenched with cold sweat, from the effort of walking. Once, they stopped, and she sat on the floor for a few minutes. She wiped her face on her shirt.

'What can I do? How can I make it easier?'

She held out her hands. 'Help me up. We'd better go on.'

'Right, and then left,' he said.

'And then the arrows – if they're still there.'

He nodded. The arrows were taken from the quills of a manticore's tail, fletched with feathers from a hippogriff, and tipped with karkadann poison. You wouldn't survive being grazed by one. They reached a turning.

'Now,' said Mal. 'Over there.'

He picked a loose rock from the maze floor, and threw it.

An arrow erupted from the wall, struck the opposite wall of the tunnel, and disappeared. He threw a stone again: this time it erupted from the opposite side. With it came a whiff of poison.

'Karkadann,' said Christopher. 'A smell I wouldn't mind forgetting.'

They dropped to their knees, then their stomachs.

'Keep your whole body low,' said Mal. 'Don't lift your head.'

They crawled forward. The movement of their bodies on the dust triggered the spring in the wall, and three knife-sharp arrows, barely an inch above their heads, flew past. Christopher forced himself not to jerk upwards.

'This now,' said Mal, 'is the hail of them.'

'Let me go first,' he said. 'Just ... in case.'

He inched forwards: and immediately the air above him was thick with shrill air as a storm of arrows flew in both directions over their heads. Christopher felt one graze his hair. He pressed his face into the ground, trying not to let the rope tangle as he crept. He could hear Mal behind him.

And then, blessedly, there was the turning up ahead – right, and he took it, and rose aching to his feet. A glow of triumph warmed him.

'Still not dead. Come on.'

They walked on. She was breathing hard now with the effort; she had one arm around his shoulder, and her left foot dragged. Minutes passed, with only their soft tread, and their breath. The dark grew greater, the lights further apart.

'Stop!' Mal cried. 'Christopher! The chasm!'

He halted in the flickering light.

'The chasm has grown! It's right there! Stop! Don't go forward!'

She had told him about the chasm, on the boat. It was a great hole, with a ledge on each side. 'They dug it so deep,' she had said, 'that you would fall for whole minutes before you reached the bottom. If you fell, your bones would never be recovered: they'd be too far to see. But there's a ledge – a foot wide – and you can inch your way around, if you are not afraid. If you fall, you die.'

Christopher stared ahead into the darkness. 'But ... it shouldn't be for another twenty paces. I was counting – thirty paces after the left turn.' He edged forwards – and then reared backwards, sick with shock.

What he had taken for a shadow was in fact a vast and terrible hole.

287

'The man in the heart of the maze – he must have made it larger,' she said. 'And look! Look! The ledge.'

The ledge along the wall now was barely two-thirds of the width of his foot. His stomach sank.

Her voice was tiny with despair. 'What do I do? My legs aren't steady enough.' She looked over the edge, and her whole body shook. 'I'll fall.'

He looked back the way they had come. They could not turn back now. 'Then I'll go on alone,' he said. 'You sit here, and wait for me.'

'You can't!' Terror rose in her; a child's terror. 'You'll die!'

'There's no other way. I'll come back. OK?'

'You aren't the Immortal, Christopher! He'll kill you!'

He looked down at the chasm, and back at Mal. 'I'm not the Immortal. But I know her. I know what you would do, if it was the other way around.'

There was silence.

'Mal, I'll come back. Just wait for me.'

He could hear her gasping with small, smothered sobs as he approached the chasm. It was a black blur, stretching down beneath his feet. He felt the taste of bile rise in his mouth. He pressed his back against the wall, and stepped, feet turned out sideways, on to the ledge. Slowly, slowly, he began to edge along, using his hands to grip at the rough stone wall as he went.

The wall of the maze now was the natural rock of the cave. It had bulges and growths on it, which made it viciously painful to press his back against, but it gave him handholds.

He remembered something he had been told once – that vertigo is not the fear of falling. It is the fear that you will jump. The blackness called to him. For one moment it felt inevitable that he would simply lean forwards, that his body would pull him into the dark.

He stopped, felt himself shake. He forced himself to keep sliding his feet along the ten-inch outcrop.

And then without warning, his sliding foot was hanging out over nothing. The ledge had ended.

He lurched. His hand shot out and gripped a knot in the wall, steadying himself.

'You're not going to die,' he whispered. 'This is not how this ends.'

There was no way forward. But on the opposite wall there were larger outcrops – sideways stalactites, some small, some a foot in length, like fists sticking from the wall. *The rope*, he thought. The rope had a loop at one end. Shaking now so hard his teeth chattered, he used his free hand to slide the rope from his shoulder.

With the other hand, he swung the rope, aiming for a protruding outcrop of rock on the other side. The first time he missed, and the rope dropped down into the darkness. The second time, again, and the third, it dropped, and each time he felt his stomach swoop as if it might pull him in after it.

He took a breath and forced his body to still itself. He thought of Mal – and of Gelifen, chewing on his hair. He thought of the unicorns. He thought of his grandfather, amid a crowd of seagulls; of his father, sitting next to his bed at night; of the half-remembered face of his mother. He thought of the blue shining world, and of what the man in the maze would do to it. He threw the rope again.

It caught. The loop held. He tugged at it; gently at first, and then much harder. He sent up one brief, wordless prayer, and launched himself out into the space above the chasm.

The rope creaked. Christopher swung in a long, fevered parabola and landed on hands and knees on the other side of the abyss.

'I'm over!' he called. 'I'm safe!' But he could hear no response.

There was no triumph, as there had been with the arrows. Mal was not with him. He got to his feet, pulled the rope after him, and went on.

He turned left, left, right. He took the two next turns – tight right and right again – and abruptly the lights stopped. Mal hadn't warned him of this. It must be new. He was in sudden, total darkness.

It was so dark that he could not tell if his eyes were open or closed. And there was something else – a chill mist, which he could not see but could feel, dampening his hands, and rising into his face and nose.

He hesitated; then he laid one hand on the wall, and continued. Left. Left. Right. Left again. It grew colder and wetter as he went deeper in. His heart clenched tighter than it had ever been. The dark closed over him.

THE GREY MIST

Christopher walked. He did not know for how long. He dared not think; only kept repeating the directions. Right turn. Left.

All there was was dark. The mist grew colder; it was on his clothes, something bitter and seeping. It smelt of dead skin. He recognised it, as he breathed it in. It was horror.

He fumbled in his brain, to make sure he still knew the way. It was there, imprinted on his memory by a thousand repetitions – but everything else was blurred.

He walked on, and on, and the minutes became dozens, and then untrackable, and he had no idea how long he had been moving forward in the dark, one arm stretched out ahead and the other on the left-hand wall.

He breathed in the mist, and a flare of jealousy went up in him; jealousy of those who were not here. The jealousy gripped at his organs, stomach and lungs and throat. Jealousy is not like anything else. It is a locust. It eats a great deal that cannot be spared.

He tried to think of his father, his grandfather, his mother, of how they would call out, encourage him, love him, but they would not be summoned up. His imagination was dead in the dark.

The mist rose and became a grey wind. It seeped into his skin. The darkness was in him, and with it misery, a dull, blunt, angry sorrow. He had already, in a short life, done such hurt.

He stumbled. The dirt beneath his feet was interrupted by something: stones, or bones. Keeping his left hand on the wall, he bent, picked one up, tried to feel the edge – but curiosity failed, and he let it fall.

It clattered, in the dark, and an animal cry from somewhere in the labyrinth went up.

He walked on. He breathed the mist, and he knew that the idea of goodness was a great con. A way to control the weak and many. Such loveliness as he had seen was an illusion. Kavil had been right: the thought cut at him. *Hope is a little lie that the powerless use to comfort themselves.*

His thoughts stuttered in his mind. *We are human rot. Rats for hearts.* He had wanted his life to matter. He had wanted there to be large, everlasting truths. It was a drab, ordinary lie to want them. Stab-stab, went the insidious little knife.

The dark was inside his nostrils. It was on the insides of his eyes. It was dread.

His heart was an iron spike.

This was the truth: the cold dust on the floor. You died: nothing mysterious. A hundred and twenty-four. *Right.* A hundred and twenty-five. *Left.* A hundred and twenty-six. *Left.*

He thought about stopping, but that too would have no meaning.

He walked on. He counted: a hundred and thirty. *Left.* He would die here: he was sure of that now.

He would walk, until he could not, and then he would sit against the wall, and he would die like that; and for a second he was so unbearably sad, it flavoured his mouth with bile – but then even that ceased to matter, the thought drained away like black sand through his hands, he could not catch it, and there was nothing at all except left, right, right, right.

Sudden hoofbeats rang down the labyrinth ahead of him.

Something came round the corner and crashed into him. He had no time to brace himself, to think, to cry out. It hit his head first, his chest a second later: something on four legs, furred, with teeth. He landed on his back, winded, could not even yell. Something tore down his arm: a claw, he thought. A horn? He could see nothing at all: blackness, and a roar. Could the thing see? Should he turn and run? But he'd lose his way.

He pulled the kitchen knife from his side – realised as he did, with a terrible lurch, that he had forgotten to take the glamry blade from Mal – almost dropped it, slashed in front of him.

He might have been screaming but it was impossible to tell. The thing was bellowing, a horn or claw came at his head, caught at his ear, cut through, and he lifted his knife and swung at it, hard. He felt something give way and heard a yowl. He dropped to all fours.

Then it was over. The thing bellowed, pushed past him, and he heard running hooves echo down the corridor.

Then there was no sound, except his heart, which beat in his ears. He wiped his face, and spat.

He felt his body, carefully, his hands shaking. His ear was bleeding. There was pain everywhere, in his chest and the back of his head, but his feet worked. His teeth were all there. He could not see his hands, but they still moved, though one was agonised: the thumb had been pulled back. He rose, took one step forward, and a thought came to him. His heart lurched as if another creature had come at him.

He had been turned round.

Or had he? Had he spun, or only dropped?

He thought only dropped.

He had to choose.

Forward. It was impossible to bear going back. So forward. Even if forward *was* back.

The adrenalin of the fight gave electricity to his blood. It gave him speed. It was not hope, but something else: it fought back at the mist. It was a kind of gritted determination. His urgency returned.

He began to run.

He stopped. Running, he could not hear if the thing was returning behind him.

He walked – and then he didn't care; he ran again.

He ran fast, faster than he had ever run, with his left hand pressed against the wall, running straight into the dark. The wall tore at the skin on his fingers. He did not stop counting.

There were one hundred and fifty-two turns. He should be ten away. Then six, five, four. And ahead – he blinked, then touched his eyeball, to check his eyes were open – light. It was a real light.

He turned left, and right, and left: and burst into the very centre of the maze.

AT THE CENTRE

The centre of the maze was a huge stone room, lit by lamps, the ceiling so high it disappeared into the darkness.

A great wave of something hot and fierce went through him. The centre of it all! Even if what was in that room killed him, he had walked the labyrinth. Unseen, unheralded; and he might die yet, and nobody would know: but even if no witnesses ever told it, it was still true. He felt a wild exaltation as he stepped into the cavern.

There was a smell: three smells, in battle. A smell of human waste, yes, and the dank mist, but beneath it the glorious living smell that he had smelt in the woods, and in the breath of the unicorn. It was the smell of pure distilled life. It was the glimourie.

A great tree grew up from the centre of the stone floor. It was tall and slim and noble, a rich brown, its leaves yellow-gold.

His eyes adjusted to the light – and then he leaped backwards, and smothered a yell of horror.

It had a face.

He forced himself to step closer. He saw it clearly: there, embracing the tree, wound into the tree, melded and merged with the tree, was a man's body; a face, half-grown into the trunk, and a body, grown the texture and colour of the tree's wood.

The face looked at Christopher, and it showed no fear. Its voice was low, and slow, and rough with disuse. It sounded of a hundred years of darkness.

'Who is this, in my arboretum?'

'My name is Christopher Forrester,' he said. He stepped, again, closer. 'Who are you?'

'I am the future of the world.' The voice rasped through the air, and grey mist curled from the creature's mouth.

'What have you done?'

'I have taken what was there for the taking.'

'Taken what?'

'The Glimourie Tree.' The face moved, shifted in the tree. 'I have taken its power into my body. Soon, I will have it all. The tree will be dead. A husk. I will be the root and source of power, and I will move into the world, and take hold of what is mine.'

Christopher fought back his panic: he pushed it back, tried to think. The man, he saw, was human; or once had been. Humans need to speak aloud. There was a hundred years of speech, pent up, bursting to erupt. If Christopher could keep him talking – if he could keep the man from directing the force of his power at him – perhaps he could think of a way to survive.

'But how did you get here?' he asked. 'Only the Immortal knows the path to the centre of the maze.'

'The Immortal, yes. And two others.'

'Who?'

He exhaled; the mist eddied, choking and acrid. 'The men who made the maze.'

'But Leonardo da Vinci, and his cousin – they took a potion. They forgot.'

'They did. But Leonardo's cousin Enzo was an intelligent man, and an angry one. Leonardo, in the Archipelago, as in the rest of the world, was the one who claimed credit. Leonardo sketched on paper; Enzo worked in stone. Enzo sweated; Leonardo merely basked.'

'And what then? What happened?'

The face in the tree turned its eyes full on Christopher. He was taking pleasure, Christopher could feel it, in his story. He breathed, and the mist rose, and with it a wind that eddied at Christopher's feet.

'Enzo grew first disgusted, then angry. And then he made a plan. Before he took the potion, he made a secret copy of the plans for the maze, and hid them. He returned home, his memory a blank, and he did not understand the importance of the plans. But he put them among his books – a child's dream, he supposed.'

The grey exhalation of mist came again, and again the air filled with the dread that clutched at Christopher's chest.

'Hundreds of years later, one of his descendants – me, Francesco Sforza – found them. I had no interest in his grubby little quarrel. But when I found what was in the heart of the maze – the tree, and its vast power – then I understood what was possible. I found a way into the Archipelago, at the equinox. I followed the plans and found my way to the island. And when I reached it, I found that the Immortal – the great protector – was gone. Think, first, of my astonishment. Think, then, of my pleasure.'

He breathed out, a rough gasp of glee, and Christopher stepped back.

'I followed the plans into the maze. I found the tree. It grew alone, unseen. It was as if it were waiting for me; as if it were waiting for someone to put its power to use. And I began to devour it – to eat, to graft, to *become* the tree. Its power is mine. Within weeks – days, perhaps – it will be mine in its totality.'

'Why?' said Christopher. 'Why, alone here, in the dark? What good is it?'

The thing that had once been Francesco Sforza turned its eyes on Christopher, and the look felt as though it charred his skin.

'It is *freedom*. The only freedom is in absolute power. Without absolute power, you will always be subject to some other man. Freedom is available only to those who are willing to take it by force.'

His voice rose, a raw hiss of disgust. 'Half the world knows it to be true; the other half only pretends not to. They play their little games, of what-can-I-do and how-can-I-help, and they know, on their deathbeds, that they wasted their lives. They changed nothing. They knew nothing. They *were* nothing. They were slaves to chance, to luck, to other men.

'But I refused to be like them. I have learned to take the glimourie into me, and control it. The tree is the source of the glimourie: it sends it out into the world, steadily. But now I have grafted its power on to me; soon I will be the source. At first I struggled, faltered, in the dark – but these last ten years, I have found the way. I get stronger daily, and the tree weaker. The glimourie – the entirety of the world's magic – is almost mine. My *breath* has power, to confound and control. My lips have the power to kill.'

Christopher took another step backwards. The wind grew stronger; it whipped through the cave.

'You must understand,' said the man. He was guttural, slow. 'I have never once had a human visitor; some have tried, but none have reached the centre. So I have had no chance to try my power at death.'

Christopher's head was growing foggy. He shook himself, hard, like a dog. Like a griffin. Like Gelifen.

He had to fight. Even if he was going to die, he had to fight first. He reached for the knife at his side, and leaped forward.

The creature thrust out a great branch of an arm, and sent him flying against the floor. It winded him, and his head smacked against the stone. He rolled over, his head spinning, and climbed to his feet. Again, he ran at the man.

This time the man did not move. His eyes glinted, and a bout of mist came from his mouth. The mist rolled over Christopher, up over his chest, his head, and he felt a great weight pressing down on him like a hand; a terrible, cold dead weight. He dropped to his knees.

'Enough,' said Sforza. 'Enough.'

Christopher crawled sideways, out of the mist. It took every piece of strength he had to get to his feet. His lips were dry, and his mouth burned. He staggered towards the man.

'This is pointless, child. This is a little play you are putting on with no audience. Nobody will know whether or not you fought. Nobody will know, or care, what you did before you died. It's worthless.'

Christopher forced himself to speak. 'It's not,' he said. He was choking; he pushed the words through dry lips. 'I'll know.'

He forced all his strength up, summoned it out of exhaustion and fear. He dodged, sideways, under the arm that came out to flick him away, and lunged towards the tree. He was fast, and he was angry – angrier than he'd ever been in his life. A branch came swinging down at him, and he dropped low and jabbed upwards with the tip of the blade. It stuck into the wood, and was whipped out of his hand. Sforza hissed, and flicked the knife away, clattering across the stone room, and the down-sweep of his arm caught Christopher across the head.

He was thrown backwards, grazing his skin on the ground. He got to his knees. He would fight, then, with his hands. He would tear and bite, if it was possible, and spit – like Mal spat: hard – until the dark came down over him. He braced himself to leap.

Through the stone room rang a shout.

'*Christopher!*'

He recognised the voice, but it was impossible. He was hallucinating.

But the shout came again, and Sforza stared over Christopher's shoulder, at an opening on the far side of the cavern.

Christopher turned; and the iron spike that was his heart unfurled, and became a victory flag.

There are many good things a person will see in a life. But few will ever see anything as good as what Christopher saw: the low-flying girl, arms out, her feet grazing the floor, sweeping into the light. She had Nighthand's glamry blade in her hand.

The sight went through him like raw gold.

She threw the glamry blade to land at his feet. He snatched it up. He leaped forward. His hand swept down in a cut. Sforza's scream ricocheted around the cavern, as he cut at the places where the tree had grafted on to the man – cut and hacked until man and tree were separate.

Francesco Sforza staggered sideways. He was tiny, and withered, and ancient, wasted by his century in the dark. Immediately the wood-like sheen to his skin faded, and turned to white-grey. He fell senseless to the ground.

They bound him with the rope, hands and feet. He was clammy to the touch.

'I know the way back,' said Mal. 'I know it like my own home. Come. Follow me.'

It was painful, and long, half carrying, half dragging the man through the darkness. At the chasm, they paused.

'We could drop him in?' said Christopher.

Mal shook her head. She gritted her teeth, and they placed Sforza on her back, and on the chill wind that still blew, she flew across the gap. On the last breaths of the grey wind, she took Christopher across, the two half leaping, half flying through the dark. But when they emerged into the sun, sweat on both their faces, the air was sweeter and softer than it had ever been.

THE IMMORTAL

They dragged Sforza, haggard and thin and the white of a drowned thing, into the sun and set him down, trussed and bound, under the thorn tree. He appeared unconscious. They moved further off, far enough away that the man's pulsating malice felt less powerful.

'Are you hurt?' he asked.

She shook her head. 'I have seen so much, Christopher.' Her eyes, in her child's face, looked ancient; there was nothing young now in her look. It was the face of someone who knows the ancient, uncompromising truths.

'Will you tell me?'

'Not all of it. Some of it. What I can. We should sit, or we'll collapse.'

They sat, the two of them, shoulder to shoulder in the sand. It was hot, but she was shivering; she drew her coat

304

around her. Her hair was a tangle down her back, and her face was filthy with sand and blood, but sitting there she radiated something infinite. She had the look of a queen to her – or not that, he thought: someone to whom a queen would kneel.

'Have we got any water?'

'I left it at the mouth of the cave.' He fetched it – he walked slowly, and he was dizzy – and gave it to her. She drank half – and then slightly more, and tried to smile at him – and he drank the rest.

'Tell me?' he said. 'If you can.'

She said: 'I have seen more than I could ever have guessed.'

Her voice sounded burned, still. She spoke low.

'I have seen horror. I have seen immoveable evil. I have seen brutality and lies. I've seen jealousy, and spite, and greed disguised as reason and sense. I have seen millions of men and women allow themselves ignorance as excuse. I have seen corpses piled in the night.

'I understand why the last knowing Immortal – the man, Marik – I know why he said: I *cannot. No. No, to the world, and no, to humankind. Humankind is not worth the horror we inflict on ourselves. I say: I will not care. I say: I will look away. I say: no.*

'I have seen the dark: dark stacked upon dark. I have seen such purposeless sorrow. I have seen fear, and dread. I have seen death. Oh, Christopher, the death!'

Her whole body, next to him, shook.

'I have lost children.

'But I have seen red dragons fly over mountains in the falling sun. And I have seen people offer up their lives to save another, as if it were as natural as breathing. I've known lovers find each other in war and famine. I have seen promises made and kept for entire lifetimes, unswervingly, as if it was easy. I've seen lions at midnight. I have seen wonder on wonder on wonder. I have seen how the world shines.

'I have seen people struggle to learn – painting, gardens, language, hand-skills, foot-skills – and I have seen them triumph. I have seen kindnesses large and wild enough to transform you. I have heard the best jokes in the world and music so sweet I thought I might fall down because of it. I have seen so much done for love, over and over. I have seen people die for love and live for love. I have seen birth, and birth again. I have known such joy. The *joy*, Christopher.'

He watched her, breathing in the warmth, and the dust of the island, and the restless beauty of the sea.

He was about to speak when there was a sudden shout.

It was a shriek of terror and of despair, so loud and anguished it froze Christopher's body. It was the jaculus.

'Look out!' cried Jacques. 'The man!'

FLIGHT

It was the most terrible thing he had ever seen. At the foot of the thorn tree, where they had tied him, the man had risen, still bound, to his knees. His face was full of dark concentration, and from all around him came a mist: a grey mist, carried on a high and furious wind. It was the same mist as in the maze: it had the same smell, of power and dread.

Christopher felt it in his ears, roaring. The wind was blowing away from the island, away from them, carrying the mist out over the sea: across the Archipelago, and beyond.

'Stop him!' cried Jacques.

The crouching man – barely human now – turned, and looked at them, and there was triumph in the look.

'Stand back!' cried Jacques. 'Children, get behind me!' They ran backwards, as the dragon gulped air and breathed a great bout of flame.

Christopher had not understood, until then, what is truly meant by fire. It was a fireball, an explosion of blue-red, and the heat of it singed the tips of his hair and scorched his eyes, so that both he and Mal had to cover their faces.

When the smoke cleared, the tree was burned to a pile of ashes. The sand, in patches, had melted into glass.

Sforza stood unscathed. He smiled; a gleeful smile. He called out to them. 'I have consumed too much for that. Your little blade will not hurt me. Dragon fire will not burn me. I am here, and the power is here, and it is mine.'

He breathed out, a great Ha! of conquest, and with that Ha! the wind grew, and with it the grey mist.

Mal looked up at the sky: up at the Somnulum. Her lips moved, and her small face, with its badly cut fringe, was vivid with unspoken thought. The scar on her cheek, from Gelifen, stood out white on her skin.

Mal's face contorted. Too much passed over it for him to read it.

But then she set her jaw, and clenched her fists, and that he recognised: he knew that gesture so well.

'Christopher! Come here. You have to listen to me.' Her voice was low and scratched and urgent.

He went to her, and bent low to hear her.

'Listen. I wanted to tell you – I don't know, a million things. I thought we had time. I thought we had years, the two of us. I thought –' A pause full of pain, a snort of breath, and she went on, faster. 'It is so difficult, to be alive. It is so difficult, and it is so beautiful.' She looked full at him, and her face was blazing. 'Listen. I need you to tell people this; I need you, when you get back, to tell them: the brutality is terrible. And yes: the chaos is very great. But tell them: greater than the world's chaos are its miracles.'

She gave a smile; a new smile. She bent, and with the glamry blade she sliced the stitches from the coat's hem, and the cloth unfurled. She dropped the blade and the casapasaran at his feet. She pulled him down to her and kissed him on the cheek, hard, almost as hard as a bite.

She whispered into his ear, one final sentence.

And then she spread her arms in the old coat. The wind lifted her, six feet in the air. She flew straight at the small, white, bone-thin man, carried on the wind of his own making.

She barrelled towards him. The man turned, scrambling to the left, then right, his mouth suddenly open with fear, but she had the agility of a child and the nerves of all eternity.

She seized the evil, crouching thing in one arm, the other still outstretched, and as he lifted off the ground he struggled, but instantly they were ten, twenty, fifty feet in the air, and the girl flew them straight upwards, towards the Somnulum.

As they soared upwards, Christopher heard the flying girl let out a great shout. It rang against the rocks as they disappeared into the burn of the great ball of light.

It might have been fear; but it sounded, as he stood watching, exactly like triumph – like joy – like love.

THE FUNERAL MARCH

Christopher told it all, later, to the sphinxes.

There had been a great burning flash – he had been knocked to the ground by it, sand in his eyes and mouth – and a single moment's pause; and then the whole earth shook. The wind screamed one last time around his ears, and dropped.

Everything was still. He did not have a grasp on time to know how long he lay there. And then from the ocean, from its depths, from the nereids, or mermaids, or, he thought, from the sea itself, there came a great thrum of music, high and sharp and joyful.

The scent he had smelt first at the lochan, the scent of something wild and pure growing, living and bursting forth, came in a great rush from the mouth of the maze. It dizzied him in its sweetness.

Slowly he got to his feet. His vision was blurred, and he saw swathes of colour that could not be there.

Haltingly, his body aching, he had returned to the boat. Jacques had been waiting. He was surrounded by a cloud of steam, where his own tears met his hot body: like a tiny kettle in the wilderness.

Christopher had climbed into the boat, and told it where to go, and lain down under the sky to sleep. As dark fell, Jacques kept his small and furious watch – but the dark did not trouble Christopher now. He had seen so much of it, and had walked through it to the other side.

He was still asleep when the boat butted against the rocks of the sphinxes' peninsula. Naravirala herself lifted him out of the boat in her jaws and carried him like a cub up the rocks, to a cave set in the ridge.

He was filthy when they found him, sand and blood in his nails and hair. They cleaned him, as best they could, by dipping him into a pool, each shoulder held between the teeth of two young sphinxes. They laid him in the cave, on a bed of straw. Naravirala visited him. She licked, with her great rough tongue, his wounds. He watched as his bruises, his cuts, the raw places where he had bled and scabbed and bled again, began to fade at the pressure of her tongue. For a full day and a night he slept.

When he woke, sometimes he stared mutely at the ground; sometimes he tried to eat; occasionally he cried, wiping water with his fists. Some of the sphinxes came and tried to ask him questions, but Naravirala stopped them, with her teeth.

'The journey has taken a bite out of part of him he could not easily spare,' said the sphinx. 'Let him be.'

Meanwhile, across the Archipelago, the news went out, from ratatoska to dryad to centaur. The word spread swiftly: of who Mal was, and of what she had done, and of what, in her great flight, she had saved. The creatures made ready. There would be a funeral march.

It began at dawn. There were no humans except Christopher. It was the greatest honour of his life that he was permitted to attend, though he did not know enough to know it.

Naravirala led the march. She carried him on her great back to the stretch of sandy ground where it was to take place: a place where land met water in beauty and stillness.

The entire clan of the sphinxes followed behind, walking four abreast, padding on vast lion feet across the sand. They moved like a silent grieving army, and all who saw them drew back in fear and awe at the looks on their leonine faces.

Behind them the nereids came, walking, their silver hair flowing down on to the sand like wedding trains. Nereids do not walk on dry land, except in cases of necessity – except now to honour the loved lost. They sang as they came, a song in their own language, so high and sweet that Christopher felt it would knock him from the sphinx's back; and behind them in the water rose mermaids, three clans, playing on their instruments an ancient tune to the fallen.

The dryads came from the wood at the edge of the sands. Erato led the way. Her tears were of sap, running down her face. They joined the song, and their voices, lower and deeper, made the earth shiver. It cut into Christopher's chest, into his lungs.

Centaurs followed, marching as one, dressed in black breastplates. They had sent their full number of trumpeters, male and female, the finest in the islands. They did not yet play. They waited for their signal.

Behind them walked a hundred ratatoskas, on silent paws, their small voices raised in song, and behind them a troop of al-mirajes, silent, their golden horns dipped low. A cluster of kankos followed. Tears shone like fireflies against their furred cheeks.

At last, from the woods came the unicorns. They came in their hundreds, silver and white and pearl. They did not come nearer, but stood at the edge of the trees, tossing their manes and sending up high whinnies to the air.

The procession came to a stop. Christopher had Mal's blade at his belt. He held her casapasaran in his palm, so tightly it bit into his skin. Naravirala dropped to the sand, and he dismounted. She bent, touched her muzzle to his face. 'Courage,' she said. 'You must bear it, for there is no other option. Courage, valiant boy.'

Then she turned, and spoke to the creatures on the sands.

'Malum Arvorian is dead, and is not dead. She is Immortal: her death is instant birth. And so we do not weep for her but for ourselves; for the sadness that is the child of our love. We weep because we will not see her face again. We sing for the bravery of her glorious heart. We will eat grief for dinner; but tomorrow, we will dine on joy for what she did.' The sphinx turned to the centaurs, and raised her head. 'Sound out, trumpets, for the flying girl.'

The trumpets sounded once, twice, a third time. Christopher felt tears run down his face as the creatures, ranged in their rows and multitudes, let out a great shout, each in their own language. They shouted out in loss and in gratitude, in grief and glory, and the sound rose up into the air and filled the ocean, and miles away a Berserker and a woman with nereid blood heard it, and wept, and rejoiced, and wept again.

THE KINDNESS OF SPHINXES

The day after the funeral march, Naravirala visited Christopher in the sphinxes' cave. He sat with his back to the mountain wall, and told her about the man in the maze, and his vicious hunger: his furious desire not to be exposed to the world's indignities, to chance and to other human people.

She nodded. 'That is why great power must never reside in only one person. It must be shared.' Her rough voice was rougher than before. 'It must be spread, among as many good women and men as can be found; not because it is kind or polite or fair, but because it is the only way to beat back against horror.'

Later, she returned, with cooked indeterminable meat, which she left at his feet. 'Do you know why she did what she did?' she asked.

He nodded.

'Could you tell me why?'

He shook his head. 'But I do know.'

'So do I, I believe. It was an act of insistence: it was insistence that the world is worth loving. The sphinxes are making songs of her already. They will sing them of you too. They will cut them into the stone across the mountainside.'

Christopher looked up at the cragged old face. It is possible to wound a sphinx, it turned out: you do it by breaking their heart.

On the day he first woke without the feeling of ache in his whole body, it was to see a green face pressed close up against his, upside down. It was Ratwin.

He yelled, and she dismounted from his head and dipped her nose to his hand, in fealty.

'Here,' she said. 'For you.' And she spat something into his hand.

'Thanks.' He sat up. 'Next time, though, it would be nice not to wake up wearing your bottom as an eye mask.'

In his hand was a tiny parcel, of brown paper and thin green thread. Inside was soft white cloth, and inside that a single golden earring. His heart dropped. He felt the blood drain from his face.

'What? Nighthand! Is he ... ?'

'No! No. It's a gesture of thanks.'

'Bloody hell! He could have chosen some other gesture! I mean, he literally calls it his coffin fund.'

'Irian did say it would startle you up and annoy you down, but he insisteds.' Her sharp little voice grew slower than usual. 'He lives. They took him to the centauride – a healer called Kentavir. She understoods the poison of karkadanns. Kentavir made him a liniment. She made it three times from the soil; the third time was in those moments after the earths shook. Had you and the little Immortal miniature not restored the glimourie, he would be dead now, I'm thinksing.'

'How's his arm?'

'It has a greenish scrofulous-meats look to it, but he says it has a certain chic.'

'And what happened to you?'

The ratatoska's eyes lit up. 'Oh, I made life bleak for the murdering centaur! I nudged his supplies overboard, and I rip-tore at the sails with my teeth. I bites him as he slept. He tried to throw me into the waves, but couldn't catch me – I climbed to the top of the mast, where he couldn't follows. When we came near land, I leaped into the water, and swam to land. I don't know where his ugly face is now. But he can't stay hidden from the ratatoskas.'

'And how's Irian?'

'She is well.' A pause. 'She is in love – which is not an easy thing, but is I thinks perhaps very fine.'

'With Nighthand?'

Ratwin nodded. 'Not an easy propositionate, but not a thin or unjoyful or dullish one.'

She brought other news: of young saplings springing

forth, and the krakens returning to their rich and silty deeps. And a nereid called Galatia sent greetings and a message to him: 'She said to say: *The water is rich again. The water is full.*'

'And ... is that true? Is all this true?'

The ratatoska raised her small, sculpted head. 'Yes,' she said. 'It's true.'

Later, Naravirala took him for a walk, riding on her muscular back, Jacques flapping alongside, up the mountain to where a stream sprang. 'It is our finest water. Drink, and it will last you.'

Together, they drank from the stream.

'Where is she?' asked Christopher. 'Mal? When she comes back ...'

Naravirala shook her great head. 'We cannot know yet. But she is already here, somewhere: of that I'm sure. And we will find out where; I imagine the ratatoskas will tell me. I know that the time will come when the new Immortal will find you. Remember, boy: everything that Mal knew and saw and loved, the new Immortal knows and saw and loved. They will know and love *you*, Christopher. Mal hasn't truly gone: she is part of an infinite soul. One day the Immortal will come for you: they will run to you and joyfully call you by name. And that will be a very great day. But for now, for you – it is time to go home.'

'Is there an opening?'

'There is. We have had lookouts posted, since first you came to the mountain with your friends. One opened: we think it opened at the moment the creature died. But it is halfway around the Archipelago, past corals and rocks that a boat cannot reach.'

'Oh,' he said. 'But then, how do I get there? I'm not Mal – I can't fly.'

'You can,' said Jacques. 'You will fly on the back of a dragon.'

Christopher looked hesitantly at the jaculus: it would be like attempting to commute on the back of a hummingbird. 'No offence, but ... I mean, it's very kind – but I'm just not sure that would be comfortable for you. Or scientifically possible.'

Jacques gave an insulted huff, which set fire to a nearby bush. 'Not me! I have sent word to a far-off cousin.'

The dragon, when it came, was the size of a small castle; and it was familiar. It was crow-coloured – black, but with petrol sheens of green and purple and deep blue – but the underside of its wings was red.

'I've seen you before!'

'She speaks only her own language,' said Jacques. 'It's a language more ancient than any invented by humans.'

The sphinx did something so unexpected that he flinched backwards from her. She opened her jaw, set her teeth around a shard of rock, and gave a great thrust downwards. There was a crack like a revolver shot and a shard of her tooth – the tip, as large as the top of his thumb – fell on to the ground.

'Take it,' she said. 'Wash it well.'

He did so. 'Like that?' He held it up to her.

'Put it in your mouth.'

'In my *mouth*? I'm sorry, what?'

'A sphinx's tooth holds language in it.'

The jaculus looked grudgingly impressed. 'It will allow you to understand any language, if you hold it in your cheek. Murder between humans has been done, for a sphinx tooth.'

Gingerly, Christopher placed the sphinx tooth in his mouth. To his relief, it tasted of very little – certainly not of sphinx breath.

'*You know of a passageway?*' He said to the red dragon. It was his own voice, but the words were new sounds. It came out harsher, rougher.

'*I do.*'

'*And it is open?*'

'*For now.*'

'*When will it close?*'

'*There is no way to know. But it smells as if it grows near the end. So bid farewell to your lion-faces.*'

Christopher spat out the tooth into his hand, and turned to Naravirala.

'She said to say goodbye.'

'I know.' The old sphinx breathed on Christopher's face, and the power of it blew his hair back from his face.

'You have done well,' she said. 'You have done better than you know, which is rare.'

'Can I take the tooth home with me?'

She nodded her great head. 'It will work anywhere in the

world.' She gestured with her body to the dragon. 'Mount.'

The dragon's back was broad as a dozen grand pianos, and as polished; it was slippery, and hard to know where to put his feet. He settled for cross-legged, and the two great wings rose either side of him.

'Hold on to her scales,' said Naravirala. 'You cannot hurt her. She is made of ancient stuff. She was alive in Mesopotamia, four thousand years ago.'

So he gripped the ridge of the scales, and flattened himself against the dragon's back, and with great gusts of wind buffeting at his ears they rose together. Mal, he thought, would have loved it, and the thought gave him pleasure.

They flew for hours – more than long enough for Christopher to wish he had brought food. But asking for a lunch break was not, he thought, something you could do with dragons.

The dragon landed carefully on a small rock of an island, with a lake in the centre of it. Green particles of light danced across the water's surface. Between the dragon and the shore, there was very little room.

'Where do I go?'

'Into the water.'

He spat the tooth into his fist, and set his shoulders.

There was a thrum of moving air, and Jacques landed next to him.

'Put out your hand,' said Jacques. 'Palm down.'

Christopher did as he was told.

The jaculus landed on his hand, and dipped its tiny head

to his skin, in a bow. Then it bit him, hard, on the pad of the thumb, and raked its claws down the back of his hand.

'Ow! Hey! What was that for?'

'To leave a scar. So you don't ever ask yourself, was it real? It was as real as you are, and you are very real.'

He did not need the scar.

His love for Mal had been the finest part of him, he knew that already. It had made him brave. It is what is meant by miracles. And though she was gone, the love burned on.

'Now go, before it closes.'

And the small dragon gave him a push, which had no effect at all, and the large dragon gave him a gentle nudge of such force that it almost catapulted him into the water, and he looked once more at the sky.

Mal's sky now, he thought. The sky belonged to the girl who had disappeared into its fire, to save the world she had chosen to love. And – the thought rose and roared in his chest with a certainty and a joy that made him shake – he would come back to stand under this sky, and they would meet again. He would make sure of it.

He turned, and took a step towards home.

THE BEGINNING, AGAIN

It was a very fine day to be born. Somewhere in the Archipelago, moments after Mal flew, a woman gave birth. The baby laughed and wept by turns, and almost never slept. Its mother adored it, and found it utterly exhausting. In its sleep, it clenched its tiny fists, and jutted its tiny jaw.

The baby had not yet control of its tongue, but even so, it was speaking; it was exclaiming, in wonder and awe and fear and joy: it was saying the same words that Mal had said as she flew.

CHRISTOPHER'S JOURNEY

The detail of how Christopher returned – how he found his way to the surface of the lochan in the darkening evening, and how he made his way down the hill, wet to the skin, to find his grandfather in the kitchen – is not, after a dragon's back, a story worth telling.

But the cry his grandfather gave – huge from such an old man – when he saw him, standing, soaking wet and scarred and smiling: that was worth hearing. It shook the trees outside.

And the roar of joy and pride his father gave as he burst through the door, to hear Christopher say, 'It's safe. The Archipelago is safe. We healed it' – that was loud enough to shake the world itself.

They had a feast: a feast of such plenty and delight that the house could barely contain it. Frank Aureate had called his son-in-law when Christopher didn't return. They had argued, and Christopher's father had broken many things in fury; and then, when the pieces had been swept up and calm restored, there was nothing the two men could do but wait.

Each day, they prepared for the boy who did not come. Each day, in hope, they had bought and cooked too much food, and each night, in silent fear, the two men had eaten alone.

And so the feast that day was enormous. The table disappeared under the food; under bowls and plates and dishes, laid out by the older man's eager hands. They ate eight kinds of pasta, pies and fruit and cheese – and seven varieties of ice cream. His father shook with joy as he piled the table high.

Christopher told them everything. His father was a good listener: he did not interrupt, and he believed what he heard. Once, he gave something like a sob; and once, he could not stop himself from crying out in delight; mostly, though, he listened. And when Christopher moved to stoke the fire, he took a sharp breath – but he did not warn his son to keep back from the flames.

Frank Aureate sat in his armchair, watching them. He listened with shining eyes to tales of wonders he had himself seen – once, long ago – and would not see again.

There was only one thing Christopher didn't tell, that night. He did not tell what it was that Mal had said, into his ear, before she flew. That was his alone.

She had pulled him down to her height, and kissed him on the cheek, and it was so hard that it was like a bite. It had left a mark.

WHAT SHE SAID

Yes. Yes, I say yes, I say yes.

Acknowledgements

In 2017 I had the idea of a girl in a too-large coat flying low over treetops. In the years since then I have built up an immense and lasting debt of gratitude. These are just some of the people to whom I owe vast thanks:

Most of all to Ellen Holgate, my endlessly inventive and brilliant editor, without whom I would still be stuck in a plot hole halfway through the book.

To the whole team at Bloomsbury, who have been truly remarkable: Alesha Bonser and Sophie Rosewell in Marketing, Beatrice Cross, the very finest Publicity Director in Britain, and Fliss Stevens for her immense skill and even more immense patience in wrangling the text. To copy-editor Nick de Somogyi and proofreader Anna Swan, to Ben Schlanker in Editorial, Laura Bird and Danielle Rippengill in Design, and Mike Young in Production: all heroic. To Rebecca McNally for wonderfully championing this book, and to Nigel Newton for his unfailing support and generosity since I first came to Bloomsbury.

To Claire Wilson, my magnificent agent, and Peter Straus

and Safae El-Ouahabi and everyone at RCW.

To Nancy Siscoe, my editor at Knopf, for her belief in the book and in those to come.

To Inclusive Minds for introducing me to Gift Ajimokun and Iara Correa-Bezzel through their network of Inclusion Ambassadors.

To Tomislav Tomić, whose illustrated bestiary of impossible creatures has given me such joy, to Daniel Egnéus for the beautiful cover and to Virginia Allyn for the glorious map of the enchanted islands.

To my friends – who I won't list here, but who know who they are: thank you. What incredible luck it is to know you. (Thank you too for not howling with laughter when I said I was writing a children's book inspired by an unfinished epic poem by John Donne.)

To the children's book community. I spent years writing a biography of John Donne, which was both a joy and a task; but I've found there's no challenge like writing fiction for children. I'm so proud to belong to the company of writers working today, whose books I admire deeply: at its best, I think children's books are where human strangeness unveils itself, and our desires are laid out, and our bone-deep jokes are told. I'm so grateful to my friends and colleagues in children's books – it's a community unlike any other.

To my family – to Mike Rundell, at whose beautiful Cornish kitchen table the griffin took shape. To my brother, Gerard, and his wife, Karen, and to my nephew and niece,

Theodore and Phoebe Rundell: impossibly brilliant creatures. And to my parents, Barbara and Peter Rundell, to whom I always will owe absolutely everything.

To Charles Collier, who read many, many versions of this book and was brilliant and witty and wise about all of them. He is also just tremendously handsome.

This book is in memory of my great-aunt, Claire Hawkins. It's easy to forget as an adult how huge an influence you can have on a small child's life simply by being funny and warm and lovingly noticing. Claire offered me a model of what people could be: she was so beloved and admired. *Requiescat in pace.*

Have you read

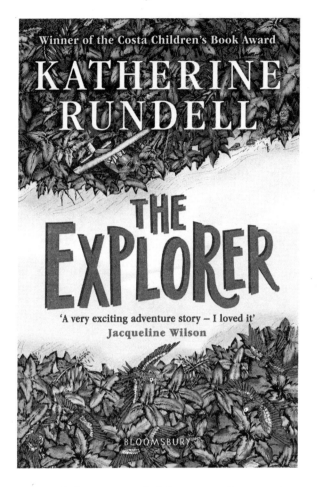

Winner of the Costa Children's Book Award 2017

'Utterly splendid ... Katherine Rundell is now
unarguably in the first rank'
Philip Pullman

Turn the page for an extract ...

FLIGHT

*L*ike a man-made magic wish, the aeroplane began to rise.

The boy sitting in the cockpit gripped his seat and held his breath as the plane climbed into the arms of the sky. Fred's jaw was set with concentration, and his fingers twitched, following the movements of the pilot beside him: joystick, throttle.

The aeroplane vibrated as it flew faster into the setting sun, following the swerve of the Amazon River below them. Fred could see the reflection of the six-seater plane, a spot of black on the vast sweep of blue, as it sped towards Manaus, the city on the water. He brushed his hair out of his eyes and pressed his forehead against the window.

Behind Fred sat a girl and her little brother. They had the same slanted eyebrows and the same brown skin, the same long eyelashes. The girl had been shy, hugging her parents until the last possible moment at the airfield; now she was staring down at the water, singing under her breath, her brother trying to eat his seatbelt.

In the next row, on her own, sat a pale girl with blonde hair down to her waist. Her blouse had a neck-ruffle that came up to her chin, and she kept tugging it down and grimacing. She was determinedly not looking out of the window.

The airfield they had just left had been dusty and almost deserted, just a strip of tarmac under the ferocious Brazilian sun. Fred's cousin had insisted that he wear his school uniform and cricket jumper, and now, inside the hot, airless cabin, he felt like he was being gently cooked inside his own skin.

The engine gave a whine, and the pilot frowned and tapped the joystick. He was old and soldierly, with brisk nostril hair and a grey waxed moustache which seemed to reject the usual laws of gravity. He touched the throttle and the plane soared upwards, higher into the clouds.

It was almost dark when Fred began to worry. The pilot began to belch, first quietly, then violently and repeatedly. His hand jerked, and the plane dipped suddenly to the left. Someone screamed behind Fred. The plane lurched away from the river and over the canopy. The pilot grunted, gasped and wound back the throttle, slowing the engine. He gave a cough that sounded like a choke.

Fred stared at the man – he was turning the same shade of grey as his moustache. 'Are you all right, sir?' he asked. 'Is there something I can do?'

Fighting for breath, the pilot shook his head. He reached over to the control panel and cut the engine. The roar ceased. The nose of the plane dipped downwards. The trees rose up.

'What's happening?' asked the blonde girl sharply. 'What's he doing? Make him stop!'

The little boy in the back began to shriek. The pilot grasped Fred's wrist hard for a single moment, then his head slumped against the dashboard.

And the sky, which had seconds before seemed so reliable, gave way.

Books to feed the imagination.
Go on an adventure with

KATHERINE RUNDELL

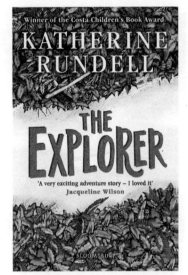

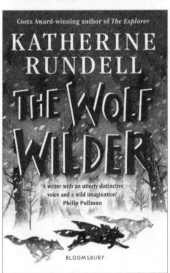

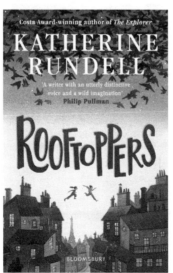

For younger readers

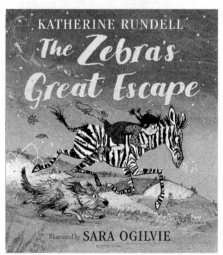